# TWO GUNS
# ACROSS TEXAS

## Historical Tales of the Texas Rangers

# Victor M. Alvarez

Black Rose Writing | Texas

ISBN: 978-1-68513-024-4
PUBLISHED BY BLACK ROSE WRITING
www.blackrosewriting.com

Printed in the United States of America
Suggested Retail Price (SRP) $21.95

*Two Guns Across Texas* is printed in Chaparral Pro

*As a planet-friendly publisher, Black Rose Writing does its best to eliminate unnecessary waste to reduce paper usage and energy costs, while never compromising the reading experience. As a result, the final word count vs. page count may not meet common expectations.

# PRAISE FOR
# VICTOR M. ALVAREZ'S
# PREVIOUS WORKS

## *Requiem for the Dead*

"Fans of military thrillers and tough, smart heroines will enjoy this high-octane adventure."

*–Publisher Weekly Review*

"A military cloak and dagger thriller, written by an authority on military protocol."

*–Authors Reading,* **Carole W.**

"An electrifying military thriller reminiscent of Mark Greaney and Brad Thor, with a plot worthy of a blockbuster movie."

*–BestThrillers.com,* **Bella G. Wright**

"Your reading frenzy begins on page one and continues to the end...well researched story as authors like Vince Flynn, Lee Child or Brad Thor bring to their readers."

*–***Rox Burkey**

"A military thriller that takes the reader on an action-packed adventure through present-day Germany and North Korea."

*–Sublime Book Review*

"I couldn't put it down. With a strong female lead and non-stop action, it's sure to please."

*–Online Book Club*

"Character-driven, fast-paced action thriller, slick compelling and gritty."

*–Artisan Book Reviews,* **Ella James**

This action-packed and bloody military tale introduces a dynamite duo."

*–Kirkus Book Review*

"Fast-paced and electrifying: this is a surefire hit."

*–The Prairies Book Review*

*The Theseus Conspiracy*

**2021 Finalist, The Best Thriller Book Awards on *BestThrillers.com***

"A psychopathic villain in possession of seven deadly nuclear bombs. A conspiracy of divesting consequences. A thriller unlike any you've ever read."

*–The Prairies Book Review*

"In this frantic conspiracy tale, characterization blends smoothly with action to produce a satisfying read."

*–Kirkus Book Review*

"The writing packs all the punches of a Tom Clancy-sequel cold war nail-biter with a modern edge."

*–Hollywood Book Reviews*

"A vivid, full-throttle military thriller featuring a villain that readers will never forget."

*–BestThrillers.com*, Bella G.

## VICTOR M. ALVAREZ
## PREVIOUS WORKS

## FICTION NOVELS

*Kill Slade*

*Requiem for the Dead*

*The Theseus Conspiracy*

*Two Guns Across Texas*

## NON-FICTION

*The Huntsman*

*No Time to Kill*

I dedicate this book to my son,
Victor Manuel Alvarez, Jr.


With sincere appreciation to my best friend Dan Russell, whose insights on all my books, I greatly appreciated. Without his help, this book would not have had the final touches required for publication.


And to my wife, Pam, the impetus I needed to complete this book.

Texas in the mid-1850s:

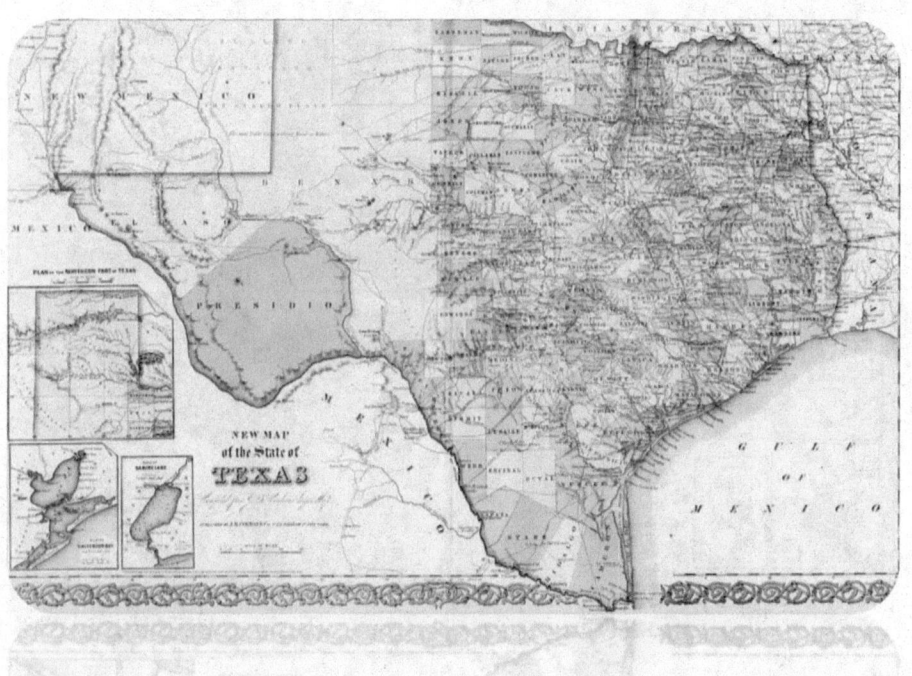

# TWO GUNS
# ACROSS TEXAS

# FOREWORD

To my new readers and those that follow my stories:

I submit here the adventures of two Texas' sons, Larry, and John Slade. It is long on story and short on plot, but it fills each story with the thrilling exploits of these two men. They're larger-than-life characters who lived in a world of violence: the Old Wild West.

What I'm about to share with you are the thrilling adventures of two guns across Texas.

It was my only son, fifteen-year-old Jonathan Slade, who expressed his overwhelming desire to learn more of our kinfolk, his great-great-grandfather, and his great-grandfather, Larry, and John Slade.

Fascinated by these forbearers, he yearned to hear all that he could about the adventurous, albeit violent and often bloody lives and times of these two remarkable Texas Rangers, so here are a few words relative to their beginnings.

Several years back, as I started relating their stories to Jonathan, I could not pull away from my position as a Deputy Sheriff for the county of Austin, Texas, and research their lives full-time. Now that I've retired, and with plenty of time on my hands, I've compiled the enormous volumes of their letters, news clippings, and other documents and preserved their stories in book form, for my son, and the Texas Rangers Museum.

The men called Slade, both father and son, are the stuff of legends. Their stories survive and have been passed down from one generation to the next. And writing it in book form, I feel it is the least I can do to honor their memory.

From all the letters and memoirs, I've read, John Slade, who was born in 1844 and passed away in 1916 at seventy-two, recounts his bloody birth. He wasn't a man of reckless blood, yet in time, much like their contemporaries—famous frontier lawmen such as Wyatt Earp and James "Wild Bill" Butler Hickok—he and his father Larry came to occupy an intriguing place in the legendary tales of the Old West.

When my father first started reading some of their letters to me at twelve, I became enthralled just like my son, about these two men who led a life and death struggle on the open plains, a rough and rowdy breed of men, alongside their women.

These two epitomized the classic ideals of manhood, standing proud and fearless in the face of adversity and danger, always giving a helping hand to those in need. Their manner was almost perfect from two men of the South.

Their guns often spoke for themselves. They were not gunslingers but trained to not just draw fast but to have an accurate aim.

Larry Slade served in the Texas Revolution and later became one of the first Texas Rangers, serving in his first post along the Sabine River, while his son, John Slade would later serve just like his father, a Ranger posted to the Austin, Texas, station.

I've written their life stories in book form. Each within their time frames of violence, happiness, and strife.

The ranch that John Slade built is still standing today. It's my home now and outback of the main house, are the tombs of Larry and John Slade, and lying beside them are the two women that stood alongside them through thick and thin.

So, with heroes and villains alike, let's return to those days of yesteryear, as I tell you the stories of the man named Larry, and his son John Slade, Texas Rangers, as they blazed their two guns across Texas.

Yours very sincerely,
John Edward Slade VI.

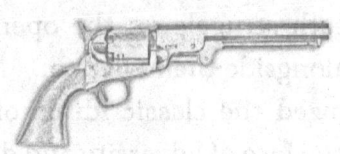

# PART ONE

# LIFE AND TIMES
## OF
## LARRY KINCADE SLADE

# CHAPTER 1

# THE HOSTILES
# AND
# THE BIRTH OF JOHN SLADE

*Slade Ranch, outskirts of the*
*Town of Nacogdoches, Republic of Texas*
*Fall 1844*

It's said that every story in life has a beginning and an end.

This is *their* story, the start of the legend of Larry and John Slade, Texas Rangers.

John Slade was born in 1844 to Martha Annabelle and Larry Kincaid Slade in a small one-bedroom log cabin built by John's father just outside Nacogdoches (*Nak-uh-doh-chiz*) — considered by some to be the oldest town in Texas—by the Sabine River and north of what's known today as Galveston in the Republic of Texas. It wasn't until John Slade turned a year old that the Republic became a State.

Larry Slade at twenty-six was a tall broad-shouldered man, with long flowing black hair that reached his shoulders, and as tan as the leather of his saddle, with a full handlebar mustache which drooped down below his lower lip.

With the end of the Texas revolution in April 1836, the Republic needed to control and defend its frontier from Mexican bandits,

Comanches, and other tribes. Life on the frontier was hard, jobs were scarce, and trying to make ends meet was an almost impossible task.

In August of that year, Samuel Houston, the first President of the Republic, authorized Colonel N. Robbins to form a fifty-man band of Texas Rangers to patrol between the Navasota and Sabine Rivers.

In September of that same year, Slade, was a cowhand for a local ranch down by the Brazos River in the town of Washington, the famous birthplace of Texas; known as the place where the Republic made their intentions to separate from Mexico and draft the constitution of the new Republic, heard the call for Rangers, and volunteered.

His first posting was with the Captain of the Cherokee Rangers. And with a compact unit of fifteen experienced Indian fighters turned Rangers, along with four Cherokee scouts, were authorized to roam between the Sabine River and Hall's Trading House for the prevention of wild Indians from stealing horses and murdering innocent travelers and settlers on the frontier.

In the intervening four years he reached the rank of lieutenant on the recommendation of his enlisted members and was later known as one of the boldest, most courageous, and vigilant officers in the service.

He took part in battles with Comanche and Mexican bandits while being wounded on three separate occasions. During a foray into Mexico chasing Comanche's, his patrol came under attack by Mexican bandits, where all but four out of the fifteen Rangers made it out alive while sustaining a bullet to his right knee that caused a permanent noticeable limp in his stride.

In late March 1840, he left the Rangers and moved back to his home on the Trinity River by the town of Nacogdoches. There he met the local schoolteacher, Martha Annabelle McBride, a petite red-haired Irish girl of twenty-one years, and after a short courtship, they married.

Because of his extensive experience as a Ranger, the town representatives offered Slade the position of town Marshal in

Nacogdoches and served for three years until his wounds prevented him from continuing in that capacity.

In the fall of 1844, with Martha's meager income as a schoolteacher and Slade's sale of horses, they grew their family from two to three with the birth of their only child, John Slade. The child was born in battle as their home came under attack by hostiles.

And so, it begins...

It was in August 1844, as Martha Slade was expecting her firstborn, her husband Larry Slade, along with five of his hired hands were packing their saddlebags and pack horses ready to deliver a hundred and twenty horses to the U.S. Calvary down in San Jacinto, Texas. Slade purchased the small spread he called home with money he'd saved from his lawman days, along with Martha's meager savings.

The early morning skies were clear and mild, promising to be another high humid day. As the sun rose over the horizon, twenty bare-chested and painted Comanches on horseback topped a rise overlooking the Slade spread.

They were there to steal the horses in the pen and kill any that may oppose them. Not since the Great Raid of 1840 when War Chief Buffalo Hump raided white settlements in revenge for being driven from their land, had a large band of Comanches dared to raid a ranch in Central Texas.

Slade, squinting against the glare of the sun, had just secured his latigo to his saddle when he turned and stared at one of his hired hands, a tall slender man, named Luke Short, who was lighting a stogie, who'd called out his name.

"Mr. Slade," he said, "we may have some trouble from up the rise yonder."

Staring over toward a slight elevation to the spot Short mentioned, he'd made out about twenty red-painted hostiles. Not wasting any time, he barked out some orders to the cowboys.

"Two of you," he yelled, staring at two of his younger cowhands, "cover the pen and the barn. Luke, take the horses around back and cover the house. Allen, stay with Luke. Dave, get inside with my wife. I'll cover the side of the house. Let's get!"

The men nodded, removed their Colt revolving percussion rifles from their saddles' rifle boots, and ran to their positions.

He wanted, above all, to be next to his wife, knowing she was due to give birth any day, but he needed to control the firing and keep his men from getting killed. He wanted to make this as fast as possible. It would take all his skills to accomplish it.

Just as he barked out his orders, the band of Comanches decked out in their war paint came riding hard and fast down toward the center of the spread. With no fence line to speak of, the ranch lay wide open: hard to defend, and easy to attack.

With everyone set, Slade, once the hostiles drew nearer, made out only three with rifles, probably taken from dead settlers somewhere along the flat plains, and the rest with bows. Good, he thought. He would concentrate his firing on those first, cutting down any further danger from that quarter, he would deal with the arrows that would fly in.

He yelled out to the two men protecting the horses and barn, "Try to take out the three with rifles boys! We'll see what fight they have in 'em after that."

Watching the white men set up defensive positions, the Comanche's rode on raising a shout, and whooping and hollering they rode down on Slade's small ranch.

The three rifle-armed hostiles led the fight as suddenly, they fired one after the other, continuing to advance, and came to within forty feet of the house. Bullets and arrows struck the side of the small dwelling.

One cowboy suffered an arrow to his left shoulder but shot the Indian off his horse and then he broke off the arrow's staff and kept on firing. The cowboys delivered a lethal barrage of fire. Three, then four of the hostiles went down dead, including two with rifles. Slade killed the last of the hostiles packing a Colt rifle. Even so, they pressed the attack.

Two lone hostiles rode hard and fast straight toward the house, and dismounting on the fly, they ran toward the front door, just as Slade stepped out in front of the Indians, and swiftly lifting his two Paterson model-5 Colts and stepping ever slowly toward the invaders, fired almost point-blank at them, as an arrow flew towards his head, blowing off his woolen hat.

Moments later, Slade heard the loud report of two Sharps rifle fire coming from the house, as Martha and Dave Preston, the youngest of the group, delivered round after round through the open windows.

Martha Slade dropped her rifle, as a series of sharp pains coursed through her body, just as Preston received an arrow through his chest and fell back dead. She screamed and yelled out for her husband, as holding onto her belly she dropped to the floor.

From the back of the house, Allen Drum and Luke Short had their hands full, as two hostiles shot arrow after arrow at their position on the back porch until Drum lost the fight as two arrows slammed into his chest. Short tried to reach Allen, but an arrow found his neck. Running into the house, the two hostiles stopped and saw Martha sitting on the floor with blood pooled around her.

She could only stare at them.

Knowing she may not have long to live, her only thought was for her baby that was being born. In a desperate act of self-preservation, she yelled out her husband's name, as tears glittered in her eyes, and streamed down her cheeks. She choked on her sobs.

One hostile drew his knife and slowly approached her just as Slade pushed through the front door. Anger and hate rushed into his heart, as he raised his two guns and fired and killed the two invaders before they could escape.

Dropping his empty guns, he reached behind his back, and drew a third Colt handgun from the gun belt at the pit of his back and approaching the two dead hostiles he shot them in the face, satisfying himself that now they were indeed dead.

Martha glanced at her husband. His face was white—with rage. She saw a part of him she'd never seen before and hoped she would never see again.

With a fierce battle still raging outside, he rushed to his wife's side and kneeling heard the cries of his son as she gave birth. Over the loud wailing of the baby, the shooting outside died off.

Once having buried Preston, Drum, and Short out back of the house, Slade patched up one of his cowboys who'd suffered a minor shoulder wound. Inside the house, Martha was sitting in her rocking chair feeding the infant as her husband walked in.

As he pulled up a chair in front of her, she said, "We haven't decided on a name for him."

"What do you think we should name him, Martha?"

With a tear in her eye, she replied, "Is it okay if we named him after my father?"

"John ..." Slade said contemplatively, "John Slade. It sounds just right, Martha."

She smiled and looked down at John who'd just finished feeding and with open eyes, smiled up at his mother.

"Think you'll be okay," Slade asked, "to ride in the wagon on the trail to San Jacinto?"

"I'll be fine," she said.

Burning the bodies of the hostiles, and after preparing the covered wagon, along with three newly hired hands Slade lured from neighboring ranches, they set out on the long ride to deliver the horses to the U.S. Calvary.

# CHAPTER 2

# THE RAID

*Brazos River, Texas*
*October 1852*

Their three covered wagons crawled through the day as one.

Eating up about ten miles a day, they'd been traveling for several weeks when they reached the outskirts of Comanche territory.

On a cold wintry afternoon, they'd crossed the Brazos River and stopped at Fort Milam in Nashville Texas, at the falls of the Brazos, for much-needed supplies and to stock up on winter clothing before the snow fell.

They were making good time, considering. Fort Milam, which was built in 1836 by Sterling Robertson's Ranger Company, when, during that same year, they came under attack by hostiles, leaving two dead.

The lead wagon, a four-wheeled, canvas-covered vehicle pulled by a team of four mules, was wrangled by Larry Slade as Martha, his wife, sat beside him. He, as usual, kept his pinto saddled and tied to the end of the wagon in case of an emergency. The two other wagons, both driven with two large solid wooden wheels, with a second smaller cart pulled behind them by a team of oxen.

These conveyances could carry five thousand pounds of equipment. But today, they hauled the household goods of two families, both from European countries, who'd made the journey crossing the Mississippi River into Texas seeking a better life in the New World.

Arriving in the town of Nacogdoches, they couldn't get anyone to guide them down to Austin during the depth of winter. When they heard of a wagon with a family of three that was making their way to Austin, and once negotiating with Larry Slade, he agreed they could travel together.

At the head of the wagon train was a young eight-year-old John Slade, riding his bronco his father captured and broke into a riding pony. Resting on his lap was his father's Warner revolving rifle and riding high on his right hip was a birthday present his father gave him just before leaving their ranch, a Dragoon .44 caliber revolver, and on his left hip was his Bowie knife.

With his favorite tan flat brim hat, with a red-colored rag bandana encircling his neck, buckskin shirt, and breeches, he rode high in the saddle. Wearing a pair of long boots, his long legs wrapped in his sheepskin chaps, stretched downward in the stirrups.

At a little over five feet and tanned to a golden hue, a firm muscled physique with long dark hair falling shoulder level, he struck a picture of surly self-confidence and unafraid of what life could have in store for him.

Martha argued John was too young to take the lead and much too young to hold a rifle and a gun. But his father was adamant that his son knew how to use the firearms having spent the last two years teaching him. And John was at the same age when Larry had gone hunting with his father.

Larry's confidence in his son was a testament to the long history of the name, Slade. He was the ultimate frontiersman that rode with Kit Carson on his expeditions; a fur trader, explorer, and guide serving time with John C. "Pathfinder" Fremont.

The Slade family had sold their ranch and property and moved to Austin, where Larry found employment as a deputy US Marshal. His assignment with the Fugitive Slave Act of 1850, called for the Marshal Service to enforce the law; to recover and arrest fugitive slaves. It was a job that paid much more than his meager ranch earnings could ever provide.

The wagon train carried three men, three women, wives of the three men, and the child, John. Late that afternoon before dusk settled in, Larry Slade called a halt. Camping by a small creek, the older Slade volunteered to go on a hunt for some game, leaving the wives in the hands of the two men; he took his son with him, to continue to teach him about hunting, tracking and the craft of a woodsman.

Riding single file, they trekked deep into the woods and roamed well away from the wagon train. An hour later, leaving their horses tied down, with Larry out in front, picked up fresh deer tracks on an old animal trail.

They walked toward a small stream when they came to a halt. John's father knelt beside the deer tracks. As his son knelt beside his father, Larry placed a finger to his lips. John knew his father had caught the scent spoor of a deer; he could smell it too. They lay on the grass and waited.

"John, this is on you," his father whispered. "Once you sight down on the game, take your time, just as I showed you, and take the shot. Think you can do it son?"

"Yes sir," the young man nodded. "I can."

"That's the spirit boy."

Moments later, from across the creek, and not more than a hundred yards' distance, a white-tailed deer broke through the woods and into plain sight. John noticed it had a reddish-brown color with a three-point antler spread. If he were to guess, it was about five to seven years old—a fine specimen.

One slow step at a time it came. The son and his father were downwind of the deer, so they could observe it undetected. Down went its head, and as it walked toward the creek, John brought his father's Warner rifle and sighted it onto the deer's neck area.

Up went the deer's head, then turning ever so to its right, the deer showed its full neck to the boy. Cocking back the hammer, he slowly inhaled once, twice and on the third time, as he exhaled, his forefinger squeezed the trigger just as the deer took two steps. A second later, the deer jumped into the air and came back down on its side.

Both John and his father sprang up and ran toward their prey. It was alive as Larry pulled out his Bowie knife and stabbed it in the heart.

Glancing at his son, he beamed with pride. "That was some mighty fine shooting, John."

A smile creased the young man's face as he watched his father. "Thanks, Dad."

"Get the horses and let's head on back."

Once the men, Oliver Stanford, and Frederick Watts, made camp, the wives Sue Helen Stanford and Evelyn Watts, made their preparations for the arrival of the hunting party. Lulled into a sense of security, they went about the business of camp life, as neither the men nor the women bothered keeping their sidearms or rifles next to them for protection.

From the surrounding woods, they were being watched by seven pairs of eyes—eyes that didn't see any weapons on or near the men. They crept through the dark brush, stopping once or twice as the folks walked about their campfire drawing near to their positions just inside the brush. They didn't know danger was in their midst until it was too late.

The Indians, a small band of Comanche, sprang forward hollering. The women ran screaming to their husbands' side.

This is what the hostiles came for, the women!

Martha Slade was nearest to her wagon when the Indians attacked!

Running to the back of her wagon, she reached in, pulled out her rifle, and cocked back the hammer, just as a hostile was running toward her. Thrusting the rifle out in front of her, and not taking aim, she pulled the trigger. The hostile, shot in his chest was flung back to the ground, just as another attacker, running, jumped over his fallen comrade when a shot rang out from inside the woods. She saw the Indian fall forward dead onto the ground and roll onto his side.

This was the scene that Larry and John came upon!

Spreading left and right, the older Slade, once he saw his wife was unharmed, kept firing as his son pulled out his sidearm and holding it both hands, shot two of the hostiles that were attempting to grab Sue Helen and Evelyn. Wounded were their husbands, attempting to save their women. Stanford sustained an arrow in his right shoulder, and Watts had one that lodged deep into his left leg. Four, then five of the hostiles met their death to the onslaught of both father and son's guns. The remaining two hostiles ran through the woods with Larry and John still firing their weapons at the fleeing renegades.

Later, with Martha's skillful hand, she tended to Stanford and Watts' wounds. After placing a hot knife to their entrance and exit wounds, she cauterized them, staunching the flow of blood.

It was a long night that kept almost all awake. One at a time, the three men and John kept watch, ever watchful for signs of hostiles or bears. With the deer skinned and prepared, they had fried deer meat and beans for dinner, with hot coffee to keep them warm.

Early the next morning it rained. First a slight drizzle then a torrential downpour all in a matter of minutes with high, cold gusting winds coming out of the north. It was a raging thunderstorm. The sky was black, thunder boomed and rolled, as lightning scrawled across the sky. It was a foul day to travel, but they had no choice as more hostiles may make their appearance and they didn't want to be around when they did.

With Larry Slade on his pinto leading the way and with rain running down the brim of his hat that seems to find its way down his back through his slicker, and John driving the wagon, with his mother under the canvas top and out of the rain, they set off for Austin once again.

# CHAPTER 3

## JAMES BUTLER HICKOK
## AND
## KATE WARNE

*Blanco, Texas*
*June 1856*

It was in 1854, after turning in his badge as a U.S. Marshal chasing fugitive slaves when Larry Slade began building up his ranch. It would be the permanent home for his family, that being his wife Martha and his twelve-year-old son, John. Slade quit his position after a fatal confrontation between a local landowner in San Antonio and two runaway slaves he was sent to arrest.

According to accounts recorded by the *San Antonio Ledger*, the landowner William Adams ordered Slade and two other Marshals off his property when a heated argument ensued.

Who started the argument was unclear, but Adams, accompanied by three other gun-hands—not backing down from the Federal Marshals—drew their weapons and fired on the lawmen, wounding a marshal.

In the heated gunfight that lasted less than a minute, one of the marshals was killed and Slade fatally shot Adams and one other man. Marshal James Baker, along with Slade, killed one of the gun-hands while another gave up the fight. It was later reported that Marshal

Slade, along with the wounded Marshal Baker, forcibly removed and arrested the wanted slaves.

Although termed a lawful self-defense confrontation by the local sheriff, Slade felt pained in having to use deadly force and killing a man who was just protecting his property—his brought and paid for slaves—unknowing to Adams of the slave's status' as wanted fugitives at the time of the purchase.

Not a man to mince words, Slade knew eventually, the North and the South would have to fight it out either in the field of battle or in the courts for resolving the slave problem which was taking center stage in Texan politics.

Now that he was done with it, he did not want to get involved anymore with any of it. His life revolved around his family, nothing more. He was not alone with his thoughts. Most of his fellow Marshals, northerners some, were of the same persuasion.

In late March 1854, fed up with Federal law enforcement, he packed up his family and moved to Blanco, Texas.

The town of Blanco is located in the Hill Country of Central Texas, west of Austin and north of San Antonio. There were two significant rivers, the Blanco and the Pedernales that flowed gently through the county which later would be called Blanco. It was near the Blanco River that Slade built his ranch.

The ranch, purchased just a short two years prior, was situated down in a small valley overlooking a high ridge, was comprised of a large family house, a bunkhouse, two barns, and a large corral all built with his own hands, and paid with funds from his position as marshal along with the help of a banknote.

With over forty acres of land, he had plentiful livestock which included over the two hundred head of cattle, several goats, and over two-hundred-fifty horses. Each summer for almost two years, he along with six cowhands conducted his cattle drive heading north following the Shawnee Trail, into Missouri. From there, they would ship his cattle to markets in Philadelphia and New York. And during the first signs of winter, he would deliver horses to the U.S. Cavalry at

Fort Davis, situated along the San Antonio El Paso Road, and to San Jacinto, in the port of Galveston.

On his last cattle drive, and once he received pay for his cattle, Slade and his cowboys rode on the first complete railroad into Texas from Missouri. Then they changed over to the Galveston and the Red River railroad. It wasn't yet three weeks when he arrived back home to his family.

Riding the train back to his ranch, he and his cowboys disembarked at Galveston station. With the sun slowly setting in the west as shadows lengthened through the station, they removed their horses from the last boxcar. Once the horses were saddled and the packhorse ready, they rode into town for supplies and some fun.

Galveston, like most big cities or towns in Texas, had its fill of gambling halls, saloons, and prostitution. It also boasted, like most other small towns, a hardware store, barber, two hotels, Western Union telegraph office, café, bank, and a livery stable.

Riding into town, his six hired hands had split up into two groups and made their way to different parts of the town looking for fun, entertainment and drinks. Being left to his own, he headed on over to a hotel with a sign that read; *hot meals, and a bath for three bits.*

"A hot bath right now would help my aching bones," he muttered.

Once he had stabled his horse, he walked over to the hotel, and twenty minutes later, he was in a room in a tub soaping down as a young boy poured warm water over him. After he left, he stayed in the tub relaxing and taking in the water. Not wanting to leave the tub, he finally got up and dressed. Strapping on his guns, he lit a stogie and walked down to the bar and ordered a steak with potatoes and a large mug of beer.

With his meal in front of him, and sipping on his warm beer, he heard from the saloon a commotion between two men that was developing into a heated argument. One, a fat grizzly man, with a dirty matted white beard, and hair to match accused a young tall, dark dapper man, wearing a dark flat pancake hat under his long flowing dark hair and a huge handlebar mustache and wearing two Colt percussion guns with white ivory grips crossed holstered under a short black jacket, of cheating at cards.

He watched the whole thing from his table, hoping it wouldn't disturb his dinner.

This wasn't any of his business. Not a lawman anymore. Let those paid to uphold the peace come and take care of it, he thought. *Don't be interfering with something that ain't botherin' you none,* he told himself. By experience, he knew that whenever someone's called out as a card cheat, blood and death were just a hair breath away.

From the bar, they heard the bartender yell out as he held a shotgun pointing over to the two men, "Y'all take it outside, gents. I don't want any shootin' in the bar."

With the trapper stepping out onto the street, the tall long-haired man left the bar and stepped out onto the boardwalk. Taking a few steps, he looked around him at the crowd, pulled his coat back exposing his two Colts, and stepped onto the street. He stood facing the trapper from about a thirty-foot distance.

A sizeable crowd of onlookers had quickly gathered outside, watching the events that would unfold. One man standing by the door said to another at his side, "That's James Hickok; he got called out for cheating by that trapper."

"You mean to say, that's Hickok, the gunfighter?"

The man nodded and replied, "The same one."

"Lordy," the man said, staring at Hickok. "I never thought I see the day."

Curious now due to the name Hickok being mentioned, Slade pushed aside his unfinished plate, gulped down the beer, and having heard the exchange between the two at the door stood up and stepped outside.

Slade stopped and stood off to one side waiting to see what would happen. Watching the crowd, he kept a sharp eye on two men, trappers by the look of them, partners he believed to the one calling out Hickok, and especially to one that was standing off to one side directly behind the shootist.

*I thought this was going to be a fair fight.*

Slade, impressed and curious, had certainly heard of Hickok and his fast guns. The stories printed in the newspaper and on store-brought Dime novels he thought may have been exaggerated. But he was soon to see for himself.

"Mister," the trapper opened by saying as he kept his right hand down by his gun holstered high on his hip, "You been too damn lucky with 'em cards. Show me ya hands. I swear that be another ace ya have upped one of your sleeves."

Hickok smiled and stared at the trapper with half-amused eyes. Placing his right hand by the handle of his gun, while gently stroking his mustache with the other, he said, "Old man, I've killed for less than that. So, draw that hog iron of yours, or shut the hell up and walk away."

The trapper wasn't a stranger to a gunfight, he'd had his share. Staring into the card cheat's eyes, he realized in that second that maybe, he'd made a mistake in calling the man out.

However, that didn't deter him from what he was about to do.

James Butler Hickok watched as the trapper slowly reached for his gun. A brief gaze of uncertainty crossed the trapper's face, and then he pulled his iron. From across the trapper, two loud booming shots resounded, one right after the other, and before anyone knew what had happened, Hickok had drawn one of his crossed holstered guns, fired, and kept it aimed at the trapper. Everyone watched as the old trapper stumbled back a pace or two, and finally fall dead on the ground.

Slade was both impressed by how quick the draw was, and the man's calm demeanor in the gunfight. It certainly was a cool and collected man who faced another with a gun. The outcome could've been slightly different.

He watched as Hickok holstered his piece, and slowly approached the trapper's body.

Suddenly, from the corner of his eye, Slade's gaze fell upon the trapper who had been standing behind Hickok, when the man drew his gun. But before he could aim and pull the trigger, Slade, already with his hand on his gun, drew lightning-quick and shot the man's gun right out of his hand dropping it beside him.

The crowd started thinning around the trapper.

Holding onto his wounded hand, and yelling with pain, the man dropped to his knees.

Seeing his gun by his side, he tried to pick it up again, but Slade fanned off two shots into the man's chest. The trapper slumped to the ground, dead onto his side.

Hickok, at the sound of Slade's gun instinctively turned and drew both his pistols and took a bead on the stranger. But Slade, glancing at Hickok holstered his gun, raised his hands over his head and said, "He tried to shoot ya in the back."

Nodding once and tipping his hat to Slade, Hickok didn't say a word.

The remaining trapper watched as his two partners were gunned down. Not inclined to die anytime soon, his hand dropped away from his gun, and peeling away from the crowd, he headed to the livery stables.

Acknowledging the nod and dropping down his arms, Slade didn't move, but he kept his hand by his gun nevertheless and just kept watching the gunslinger's movements as he turned to the crowd, maybe expecting some trouble from that quarter.

Holstering his two guns, Hickok—himself a onetime lawman—wandered over to his horse tied in front of the saloon and grabbing the reins he put foot to the stirrup, threw his leg over the saddle, turned his horse around, and stopped to face Slade.

Calmly, while not evidencing any regrets for killing a man, Hickok said, "If you're ever around Deadwood out in Dakota Territory look me up."

Turning his horse back around, Hickok spurred his horse and at a gallop rode out of town.

It would be a few years later that James Butler Hickok would come across another man named Slade.

Two days later, Slade and his six cowhands were apporaching his ranch.

It was early June, midday, the sky mostly clear of rain clouds, as the heat rose off the landscape in shimmering waves, with no wind to speak of.

Topping the ridge, they overlooked the ranch. It was as peaceful as the day they left. But Slade noticed something was out of place. There was a strange horse tied up in front of his house.

He removed his bandana from around his neck, then removed his hat and swiped at the sweat cascading down his face. Replacing his hat, he reached into his saddlebags and pulled out his binoculars, training them on his house.

"A visitor," he said out loud, not glancing at his hired hands as he replaced the binoculars.

Jesse Anders, his assistant trail boss, reining up by Slade's right, said, "Anyone you know, boss?"

There were three people on the veranda, Martha his wife, John his son, and a woman he'd not seen before.

"Wife and son," Slade replied. "The other a woman, ain't never had the pleasure. Let's get on down. I'm curious as to the visit."

Martha Annabelle Slade and her young son, John, saw riders coming from afar. They were only a speck in the distance, but staring through the sun-drenched land, she knew instinctively it was her husband and the hired hands back from the cattle drive.

Martha and John were sitting on the veranda, enjoying a conversation with their visitor, who'd ridden from Chicago just to talk to her husband. Martha was about to ask her a question or two but decided to let Larry ask any questions as to why the lady was there.

Later, as they all sat around the fireplace, the visitor noticed the boy staring at her cross-holstered gun and volunteered to show him how to shoot from the holster, with the permission of his father.

Smiling at his son, Larry Slade gave his permission and said, "Mind your manners, son."

"I will, sir," young Slade replies, with a large grin on his face.

Once outside, with young Slade and his father, watched as picking a tree, the visitor pulled a deck of cards from her coat, drew an ace of spades, and affixed it to the tree.

"Here," she said, glancing at the boy. "Let me show you."

Staring straight at the target, the visitor's hand flew in a blur of motion, went to the gun, drew it and holding it by her side, instead of pointing it straight out in front of her, fired and as quickly returned it to its holster. The bullet hit its mark, as it struck the center of the ace of spades card about seven feet distance.

"Mighty fast shooting, Miss," John said with eyes held wide open.

"Want to learn to shoot cross holster?" she asked the young boy.

"Yes, please," he replied, keen to learn the rudimentary method of fast draw shooting.

The father then watched as his boy buckled on his gun belt, straightened on the target, drew, and fired in one smooth motion. But he missed the target altogether.

"It takes practice," she said, "lots of it. But you'll soon be able to do it."

Smiling, the father watched his son standing beside their visitor who called herself Kate Warne, out of Chicago. Showing him how to fast draw and shoot from a crossed holster brought back a recent memory of once seeing someone else using the cross-holster draw.

He had seen one other person draw from a crossed holster— James Butler Hickok, but much faster than Kate Warne, he surmised and much faster than him as well.

Watching her, he saw a slender, brown-haired young woman, about five-eight, graceful in her movements, and a little self-possessed. She wasn't that all good looking like his wife, but she had what he thought a quiet intellectual cast.

It was her face that gave it away. Wearing a dark sack coat loosely fitted that reached to mid-thigh over tan trousers and boots, with a soft crowned brown hat; she was quite stunning to watch.

Shaking his head, he returned to sit by his wife. Striking a match to his stogie, he inhaled and slowly exhaled the blue aromatic smoke while staring over at his wife who was busy knitting, not paying the least amount of attention to her husband.

Larry then asked the visitor the purpose of her visit, to which she laid out the reason:

She explained that she was given the assignment by the Pinkerton Detective Agency, as the first woman hired as a detective, to capture an outlaw that has been operating out of Round Rock robbing stagecoaches and she needed Larry to help track and capture the outlaw. She had asked the U.S. Marshals service for an experienced tracker, and they gave her his name.

"You think I shouldn't go, Martha?" he asked, tilting his head ever slowly in her direction.

"That's up to you," she said, as she raised her head and held his gaze, "You just arrived from a long cattle drive, and you haven't seen your son or me for a while. Shouldn't you at least stay put for a week or two?"

Her eyes seemed different somewhat, he thought. Was she afraid something would happen to him? No, they seemed far away, haunting somehow.

Nodding, he sat back and glanced away from his wife. "If that's your wish, I will."

Martha raised her head to her husband, knowing quite well he'd already decided to travel with the young lady. Nothing she would say was going to change that. But she was worried, more worried than she cared to admit to him. He was getting up in years, and he couldn't be doing this type of work for much longer, she thought.

He smiled at his wife and took a deep breath. "She'd traveled a long way to see me, I give her that. The job would be for at least one, maybe two weeks. The most astonishing thing about her is that she is the first lady ever hired by the Pinkerton agency, and that made me most curious."

Besides, he needed the money he'd be getting for this job, as it would help to pay off part of the house and still have some leftover for things his wife had always wanted.

Abruptly placing her knitwork on the side of her chair, she stood and glanced at him.

"I'll get your pack roll together," she said in a measured tone.

Slade simply nodded his reply.

## CHAPTER 4

# THE PINKERTON DETECTIVE

From the open doorway of her ranch, Martha Slade watched as she saw her husband and the Warne woman ride out of sight along the sand-filled trail. With her son John by her side, she silently prayed that her husband would finish the case much earlier than they anticipated.

With the detective from the Pinkertons, she'd been hesitant in having her husband out on the trail with the woman, any woman. Strong was her conviction. But she knew her husband. Knew he would always be faithful no matter what.

She bit her lip. That wasn't what bothered her about the arrangement; she agonized over the fact that with a woman by his side, he could get himself killed. And if that occurred, she wouldn't be able to live with herself.

By her side, young John turned his gaze onto his mother. "Ma," he said smiling, "Pa will do just fine." As if he'd been reading her thoughts; so, in-tuned the youngster was with his mother.

But then, the boy, standing eye to eye with his mother said, "What do you think of a woman being a detective or lawman, Ma?"

She waited to reply, as she smiled placidly at her son. "I for one John, don't think women are ready for it, maybe in the far future. But time will tell."

Turning back inside the house Martha and John both said a silent prayer for both of them.

They were traveling in a northeasterly direction into what was known as Comanche territory and no man's land.

With the Comanche's now occupying the land since the Tonkawa, Kiowa, Yojuane, Tawakoni and Mayeye tribes had been removed from their lands by white settlements, the Comanche's started raiding those settlements, trying to take back some of their homelands.

Kate mentioned to Slade that they should start searching in or around the small town of Round Rock, about a half a day's ride. She also mentioned that it was the last known location for the robberies, as she was led to believe from reports from several local lawmen.

Warne had yet to give Slade the whole story as to the outlaw she was instructed to stop and bring to justice. But he was in no hurry, not yet though. There's plenty of time for that on the trail. But soon, she'd either have to open up to him, or he'd have to ask.

When they left his ranch, the weather was dry and hot, and the sky was clear of any rain clouds. However, after only two hours into their travel, the clouds to their immediate front were lower to the earth and beginning to turn black.

"There's a storm brewing up ahead Kate," he said. "We need to seek some shelter soon."

Kate looked about her, only seeing flat lands with no possible place to get away from the coming rain. Glancing at her tracker she asked, "Where do you recommend we find shelter?"

"Let's keep moving," he said in a reassuring tone. "I recollect an old, abandoned shack just a short ride ahead if it's still standing."

"Think we'll get to it before the rain comes?"

Suddenly, as if in answer to her query, the wind picked up blowing hard against their exposed bodies. He saw the rain clouds slowly dropping lower from the sky, holding the promise of rain. If they spurred their horses, he thought, they should be able to reach the shack in time before the rain fell. But, with her riding an old mare more half-broke than old, the chances were slim to none that they'd make it to the shack in time.

The small old building, from the last time he'd run across it, was in bad shape. It was located about half a mile straight into the rain clouds and situated on top of a small butte. If it got too dark, he'd miss the cutoff.

Slade drew rein and dismounted. Rummaging in his saddle bags, he pulled out his rain slicker. Then gazing up at Kate he asked, "You pack a slicker?"

"Ah, no, I didn't," she said lowering her face from him and biting her lower lip, and thinking how stupid she'd been for forgetting her raincoat.

"Christ!" was all he said. Walking to her horse, he passed his slicker to her and walked back, jumped up in his saddle, and checked to see if she'd donned the coat. Watching her button, it up he turned back around and waited until she'd finished.

A few seconds later, he turned in the saddle and said, "I want you to spur your horse and give it its head. Stay right behind me, don't veer right or left. Ready?"

Kate frowned, gazed at Slade, and said, "No, but I guess I have no choice."

"Let's go then," he said, as removing his hat, he struck his horse's flank and gave it his head.

Watching as Slade's mount slowly increased its speed, she did the same. Removing her hat, she strongly struck the horse's flank, and digging in her spurs the horse reared up suddenly as she held the reins for dear life, and once landing on its front legs, sped off after Slade who was way ahead of her.

"Damn!" she muttered through clenched teeth as she shoved her hat back on.

Just before reaching the cutoff to the shack, he turned in his saddle and cast his eyes on Kate who was lagging far behind. Reining in his horse he cut his speed in half and waited for her to catch up.

With darkness rapidly descending he heard her horse approaching as once again he cast a glance behind him and saw she was almost upon him. Bringing up his coat's collar, Slade slouched his hat down on his head, and riding low in the saddle, he dug in his spurs, as the horse rapidly sped off in full gallop with Kate right behind him.

In the fading daylight, he caught sight of the turnoff just as the storm suddenly broke, drenching the landscape that poured down on them with such force and ferocity that they had to slow their mounts.

It was a raging thunderstorm that fell and slowing down to a gait lightning scrawled across the darkened sky making visibility more difficult. Thunder boomed just above them and lightning struck the ground behind them and surprisingly it outlined the shack briefly to Slade.

"Come on, keep close, we're almost there!" he yelled out to Kate, hoping she heard him through the storm.

Kate did hear him. Drenched, due to the wind blowing the slicker open, tired and hungry, she spurred her horse and got in step with Slade who rode right in front of her.

Coming around a short bend in the road, Slade saw the shack just ahead. Approaching it, he drew rein, and not waiting for Kate, he dismounted leading his horse into the shack just as Kate reined in front of the building. Seeing what he'd done, she followed suit.

Once inside, they unhitched their saddles, removed their saddle bags, rolls and dropped them on the wooden floor. He looked around for wood and spied two broken-down chairs in a far corner. Once he had them, he broke the wood and started a fire at a place where the floor was bare of wood and where the rain wasn't falling through the cracks of what was left of the roof. Minutes later, with the raging fire heating them, Kate placed her saddle on one side of the fire, as he placed his on the other side.

Rifling through his saddle bags, Slade found his coffee pot, coffee grounds, and with his canteen of water started brewing some much-needed coffee.

Grabbing her saddle bags, she walked to a part of the shack that was cloaked in darkness, and said, "I'm going to change into some dry clothes, Larry." Once there, he watched as she used her blanket and strung it over an exposed wooden beam, giving her enough privacy to change.

Slade couldn't see why she'd wanted to change. Hell, he'd given her his slicker to keep her dry. *Guess you'll never know what a woman thinks from one moment to the next, especially one that's come from Chicago,* Slade thought shaking his head with a breathy chuckle.

With coffee ready, Slade sat down on his saddle, lit a stogie, and sipped on his coffee. As he was getting himself dried off, he decided to open her up for some much-needed information, which he thought she was holding back and gain some insight into the young detective as well.

He glanced over to where she was dressing and said, "So, what's a young lady like yourself doing working for the Pinkerton's and a detective to boot?"

A faint sigh came from behind the blanket.

Deflecting his comments, Kate rather asked, "My contacts said that you rode with Kit Carson as his tracker. One account told of you back in '33 fighting alongside the Ewing Young's expedition to the Rocky Mountains. Heard tell you took a scalp or two and killed some hostiles."

Stubbing his stogie on the wooden floor, Slade closed his eyes and remembered what transpired that day so long ago. He'd lived and fought for years among the Indians. Opening his eyes he stared down at the floor and said, "Wasn't cut and dry the way you put it. And it wasn't my best day."

Kate raised her eyebrows. "Do tell."

He remained very still as if remembering would cause him shame. Raising his head, he said, "Hostiles, I later identified as Crows, broke into our camp and stole nine horses. I along with Carson and three other trappers followed their trail. During the pursuit we lost two men, but once we found the Crow warriors, we opened fire, killing every hostile. I remember Carson getting his first scalp, along with one of the other trappers. I didn't join in. Not right."

It seemed as if a great time had passed without even a word between them when Kate pulled down her blanket and walked briskly toward the fire.

Watching her stroll in and reaching the flickering light of the fire, Slade was stunned by the young woman as the clothing she wore outlined every curvature of her youthful body. She had styled her hair into a ponytail. Halting in front of the fire, she placed her hands on her hips, dropped her blanket on her saddle and glanced down at him.

She lowered her eyebrows. "I see, and by the way, I'm not young," she said, her voice reedy. "I'm twenty-three and able to take care of myself."

Sitting on her saddle, they remained silent.

Kate was always annoyed when people pointed out her age. As if being young and a woman would be out of character in law enforcement. She just laughed at them. She'd always aspired to be a police officer, ever since reading about detective stories in the Dime novels and in the newspapers. She knew right then; this was what she wanted to do.

A smile that accompanied her answer spread across his lips. And he wondered what type of training she had received to be tangled up with bringing in a desperate outlaw; probably, not enough, he thought for one so young.

"How did the Pinkerton's hire you? It's my understanding that they hire only men."

"Well," she began, "When my husband died at our home in Erin New York, I packed my bags and moved to Chicago in answer to an ad in the newspapers from the Pinkerton's, who were looking to fill the positions of detectives."

She paused, and then said: "I didn't know there were no women police officers, let alone detectives in the entire country." She paused again. "When I walked into their offices in Chicago,

Mr. Allan Pinkerton was surprised that I was not looking for clerical work but wanted to be a detective. It took quite a convincing argument on my part, so he hired me on the spot."

"Did they ... train you?"

"Yes, two months of it," she replied smiling. "Then he gave me this assignment and put me to the test."

Curious now, Slade nodding glanced over at her and raising an eyebrow noticed she was staring back at him. "So, what did you say to convince Pinkerton to hire you?"

"I pointed out to Mr. Pinkerton," she explained. "That I can be placed in a position of confidence of any person suspected in an investigation to root out possible involvement in a crime and worm out secrets where it would be impossible for a man." She paused and smiled,

"And I know we women have a keen eye for detail ... among other things."

Slade turned his grey eyes toward her. "That's rather a unique point of view ... about police work."

Warne laughed. "That's just what Mr. Pinkerton said."

They fell silent.

The rain had grown in intensity and outside it was almost pitch black. The wind was blowing through narrow cracks in the windows and walls, making them raise their voices a few octaves to be heard through the howling wind.

"Well, get your cup and I'll pour you some coffee."

"I'd like that, thank you."

Once she had a steaming cup of coffee in hand, he finished his and glancing her way once again said, "So, how about you tell me what you know about your outlaw?"

Taking a couple of sips on her coffee, she finally said, "Well, he's been described as a man of medium height and broad-shouldered, black hair with blue eyes. The color of his eyes differs in the telling."

"That's not much to go on."

"Tell me about it," Kate said. "The outlaw seems to know when a shipment is due on the Overland Mail and Express Company stagecoach. So far there have been three holdups totaling about twenty thousand dollars in gold bullion and another three thousand in coins."

"Have other outlaws been seen in the holdups?"

"I don't believe so, but there have been no witnesses to the contrary."

"How is he stopping the stage?"

Kate had to think about it before answering. "He places large tree trunks on the route."

"What, in the same location?"

"No, he selects the route in which to place them."

Thinking it over for a minute, he said, "He must be operating with a wagon in which to haul the trunks in. He wouldn't have enough time to search the area for any. If he's behind the operation, he is privy to what the express company is carrying and when. It's safe to say that he is operating out of a town, which I believe the nearest is Round Rock."

"I never thought of that," Kate said.

"Anything else I should know?" he asked pouring himself another cup of coffee.

"Yes, he's killed two guards in his last holdup along with the stagecoach driver."

"So, a killer as well, this is not going to be easy."

"What do you have in mind Larry?"

Slade leaned back on his saddle. "Let's roll this over to you, Kate. How would you handle it? Remember you're the detective. Think about it for a minute."

She rubbed her hair and flicked a couple of loose strands back. "From his method of operation," she began, "he seems quite familiar with the area. Maybe he's working with others in the town that may be providing him the information."

He gave a slight bow of his head. *She is smart, I have to give her that* he thought. "So far so good, Kate. What else?"

She shook her head and shrugged. "Ah, I can't think of anything else."

"Alright then, how would you start your investigation?"

Thinking it over, she was at a loss as to where to begin.

"I see your hesitation."

"How would you handle it?" Kate finally asked not at all embarrassed at her lack of detective work. This was a learning curve, and who better to assist her in that than the famous tracker, Indian fighter, and U.S. Marshal, Larry Slade.

"The first thing I would do is talk to the Sheriff," he explained. "Give the description you have and see how many suspects fit the bill. Then, slowly whittle the suspect list down to one or two and follow their every move. Finally, you can act as a widow just arrived in town and get sufficient evidence on our suspect to take to the Sheriff for prosecution. Or catch him in the act of a robbery. I'll leave that up to you. You game?"

She nodded at his wisdom. "Yes, you make it sound so simple."

Slowly, he rose from his saddle, glanced around the shadowy shack, lit only by the flames of the campfire. He knew he was taking on a lot of the work, but that couldn't be helped. She needed to get herself completely involved if she wanted to be a detective. He took two steps toward the entrance, stopped, and turned around to face her.

"It's not simple" he finally said. "But it's going to take at least a week or more to catch our killer."

Walking back, he laid out his blanket and said, "Let's get some sleep. We have our work cut out for us in the morning."

She laid the blanket onto the hard floor and wrapped it around herself. Turning so she faced Slade, she watched him take his gun and holding it on his chest keeping an eye on the entrance to the shack. Will he sleep too? The thought ran through her mind. She felt safe around him. If he wasn't already married she would have loved to snuggle up to him *and* ...

Slowly she closed her eyes, as sleep finally overtook her.

The next morning, Slade standing at the open-door way to the shack, saw the flat country ahead of them through the bleak pale light of the early overcast morning. Just outside the shack, he had their horses ready.

Not spending any time on a campfire, he wanted to be in Round Rock early. He'd awakened Kate and had her ready herself for the ride. Then he explained his plan to her. She understood her part and was satisfied with it. It had a good chance of working.

With the horses saddled and ready, Kate walked outside, stood next to Slade and said, "I'm ready."

"You know what your part is in town, Kate," he said. "Maybe we'll get lucky and finish it off in a few days."

"Hope springs eternal," Kate said smiling.

"I reckon."

Slade gestured to the horses. "Shall we?"

She smiled and stood in front of him, and before he knew what was happening, she kissed him on his lips.

"Ah, what was that for?"

She lowered her head, and softly whispered, "For helping me through this."

At the outskirts of Round Rock, Slade and Warne separated. He would ride into town from the west side and Kate from the east, giving the appearance of not knowing each other. They'd planned on meeting in secret at midnight once they were established in the hotel and give each other their information.

The town of Round Rock formed in 1851 is situated on the banks of Brushy Creek, near a large anvil-shaped rock in the middle of the creek. The round rock marked a convenient low water crossing for wagons, horses and cattle. It was a small town of about four hundred with four cattle ranches.

It was a booming little town. It had a school, a church, two mercantile stores, on either side of the town, a post office and a telegraph office. Besides the Overland Mail and Express stagecoach, the Harris Stagecoach Inn located at the west end of town by the second hotel served the stagecoaches that carried mail and passengers from Waco, Austin, Blanco Creek and New Braunfels to San Antonio.

Arriving at the edge of town, he rode slowly as his horse's hoof beats splashed through the wet soggy streets. Staring left then right he passed a small church on his right, then further on the Sheriff's office and jail was on his left side. The town also boasted two saloons, a small café, two livery stables and two bakeries.

Not stopping, he continued until he reached a two-story hotel with a veranda that seemed to encircle the upper part of the building. Early morning shoppers and shopkeepers were out in force, getting ready for their early morning customers. He observed the café filling fast.

"That's my next stop," he muttered to himself.

When he came to within a few yards of the hotel he stopped and dismounted. From across the street at the saloon entrance, two men stared at the new arrival. One was a deputy and the other a local cowhand. The deputy, a tall leggy man with long black hair and sloped shoulders, stepped onto the boardwalk, stared long and hard at the stranger and meandered over to the jailhouse.

Riding in from the west-end of town, Warne slowly made her way to an open stable just at the beginning of the street she was on. Turning into the stable, she reined in and dismounted as a boy of about twelve approached her from inside.

Smiling, she asked, "Can you take care of my horse son?"

"Yes, ma'am," the boy said in a soft Southern twang. "My Pa, the owner, is at the café having breakfast. He should be back soon."

"Is there a hotel in town?"

"There's two, but the one down the street is the best."

"That's where I'll be," Kate informed the boy. "Tell your Pa I'll be back to settle with him in a few hours."

Taking the horse's reins, the boy said, "Yes, ma'am."

Removing her saddle bags, she let the boy take her horse into the stable as she started walking down the street. She saw the hotel sign towards the center of town; the Round Rock Hotel. Aptly named, she thought. It didn't take her long as passing several towns folks with children on the boardwalk she was greeted with kind gestures.

But, from the other side of the street, Kate was being watched from the entrance of the saloon by a tall cowboy who was leaning on the door jamb. The man had a wide sombrero, large red bandana around his neck, dirty black coat and he was wearing chaps. He'd just finished his smoke and flicked the butt onto the street when he caught sight of her walking into the hotel.

"Why look at that, someone new in town. Good looking, too," he muttered.

Stepping out onto the street the cowboy slowly made his way to the hotel. He intended to strike up a conversation with the woman and maybe, just maybe get lucky with her. One thing he was sure of— she seemed alone.

# CHAPTER 5

# FIRST KILL

Luke Mitchell, a local cowhand with the Simmons spread about four miles out of town, increased his wobbly drunken steps, aching to have himself the woman, as he watched Kate Warne disappear into the hotel.

With too much to drink, Mitchell had been in town for a few hours, gambling, spending his wages, and without a woman for the last month or so while on a cattle drive, and no saloon whore to spend time with, he was hedging his bets on bedding down with *her*. With a broad smile on his lips, he opened the hotel door, took three steps in, halted, and watched as she stood at the registry desk.

Removing his sombrero, he stared and wondered what she would be like in bed: Would she be *tough, submissive, or unwilling?* Christ, he couldn't wait any longer to find out, although Luke liked them tough and unwilling. Slap them around a couple of times he thought, and they would give up everything.

He worked for a living. Driving cattle month after month, making good wages. With no family to speak of, he was always by himself, unless he had a saloon girl to keep him company whenever he was in town. This wouldn't be the first girl he'd forced himself on and wouldn't be the last. However, to his credit, on those occasions, he'd left money on the bed.

Oh, he worked alright. A man had to work to earn his keep, eat and have a roof over his head. However, he considered himself a proud man... more or less. He needed to play every so often and have the feel of a woman in his bed, like today. He wanted company and he figured she would provide it.

Still staring, Mitchell found a chair towards the far wall, sat, and waited. A few minutes later, having registered, Warne picked up her saddlebags, turned, and headed for the stairs, just as Mitchell rose and slowly followed.

Keeping about ten paces behind her, they made the top landing of the second floor. He halted and watched his prey as she arrived at the door to her room; with a quickened pace, in an instant he reached her side. As she inserted the key in the door lock, he stopped beside her, and reaching for her saddlebags said, "Here, let me help you with your bags."

Turning slightly to see the man looming over her, Kate smiled, smelled the powerful odor of alcohol and replied, "That won't be necessary, sir. I can manage. But thanks anyway." She didn't feel any perception of apprehensiveness from the man. Although, she felt the stranger was uneasy and tensed. *Maybe,* she thought, *he isn't accustomed to speaking to a woman.* She showed a quick smile to her thoughts.

Glancing up and down the hallway, he saw his chance. As she opened the door, and as she bent to pick up her bags, the cowboy pulled out his gun, cocked it, grabbed her left arm, and shoved the gun into her back while pushing Kate into the room. "Do something stupid," he said, "and I'll pull the trigger!"

Fearing for her life, and afraid the man may be drunk, she hesitated. *If I turn too fast, his gun will go off and I'll be injured or killed. If I play it out and see what he wants, maybe he'll leave an opening I can take advantage of.* That thought raced through her mind. However, she had reservations about that line of thinking.

Warne had stayed alive because she was a cautious person. Living in Chicago in one of the most dangerous neighborhoods she was made to always keep an open eye on her surroundings and those around her.

So, to her dismay, she'd realized he'd taken her completely by surprise. Anger swelled deep down in her soul; angered because she didn't register the danger until it was too late. So, she made it a challenge of sorts. It would be a game in which one of them would come out alive.

Once in the room, as Kate turned to face the cowboy, she gazed into his eyes and saw an uneasy, but calm person in front of her as if he'd waylaid women before.

Mitchell without losing sight of her hands closed the door behind him and said, "Easy like now, pull your iron and drop it on the floor." He spoke urgently, raising his voice with authority.

She did as she was told. Slowly she grasped the gun handle, held it out in front of her, and dropped it on the floor.

"Now kick it over to me."

Once again, she did what he wanted. However, with her arms by her side, she slowly turned on her right side and pulled up the ends of her coat. Grasping a gun holstered in the pit of her back, she slowly pulled it out, and held it by her side away from his direct line of vision.

Stalling for time and looking for a way to distract him she said, "I've got money if that's what you want. Here, let me get it for you." She took a step to her left and slowly cocked her gun.

"Bitch, move again, and I'll plug ya!" Luke said. "Nope, I don't want your damn money. What I want *is* you!"

Staring straight at the man, she said, "Listen, I've got about a hundred dollars in my back pocket, it's yours, just leave."

He took two steps toward her. "I want a piece of your ass, woman. Don't you get it?"

Fearing he would grab her, and before her attacker knew what happened she suddenly took another step back, raised her *James Warner* pocket revolver to her side and fired a shot. The .28 caliber bullet plowed into Mitchell's chest close to his heart, but in his drunken state, he dropped his gun arm to his side.

As the gun clattered onto the floor, he gazed down on his chest. Placing a hand over the bullet hole, his hand came away with his blood, and cocking his head to the side said, "You shot me!" Shock and disbelief spread across his face. Staring back at her, she saw a quizzical look come over him. He met her stare and on unsteady legs, he came straight at her.

One, then two steps back Kate took, trying not to let the *asshole* grab her.

At arm's length he raised his arms in an attempt to grab her once again. Kate fanned two more shots in quick secession. Two of those bullets struck on or near his heart. The last bullet struck the center of his neck. Instinctively both his hands grasped his neck trying to staunch the flow of blood as it sprayed everywhere like an angry gusher through his fingers.

Spitting out blood, Luke Mitchell halted, slumped to the floor onto his knees and as his head dropped to his chest, his big arms dropped to the floor. A tremor ran through his body and

taking one last breath, death came swiftly. His body shifted to its left as it slumped onto the floor and it rolled once, coming to rest on its side.

She just stood there in the gloomy hotel room, not used to seeing death before her very eyes or her administering the death blow. This was the first person she'd ever killed outright. Her hands were shaking, tears rolled down her cheeks. Not tears for the bastard that attempted to rape her, but tears of joy, knowing he failed in his attempt.

Wiping at the tears, she tried to stay calm, and swaying somewhat she let her anger subside. Taking three steps back, her legs struck the side of the bed. She quickly sat. She heard several loud footsteps outside her door. Suddenly, the door flew open, and standing there was the town Sheriff and two of his deputies with drawn guns aimed directly at her.

Walking into the room, the Sheriff, Dan Clark, a man of medium height, wearing dark baggy trousers, a dark vest over a white shirt, a flat-brimmed hat and a thick black mustache that sloped down to his chin looked at her and the corpse on the floor. She looked back at him not saying anything.

She seemed young, no older than twenty, Clark thought, and he also saw she was trying to get herself together. She stared up at him and tried to smile. The Sheriff smiled back and nodded, keeping his gun aimed at her chest.

"Please, lady," he said, "drop your gun!"

Kate opened her mouth to say something, stopped, and without a word, dropped her gun onto the bed.

The Sheriff's office was situated on the east end of town. It was a two-story structure. Out front, the sign read: Sheriff's Office and Jail. Two picture glass windows with bars on them looked out onto the busy streets. The jailhouse was a plank-floored large space with a second floor. An iron-barred door led up the stairs where a second iron door led into three jail cells, all unoccupied at the moment.

A deputy was standing guard at the front door and Kate Warne was standing by the Sheriff's desk waiting for the Sheriff to pour himself a mug of coffee from the potbelly wood burning stove that was in the far-left corner.

With a coffee mug in hand, Sheriff Clark gradually walked toward his desk, came around it, and sat on his old wooden back chair he'd kept around since first arriving in Round Rock a few years back.

Kate gazed around the jailhouse. To one wall were several wanted posters, a rack of rifles and two shotguns, and the Sheriff's wooden desk with two chairs in front.

Clark shook his head and frowned. "Please pull up a chair," he said to the pretty young lady standing by his desk. "You have true grit, Miss Kate, I give you that, to have gone up against an armed man the way you did."

She measured her response and spoke for the first time. "It was either me or him Sheriff. I didn't feel like being raped or killed today."

Clark smiled, intrigued by her answer. "Still, you're very lucky to be alive."

Shrugging and nodding, she lowered her head.

The lawman lowered an eyebrow. "There won't be any charges brought against you, Miss Kate. It was purely self-defense."

Still sitting, Kate raised her head. "So, I'm free to go?"

He nodded. "Uh-huh, guess so. Just another question, though."

Kate waited and immediately knew what the question would be.

"What brings you to our town?"

*There it was.*

Keeping quiet for a second, she smiled, remembering her background story, as she and Slade had put together. "I'm a widow and I'm looking for a friend of my late husband. They have not seen each other for several years and I'm filling his last request to let the friend know of his passing. I was told he may be staying in this town."

The Sheriff shrugged. "Well, do you have a name?"

Quickly, Kate had to think of one, or the Sheriff could get suspicious. She blurted out, "Tom Mooney."

Squinting, Clark lowered his head, thinking. "Don't recollect anyone by that name." Raising his head, he met her stare. "You have a description?"

"I don't have much, only that he's of medium height, broad-shouldered, black hair, and blue eyes."

Sitting back on his chair, Clark said, "Well, there's Billy Grey. He has a small spread several miles outside of town, east of here. Don't recall him having blue eyes, though. Then there's Andrew Tucker, he's been around a year or two. He works over at the Overland Mail and Express stagecoach office and at times at the Western Union office. He fits the description."

Kate winced. "That's good news. Thank you, Sheriff."

# CHAPTER 6

# THE OUTLAW
# ANDREW TUCKER

A crowd had gathered on the sandy street in front of the hotel, as they waited to get a closer look and learn the aftermath of the shooting. Women, some wearing Victorian clothing, and others with blouses, skirts, and boots, stayed away from the hotel's front entrance; instead, they stood on the plank boardwalk and under the awning shading them from the sun's scorching rays.

But while the crowd was murmuring of a woman killing a man, and waiting on the identification of the dead man, Larry Slade, in a blue shirt and tan cowhide vest, and faded black boots, was sitting across the street by the town saloon door, waiting for the crowd to disperse so he could make his entry into the hotel and his room.

Minutes passed when through the hotel's front door, two burly deputies carried a man's body as a buckboard pulled up behind the crowd. Another deputy, tall and stocky, walked to the front of the on-lookers and shouldered his way through.

"Move out of the way, folks!" the deputy yelled out. "Go on now, get on home."

Once a clear path to the buckboard was established, they carried the body unhurriedly forward. As it passed through the crowd, someone exclaimed, "That's Luke Mitchell out from the Simmons' spread ... the old man ain't gonna like this."

Someone, a women's voice said, "Had it comin' to him, for forcin' himself on a woman."

As the crowd thinned, Slade from across the street heard it all. Lighting a stogie, he blew out blue smoke with a smile on his face. "She's done well," he whispered.

Seconds passed as he turned to the other side of the street and spied Kate Warne, leaving the sheriff's office. She stopped on the boardwalk and looked up and down the street. As her eyes scanned the crowd, she found Slade looking at her. She gave him a nod and a smile and walked over to the hotel.

The crowd had thinned to two, as Warne made her way toward the clerk's desk, while Slade ambled over onto the other side of the desk, a good six feet away. Leaning on the desk, he waited as the clerk, a well-dressed white-haired man in his fifties, addressed her.

"I like to change rooms, please," Warne said, not waiting on the clerk.

"That's no problem, lady," the clerk answered. Turning around, he faced the key rack and pulled a key on a ring. Coming back around, he gave it to her. "Please sign the register again. The room is 216 on the right top of the stairs."

Now that he had her room number, Slade left the clerk's desk, sauntering up the stairs then to his room directly across from her.

Still reeling from her near-death experience, Kate, having changed from her bloody blouse, stood in front of a porcelain basin and washstand in her room, poured water into the basin from a water jug, and splashed the cold liquid onto her face. After reaching for a towel from atop the washstand, she heard a soft knock at the door.

Her small room comprised of an open curtained window, two wall-hooks to hang clothing, the washstand chair, and a bed was a far cry from what she was normally used to in Chicago. Her room in her parent's house was three times larger than this flea-bag room. She hoped the case didn't last much longer; she was already missing the big city life.

A second knock sounded.

Slowly she moved to the bed, grabbed her gun, cocked the hammer, and walked to the door.

At the door, she said, "What do you want?"

From the other side of the door, she heard, "Kate, it's Larry, let me in."

Kate unlocked the door, opened it wide, and as Slade stepped inside, she closed the door behind him. Walking past her, Larry quickly saw she wore a red plaid shirt and denim, while her hair cascaded down past her shoulders.

Stepping into the center of the room, Slade turned around and faced her. She looked slightly pale. There were dark shadows under her eyes, as though she'd been crying.

Before Slade could say a word, she asked, "Did you hear about the shooting?"

He watched as she shuddered slightly. Without a word, he pulled up the chair and sat down. "It's all over town. Nice to see you're still alive."

She barely reacted. Kate walked to the edge of the bed, placed her gun atop the bed, and sat. With bowed head and in a hushed voice she said only, "I've never killed anyone."

Slade reacted. He stood and sat by her side. "Let's hope you don't go through that again."

Laying her head on his shoulder, she held back tears and kissed his cheek. "Thank you," she said, "for being here. I feel a lot better now."

*That's the second kiss she's given me.*

Knowing there wasn't anything to it, he felt as if a fatherly bond was growing between them.

Larry rose, walked to the window, pulled a stogie, and fired it up with a match he fished from his vest. As he sat back on the chair, he exhaled the blue smoke. "Saw you leaving the sheriff's office," he said. "Did you get anywhere with him?"

"Interesting, how your intuitive reasoning drew results," she said, "Yes. And the sheriff did divulge the name of a person fitting the description. And the kicker was the man works over at the Overland Express and the Western union offices."

"Now we're getting somewhere," he said, inhaling and letting out smoke. Placing on his hat he walked to the door. Grabbing the doorknob, he turned back to her. "Stay here, get some rest. I'll take a look at the man. Did you get a name?"

Standing, she shook her head and frowned. "I'm … I'm coming with you, Larry."

He shook his head. "That's out of the question, for now. I'll scout around and take a look-see on our man, find out anything I can; see where he beds down, and then we'll take it from there. So, does the man have a name?"

"Oh, yes, sorry. His name is Tucker, Andrew."

Slade would approach it as a hunter stalks his prey, ever watchful until the prey shows itself to the hunter. For one accustomed to stalking, having learned the craft from the Apaches, known to be the greatest trackers and hunters of the plains Indians, he could wait for hours without showing his hand.

Slade saddled up and left the stables. He rode slowly to the edge of town, onto the side of another hotel a hundred yards from the train station. He reined to a halt in front of the hotel. Dismounting, he tied his horse to a hitching post and walked up three steps onto the boardwalk.

Under the awnings, he grabbed a chair, sat, and set his vigil waiting for the man named Tucker. From time to time, he gazed over at the station house. Twice he saw his prey, leaving the station but returning soon thereafter. Nothing suspect with that, he reasoned.

Lighting a stogie, he waited. He waited for the time Tucker would get off work and lead him to his wherever he called home. His plan was simple in its execution. He would search Tucker's house for evidence that could incriminate him. Then he would join up with Kate and hope they could catch him in the act and let her make the arrest.

Having learned from the desk clerk at his hotel that the train wasn't due for about forty-five minutes, the last one for the day, Slade reckoned he had only to wait until after the train departed to follow him.

At one point Tucker left the Overland Express office and made his way to the Western Union office. On his arrival, the telegraph clerk, Sam Culpepper, smoking a pipe, looked up as Tucker entered. Culpepper was a friendly old man, who appeared to be in his late seventies, but one couldn't tell by the absence of wrinkles on his face. He loved to talk and crack out jokes.

"You're kind of early for your shift, ain't you Tucker?" Culpepper asked.

"Just came in to see if anything worthwhile is coming through the station."

Culpepper kept Tucker informed of any sizable high-value payroll shipments carried by the express stage, and if it was guarded. It was Tucker's job as the station master to ensure the safety of the payroll shipment whenever it stopped at the swing station once it left the main station.

Culpepper removed his spectacles, cleaned them with a rag from his desk and placed them back on. Shuffling through several sheets on his desk, the old man said, "I reckon there is one for ya. Give me a minute to find it."

Tucker waited for old man Culpepper to rifle through his papers.

"Ah, here it is," Culpepper exclaimed a second later, placing the sheet on the countertop.

Taking the telegraph sheet, Tucker read:

*Station Master, stop, payroll shipment coming through tomorrow on the evening stage, stop, provide security for the guards and shipment, stop.*

Nodding his head, and as he finished reading the wire, he pocketed the sheet, gazed at Culpepper, and said, "Thanks, old man."

Still nodding as he stepped out of the Western Union office and with the sun slowly casting its shadows on the dusty streets he reflected on the dangers of robbing stages and his violent beginnings ...

... Andrew Tucker knew someone, someday, would put two and two together and find out he was the one behind the stagecoach robberies. But no one in town suspected him. Not even the sheriff. The lawman wasn't very smart and really couldn't care less since the robberies weren't committed in the city limits. Tucker made sure of that. Along with his two partners they had a great business going and he and his partners, both towns' deputies, were getting rich from the robberies.

Tucker himself having dropped out of school at the age of seven never returned to school, to live the minimalist lifestyle. It was through being a cowhand where he made a good living. But the lure of being an outlaw grew into him and with the knowledge he gained in prison, he hoped to make a better life for himself.

Born Joshua Goldsby in the town of St. Charles, in Western Missouri, when at the age of fifteen, Tucker was convicted of murdering his parents. At the age of twenty and while serving his time in prison, he along with two other inmates broke out of the Missouri State Penitentiary just west of the Mississippi River in Jefferson City. After roaming from town to town he changed his name to Tucker and fled south into Texas.

It was in prison where he met an old man and befriended him. From his friend, Tucker learned all there was to robbing banks and stagecoaches. The old man and Tucker became close friends, but before his escape the old man passed away in his sleep.

Now, he had to alert his partners, Ed Black and Slim Wilson, of the next shipment. He hoped it was a sizable amount, for he planned to quit once he had the sum of forty-thousand dollars saved and book passage on the next steamer heading for Europe.

With the late afternoon sun gradually ending the day, Slade heard the Overland Stage approaching. Slowly it came, rumbling down the back streets of the town and stopped at the Harris Inn station. He spied Tucker waiting on the platform as passengers unloaded the coach.

After an hour had passed, Slade watched as Tucker, walking from the Harris Inn, headed toward him; minutes passed as Slade watched Tucker walk through the dusty street. He passed Slade's position, heading toward the other side of town. Slade rose and stepped onto the street, unloosed the reins from the hitching rail, put boot to stirrup, and mounted his horse Slade turned his horse's head and followed Tucker at not much more than a trot.

# CHAPTER 7

# GUNFIRE UNDER THE TEXAS STARS

Larry Slade felt the cool current of air fanning his face.

Nighttime shadows were slowly rolling in, and as he stared up into the sky, he saw millions of stars coming into focus. The evening wind was a welcoming visitor after the scorching heat of the day.

He was standing by his horse about two hundred yards from the livery stables entrance, waiting on Andrew Tucker to make his appearance. Earlier, Tucker had disappeared inside the stables. Slade waited between Clancy's saloon and the town's water tower, far away so he wouldn't seem suspicious to anyone, least of all Tucker.

Five minutes later, Tucker, riding a brown Chestnut, slowly trotted forward. Riding in the center of the street, he headed straight to Slade's location. Before Tucker reached him, Slade walked around his horse, showing his back to him, and busied himself with his horse's saddle cinch.

Riding past Slade, Tucker paid little attention to the cowboy. Hell, he thought, *just another drunken cowpuncher*. He'd seen too many of them in this town.

Slade turned away just as Tucker rode past him. Walking around the other side of his horse, he would wait several minutes before mounting up to follow. However, he noted the direction that Tucker had taken, due north.

Through the grainy evening darkness, he saw Tucker disappear. Not waiting any longer, he hopped up onto his saddle, swung his horse around, and nudged it forward following the suspected stage robber.

Twelve miles out of town, Slade pushed his horse faster, as he tried to maintain visual contact with Tucker. Two miles further on, down a rocky and hilly trail, he slowed, catching sight of him through the moonlight, as the man rode through what he believed were sand flats, but he couldn't be sure due to the darkness.

Through the high rocky terrain, Slade had to slow his horse, careful not to let his mount injure itself in the darkness.

Later, losing sight of his prey once more, Slade, his attention riveted on the trail, rode through the sand flats, keeping his horse at a slow gallop, when with knitted brows he saw dim lights over the horizon. From this distance, he could not distinguish what it represented; it could be a campfire, he reasoned, but he doubted it.

Dismounting, he knelt struck a match he grabbed from his vest, and saw from the flickering light, some fresh deep hoofs of a horse as if it rode at full gallop. The tracks seemed to lead straight to the lights. He stood and gazed out over the horizon. "I think we know where he went, horse," he said, gently stroking the side of the big animal's head.

Mounting, he gently spurred his horse forward down the outlaw's path, maintaining a steady pace. He rode up onto one of the many high hills and more rocky terrain.

Ten minutes later, when he topped a hill, he halted and stared down into a small valley with a stream running through it, and through the moonlight roughly about a third of a mile away he could make out a dilapidated and cluttered ranch house, a barn, windmill, and a horse tied up in front of the main house.

As Slade rode down the hill, he spied a small hillock two hundred yards in front of him and away from the trail leading up to the ranch. Dismounting, he tied his horse to a tree and unhurriedly topped the hillock from where he was able to survey the ranch from a better vantage point.

Lying on the grass, he gazed at the ranch and was deciding from where to sneak up to the side of it when he heard horse's hoofs approaching hard and fast from somewhere in the near distance.

Slade cocked an ear to the sound. He thought, maybe he heard two horses, but couldn't be sure.

Then, from closer to his position, he heard a soft low whicker noise from his horse, warning him of danger. He instantly turned around, drew his gun, and quietly waited.

It must be an animal, he thought.

Suddenly, he heard scraping sounds and a shadow appeared over the hillock. Aiming his gun at the shadow, he cocked the hammer and heard a female voice softly calling his name. "Larry, it's me Kate, don't shoot. Where are you?"

Slade froze. He was almost in shock. "Damn it, Kate, you were supposed to stay in town!"

The woman had stopped the moment she heard the cocking of his gun. Kate walked forward, stopped again, and stared down at him. "It's my case, Larry. You can't keep me away like that."

"You're here now," Slade replied grimly as his shock wore off. "So, there's nothing I can do about that, so come on over beside me."

Just as Kate lay beside Slade, two riders came into view riding down the ranch trail and over toward the front of the ranch house. They watched as the two men tied their horses to a hitching post and made their entry into the house.

"Well, look at that," Slade said. "Those are two of the sheriff's deputies."

"How can you tell?"

"One, tall and burly, and the other sloped shoulders, yeah. The burly one is the same one that helped carry the man you killed out of the hotel."

Kate shook her bowed head. "So, do you think they're mixed up with this?"

"I reckon they are."

"What now?"

Slade shrugged.

"I want... I'd like for you to stay here and watch my back, while I go up to the house, and have a look-see. Think you can do that for me?"

To this, Kate nodded her head, and looking up and down with no reply for several seconds she creased her brow, and asked, "Hmmm, do I have a choice?"

Larry Slade caught the threat of it and cocked his head to the side. "We all have choices, Kate. But if you follow me down, and something happens, gets you killed or seriously wounded, I couldn't live it down."

"So, what... what exactly is it you want me to do, besides not going down with you?"

He took a few shallow breaths. "If you see me running back to you, and those three are shooting at me, I want you to cover my escape."

The woman nodded. "I can do that."

"Good."

Slade surveyed the ranch.

The only way he could make his appearance without being noticed or spooking their horses was to make his way toward the rear of the house, search the barn and then sneak over to the back of the ranch house.

Slade in the dimness fell silent. Standing, he gazed down at Kate. "Watch for my return."

For a long moment, she didn't say a word. "You know you're crazy, doing this by yourself."

"Reckon so."

Without another word, he turned his back to Kate, and slowly retreated down the hillock.

Slade sprinted the short distance through the darkness, glancing now and then at the house and the horses. If he spooked the horses, maybe, just maybe no one in the house would be alerted; a big maybe. The only sound was the faint moaning of the wind. The area seemed barren; tree branches knocked themselves against each other in the stiff winds.

He ranged about two hundred yards before making the outskirts of the barn. He stopped and stared at the house. From his vantage point, he saw the entire side of the ranch. There, a back door to the barn was left wide open. Through it, he made his slow way into the darkness inside.

Fishing his last match from his vest, he struck it on a wooden post, and through the momentary light, he saw several large tree trunks stacked up against a far wall, a buckboard, and two horses. Shaking the match out, he felt that was all he needed to see. This could prove beyond a shadow of a doubt the guilt of those in the house.

At this he paused. Should he stop, he thought, leave, and have the county Marshal join in and arrest these three? No, he wanted to catch them in the act, leaving nothing to doubt. And he owed Kate an arrest. But how was he supposed to do that, with no firsthand knowledge of express shipments? For that, he would spy on those in the house.

The three outlaws were together in the house. Were they planning another heist? It could be, he reasoned. "Let's hope luck is still with me," he murmured.

Within minutes he reached the back of the main house and found the back door slightly ajar. Here he paused listening, silent, and motionless as he distinctively heard the three in conversation just a doorway away, along with the crackling of a fireplace to his left.

With utmost stealth, he ventured inside, past the door, and found himself in a small storage room with a bed; the room's door was open from the inside. He flattened himself against a wall. Then, he heard a gruff voice; he assumed it was the burly deputy. "So, you want me to board the stage as before and wait for it to stop, get the draw on the guards, and watch as you two ride in and do the rest?"

Tucker replied, "That's the plan."

The gruff voice of the deputy, asked, "What stage?"

"Tomorrow on the evening Overland Mail and Express out of Austin."

"What's the take this time?" asked the burly deputy.

"Enough so we could retire with."

"Damn, that much, eh?"

"Uh-huh!"

A low slow voice, Slade thought was the deputy named Slim, asked, "How much is our split this time?"

"Um, same as before, we ain't changin' our agreement now."

Hearing enough, Slade took a slow step back, and just as his boot put pressure on a loose board, he heard the distinct creaking noise, not loud, but enough so that those in the house may have picked up on it too.

Instantly, he heard the gruff voice of the deputy. "Did you hear that?"

"Sounds like it came from the other room," Tucker instantly replied.

Without the slightest hesitation, they drew their weapons. Two of them slowly approached the room's door, while the deputy named Slim, ran toward the front door.

Slade heard them coming and ran out the back, sprinting toward the woods directly to his right. Fast behind him, the two-stage robbers saw their intruder's shadow through the darkness just as they stepped through the door. Slim running out the front door, heard and saw a shadow running, as Tucker and Black started shooting at the running figure.

With guns blazing, the hot lead kicked up the dust and dirt on Slade's left side and behind him, as a few slugs buzzed over his head, but none did any damage. Then he was out of range of their fire and still running when suddenly, from Kate Warne's position, he heard rifle fire aimed at the outlaws. Her shots forced them to seek cover back in the house. Kate could not get a clear shot at them, so she'd fired at their muzzle flashes.

Safely inside, they assumed the intruders were scavengers who, from time to time, came in the dark and stole from the ranch. Twice Tucker had to purchase new horses when two were found missing. They never found out who robbed them.

"Damn ... ah, are we still on then?" Deputy Ed Black asked.

Tucker, sobering up fast, said, "By God, nothin' gonna keep me from gettin' that money!"

"Fair enough," Black replied.

"You best be gettin' on. You have a long ride to Austin."

# CHAPTER 8

## WHEN THE GUNSMOKE SETTLES

By candlelight, as his shadow moved with him through his room, and from across the hall from Kate Warne, Larry Slade unbuckled his gun belt, removed his hat, and laid them on the only chair by his bed.

Stripping off his vest and shirt exposed a well-built muscular body. Small, well-defined puckered scars of five bullet holes on his chest and two well-healed jagged scars made by a knife in the side of his back were visible, attesting to the rough life he'd lived throughout the years.

He'd killed more men than he could remember. Some that deserved it, a few that were downright killers, with many Indians along the way. He'd been in fights that he never started but would always finish, and a handful he had started.

Walking over to the mirror, staring back was a no-nonsense man with a deep tan, a cleft chin, ocean blue eyes, and a strong angular wrinkled face. And at thirty-eight, he was a man that had aged too quickly. Observing the many wounds on his body, he knew where and when he'd received them and from whom and gave thanks to the *Almighty* for still being alive.

The small room he was in consisted of an iron-framed bed and thin mattress with a pillow, a dresser, washstand, and not much else. *At least it was better than lying beside a campfire, sleeping on the cold or wet ground, and staring up at the stars*, he mused.

Sitting on the bed, he removed his boots and socks but kept his trousers on. Walking to the chair, he grabbed his Colt, laid it under the pillow, and laid down to rest.

Staring up at the ceiling, he recounted the events of the evening: He and the Warne woman had fled at full gallop through the darkened landscape, thinking Tucker and the deputies would be out chasing after them. But after several miles and stopping once or twice, they did not see anyone behind them, so they reined in their horses to a slow trot.

During the long ride back to town, Kate would keep in stride with Slade's mount. At one of those times, she asked, "Did we get anywhere back there?"

"Sure enough," he replied, using as few words as possible. "They plan to rob the payroll shipment from the Overland Mail and Express stagecoach out of Austin. A deputy will be on the stage already. Their plan calls for Deputy Black to get the draw on the guards just as the stage is coming to a stop, and once that's done, it's up to Tucker and Deputy Slim Wilson to ride in guns a-blazing."

"That's a bold plan," Kate said.

"Hey, seems to have worked well for them in the past."

Kate nodded. "It would seem so."

A slight pause as they rode side by side.

Kate asked, "When will they hit the stage?"

"It appears, that be tomorrow, on the late evening stage."

"So, we have time to plan."

Slade nodded with a trace of a grin. "Reckon so. About that, Kate, I've been thinkin' ... here's how we should go about it.

Looking over at Slade, she shrugged. "I'm all ears."

After detailing his plan, they agreed they should sleep on it, and go over it again in the morning.

His plan was also a bold one. And if it worked, they should have the outlaws in jail before dinner time. The element of surprise played in their favor.

Once back in town, they fell back into their hotel rooms, and both used the bathhouse in the back of the hotel. In the capacious dining room, he had a late-night dinner as he sat apart from Kate. Afterward, they called it a night, as they separately returned to their rooms.

Now, rising from the bed, he walked over to the washstand, blew out the candle, and walked back to the bed. Once again, he plopped onto the thin mattress, as he carefully reviewed the plan he'd outlined to Kate.

Slade was a cautious man, not anyone's fool. He couldn't bring the three outlaws in by himself, he knew that much. But with a woman, any woman by his side, he just didn't know.

In his estimation, Kate wasn't a wild woman. She had spunk and tenacity coupled with smarts, he'd give her that. And it showed when attacked by an armed man and surviving it. Most of all, she was right there when he needed it as he fled through the woods, with her rifle blazing away, covering his retreat.

With an audible sigh, he drew his blanket over himself and smiled as his thoughts revolved around his wife and son back home. It was a pleasurable memory; of time spent with Martha and John, his son, just before departing with Kate. Within a few minutes, as he turned on his side, he fell into a deep sleep.

In the early morning light, Larry Slade woke up hungry. He stood and stretched, and after dressing and strapping on his gun belt, he stepped up and stood in the second-floor window room and pulled open the curtains. Gazing up through the growing heat, the strong eastern winds, and the slowly rising sun, with its orange and crimson colors, he saw a clear blue sky. With no clouds in sight, it promised a hot and humid day.

He gazed out over the barren hills. To the east were the salt flats, and as his eyes dropped onto the busy streets, riders made their slow way through the dusty Main Street. Tumbleweeds tossed about by the winds crawled across the dirt-ridden sandy street, and open buckboards were full of families, rolls of concertina wire, and lumber, as they made their way out of town.

Turning his back to the window, Slade sauntered over to the chair and grabbed his hat. Just as he faced the door, he heard the door across from his room close loudly.

Slade nodded and arched an eyebrow. "She must be up and about too," he muttered.

Once he left his room, Slade donned his hat and ambled down to the dining room.

Slade opened the café door and stepped into the diner, stopping at the threshold. He made a quick scan of the interior. Sitting alone at a table was Kate Warne, just a few feet from him, waiting for her order, he guessed. Across the other end of the room, Sheriff Dan Clark was having breakfast with a deputy, a sloped-shouldered man he'd seen before, and believed was the one they called Slim at the shack last evening.

As Slade took a seat at an empty table at the other end from the sheriff, a pretty young waitress approached him, menu in hand. Not reading it, he ordered steak and eggs, taters, and hot coffee.

Waiting for his breakfast, Slade looked around the room once more. Meeting Kate's eyes, he tipped his hat and smiled. As she smiled back, she felt other eyes on her. She turned ever slowly and stopped when she spotted the sheriff staring at her, holding a cup of coffee, and smiling.

Without warning, Clark stood, wiped his mouth with a tablecloth, and started over to her table. Still looking at him, Kate smiled and waited as he approached.

Clark stopped close to Kate's chair. "I was about to go lookin' for ya, but here you are, young lady."

Kate asked, "Oh, why is that Sheriff?"

Clark, ever since he'd spoken to her, believed she may not have told him her entire story of why she was in town and asking about

Tucker. Something just didn't sit right with him. "I'm a little curious to know if you'd met Mr. Tucker yet."

"No, I haven't, I've put it off until today. Did some riding around your town, and I've been thinking of maybe calling this my home? It's a nice quiet town."

Frowning, Clark sensed a change come over the woman. Was she telling him the truth? "I see. Well, that it is … peaceful and quiet. You'd be welcomed into the community if you decide to stay."

"That's so kind, thank you Sheriff."

"You have a nice day young lady."

"Thank you."

As the sheriff walked back to his table, Slade kept an eye on him and his deputy, while keeping a hand on the butt of his gun. He'd heard their conversation and was inclined to believe something may have prompted the visit. What that could be, he didn't know. But his gut feeling was that the sheriff was just digging deeper into her story. Was the sheriff getting wise to her real agenda, or was it idle speculation on his part?

By tonight, it wouldn't matter one bit, Slade thought.

Once Sheriff Clark was seated, he turned to Deputy Slim Wilson. "Somethin' not sitting right with me 'bout that woman; I want you to keep an eye out for her and report back your observations."

Wilson stared briefly at Kate. She's pretty, he thought. Turning back to the sheriff, he said, "Yes, sir."

Slade, ever conscious of the conversation, was gazing at the sheriff's table, and out of the corner of his eye, he saw Wilson staring at Kate. Yeah, he thought, something's not right.

After breakfast, Slade and Kate cautiously locked themselves in her room. Slade closed the room's window and curtains.

The first order of business was the meeting Kate had with the sheriff. With Kate sitting on the chair, hands on her lap, Slade paced the floor, hands clasped behind him. Once he stopped, he asked, "What do you make of the sheriff's conversation, Kate?"

Kate leaned back in her chair. "I just don't know, Larry. Do you think he knows something?"

This could be a serious problem for both of them. He remembered as they came out of the dining room, that Deputy Wilson also stood and had followed Kate as she departed.

The troubling part was she had seen Wilson as he strode briskly past her on the hallway of the second floor. So, they were following her, not a good sign. Did they suspect him as well? He didn't think so; this whole thing was centered on her.

Was the sheriff being overly cautious of a new person in town? An unknown quanity he had to get a fix on before anything else happened to her or anyone else in town. Or was the sheriff just doing his job?

For a moment Slade didn't speak. "I think he's just trying to get a better handle on you," he finally said. "The lawman in him seems to think you could be trouble. You killed a man in your room and he thinks something else may come of it. I don't think there's anything else to this."

"Okay," she said, turning to face him as he stopped talking. "What now?"

A long sigh followed as Slade stared down at her. "Well, stay put here until we're ready to leave later on. It wouldn't do for you to be seen walking around town. After tonight, this won't matter anymore."

Kate frowned and looked down. As much as she hated to admit it, he was right. "I ... I think you're right."

"Good, let's talk about my plan."

It didn't take them long on deciding the course of action they would take. Once that was done, she slowly rose from her chair and walked him to the door. Opening the door, a crack, she peered up and down the hallway and didn't see anyone.

Slade started to the door and stopped. Standing still he gazed into her eyes, "I just..." he began, but she cut him off.

"I know," she said. "You're just looking out for my welfare. I thank you for that." She gently squeezed his hand, tilted her head to him, and held her stare for a moment, ever hopeful he'd kiss her. When the kiss didn't come, he slowly slipped out of the room making his way down onto Main Street. He had provisions to purchase for their plan.

Kate stood with her back to the door and gave thought to the kiss that wasn't. She wanted badly to be kissed by this remarkable man. Why he didn't was remarkable in itself ... married and proud of it. Will she ever meet someone like him? She could only hope.

At the hotel lobby, Slade noticed Deputy Wilson sitting, ostensibly reading a newspaper. As he strode past him, the deputy didn't pay much attention to him.

The hallway was dark as Slade and Kate carefully made their way out of their hotel rooms, and closing the doors behind them, they met in the center of the hallway and stared at each other for a second; she with a smile, and he with a frown.

Slade sauntered for the back of the hotel, as Kate followed. Down the back stairs, they made their silent way, not saying a word to each other until they would reach the stables and their horses; just as they'd planned.

A few minutes later, they reached the livery stables through the back dark alleyways, not meeting anyone along the way. All was still as the silence of the late evening reigned throughout the town.

Kate said, "We're in luck, Larry. No one is about this late at night."

Slade nodded and smiled.

Not typically a superstitious person, he still believed the element of surprise played in their favor. "That could well be a damn good omen, Kate."

Once they had their horses saddled, and leading their mounts, they walked behind the livery stables. Peering out into the darkness, Slade didn't see anyone. Once out of earshot, they mounted putting spurs to their mounts. Out through the cold dead of night, they rode, as the Pinkerton woman kept the pace set by Slade.

By the time they reached Tucker's shack and lying on the ground beside each other and while gazing down on the house, they saw by the bright light of the full moon, a buckboard sitting in front of the shack packed with several long logs, and two saddled horses tied behind it.

"Guess we arrived just in time," Kate said, observing the obvious.

Slade nodded. "I reckon," he replied, hunkering lower, not taking his eyes away from the house.

It occurred to Slade that maybe an hour may have passed when activity down at the shack picked up. The front door was thrown open and out first came the deputy named Slim, carrying a rifle. Seconds later, Tucker ambled out the door, closed the screen door, and made his way to the side of the buckboard.

Both of the outlaws stepped onto the wagon's seats, with Tucker doing the driving. Moments later the wagon was turned around, and they slowly made their way away from the shack.

Rising from the ground, both Slade and Kate ran to their horses as they followed the wagon. Five minutes later, he judged, out in the near distance he saw puffs of dust as he caught sight of the wagon; it was only a matter of hanging back and keeping a careful enough watch to avoid detection.

They rode in silence, each consumed with their thoughts. Each knowing that their plans could instantly turn to shit once the shooting started. And no matter how he looked at it, bullets were gonna fly.

The Overland Express Concord stagecoach built by the Abbot Downing Company of Concord New Hampshire, was old but still as sturdy as the day purchased, roughly six years ago, as it rumbled across the sand flats, its six-horse team kicking up dust and sand, all along the way.

The coach's leather window shades rolled closed prevented sand and trail dust from seeping into the passenger compartment. Without springs, the coach was suspended by old worn-out layers of leather straps. Painted two-tone red and black, with yellow painted wheels, the paint was fading and peeling away. Painted just above both doors in yellow was: *Overland Express and Mail Stage Line.*

Next to the stage driver was a guard sitting next to him with a shotgun and sitting atop of the stage facing the rear was another guard with a rifle on his lap. Two more guards rode inside the passenger compartment. An express box sat positioned down in the well, between the driver and the shotgun guard, beaming with the payroll shipment of forty-thousand dollars.

Deputy Ed Black, wearing a sweat-stained Confederate Cavalry hat, dark britches, rawhide chaps, shoulder-length rawhide jacket, and an oversized red bandana, had just positioned himself under the light of the full moon and about twenty miles out of Austin.

On his arrival, he removed his saddle, blanket, and bit from the horse, gave it a good whack on its rump, and watched as the horse galloped away. Placing the saddle in the middle of the trail, he removed his rifle from the scabbard, cradled it across his middle, and sat to wait for the stage to make its appearance.

The only thing moving in the vastness of the open flat country was the stage. Out in the far distance, a coyote howled. The land was desolate, with no trees in sight for miles. The chill night wind, only the desert can bring, whispered through the stage driver's sunburned face, bringing tears to his eyes as he wiped them with the sleeve of his coat.

Old man Tom McCoy chewing on a wad of smokeless tobacco and just at his prime of sixty-two grabbed hold of the reins of all four horses, as he leaned forward in his seat. This wasn't the first time he'd ridden the stage. He had eight years of experience, and only two holdups to brag about. The old Concord stagecoach creaked and swayed down the well-defined trail, under the wide and starry night sky.

The moonlit trail made it strikingly possible for McCoy to see the way ahead of him and to both sides of the trail. McCoy meandered straight down the trail. He knew up ahead a sharp turn came around a narrow bend. And he knew he had to slow down to negotiate it. Unable to see around the bend, he slowed almost to a crawl.

Suddenly, coming out of the turn, he pulled back on the reins, bringing the stage to an abrupt stop, and set the brakes, for a lone figure stood center of the trail, rifle cradled, and saddle on the ground. The shotgun guard stood, cocked back the two hammers, and pointed his weapon at the stranger. "What the hell, mister!" McCoy said. "What are you doing in the middle of the trail and at this time of night?"

Just then the two guards from the passenger compartment jumped out and leveled their rifles at the stranger and the guard on top of the stage, cocked back the hammer of his rifle and aimed it too at the tall stranger.

"I ain't a holdup man, mister," Ed Black roared out for all to listen. "Lost my horse to a gopher hole, back yonder had to put it out of its misery. Could use a ride to the town of Round Rock, or close by."

"Who are you, mister?" McCoy shouted down.

"I'm a town deputy sheriff," Black replied, slowly dropping his rifle to his side, and opening his coat enough so they could see his badge.

McCoy grunted and spit his chew out to the side of the stage. "Deputy, you say?"

"Yeah, that's right, how's about that ride?"

"Sure, tuck your belongings inside and make yourself comfortable. I couldn't leave a man out here stranded. We could use another gun though, in case we get into trouble, and such."

"Much obliged."

"Kate, stay back with the horses," Slade said. "Don't let anything spook 'em. I'll get over and see where they are setting up their ambush. This won't take long."

She replied almost in a whisper, "You best be coming back, I can't do this alone."

"Don't worry, I'll be right back."

Earlier they stopped far away from the outlaws when they saw the wagon pulling onto the side of the road, just enough so one could see it.

Slade waved his right hand at her, and with a sigh turned his back and proceeded to where the outlaws were setting up. Minutes later, just up ahead, he heard them talking. Slowly he crept low as an Injun would and saw them lugging the tree logs and placing them on the middle and sides of the trail.

Slade stopped and dropped to the ground, wondering how they planned to rush the stage. He figured they would come from both sides of the stage at once. It was what he planned to do with Kate.

Waiting, he got his answer. Just as they finished, Slim Wilson mounted his horse and rode across the trail, while Tucker also mounting stayed on his side. Slade noticed they were planning to rush from both sides. He smiled. Crawling away back the same way he'd come, he made it back to Kate's side.

"They are using the same plan as us," Slade said.

"We're still sticking to ours Larry?"

"Oh yeah," Slade replied. "Let's mount up, you take the other side of the trail and I'll stay this side. Ready, Kate?"

Kate drew her Colt, half-cocked it, and re-holstered it. "Let's go."

"Kate, make sure you put distance between you and the deputy. Once the shooting starts, that's our cue to engage."

"I'll be ready."

An hour later, as the two guards were fast asleep across from him, Deputy Ed Black drew his sidearm, clicked through the cylinder making sure six cartridges were loaded, and held it on his lap as he steadily watched the guards' movements.

Seconds passed, and as McCoy, the stage driver saw what he believed were felled logs across the trail he slowed and pulled up reins. Momentarily confused, he shook his head, and then seconds later, he recognized it for what it was. Immediately he scanned left and right of him. "Son of a bitch!" he yelled out, "It's a hold-up!"

Pulling the reins to the left he tried to go around but side logs kept him from that. He had no alternative but to bring the stage to a halt. Just then the shotgun guard raised his weapon and looking around wondered when the outlaws would make their appearance.

He didn't have long to wait!

This was Black's cue. Quickly he raised his Colt and fanned off two shots, instantly killing the sleeping guards. Black then aimed the gun at the top of the stage and fired off the remaining four shots killing the guard above him. That left the shotgun guard and the driver.

McCoy and the guard sitting beside him were confused, wondering where the loud gunshots came from, and wrote it off to the two guards in the passenger compartment who, in their haste, started shooting out into the night.

Quickly reloading, Black sat back to wait for his two partners.

Suddenly, from both sides of the stagecoach and firing in the air, Tucker and Wilson arrived at full gallop just as the shotgun guard aimed at the horsemen on his left and let fly with both barrels.

Wilson, unhurt from the blast, and drawing closer to the stage, fired off three gunshots of his own at the guard. Two rounds impacted squarely in the guard's side and one entered the side of his head as he was flung off the stage, landing with a dull thump and a large puff of dust.

Almost simultaneously, several things happened: Tucker arrived next and fired, wounding old man McCoy. Stopping in front of the stage, Tucker quickly yelled out, "Throw down the express box, old man!"

"Go to hell!"

"I'll bury you where you damn sit, hombre!" Tucker shouted, pointing his gun at McCoy's head.

However, suddenly forgotten was the express box, and the driver, as Tucker heard horse's hoofs from his right. Quickly turning his head to the noise, he caught sight of some rider hell-bent for leather approaching, while a bullet from Slade's gun sailed over Tucker's head. Just then, Ed Black jumped down from the stage and joined in the gunfight.

But, just as Black turned to face the rider to give cover to Tucker, Slade's horse got spooked, stopped, and rearing up on its back legs lashed out with fear. Slade, with a gun in hand, fired off a shot that dropped Black where he stood just as his horse dropped to all fours.

Putting spurs to his horse, he fired at Tucker, who had turned tail and galloped away. Slade clinched the reins between his teeth, cleared the spent cartridges, and reloaded his gun on the fly. Aiming carefully, he fired off two shots. One of his shots struck Tucker's horse, and both rider and horse went head over heels to the ground.

Meanwhile, from the other side of the trail by the stage, Wilson heard another horseman fast approaching his position. Wilson turned his horse facing whoever was approaching when through the moonlit night, the rider came into view.

Out of ammo from his sidearm, he removed his rifle from its scabbard, and did the unthinkable; he spurred his horse straight toward the unknown rider while working the rifle's lever-action, firing a continuous barrage of bullets.

Caught by surprise by the outlaw's daring move, Kate slid to the right side of her saddle, not affording the outlaw a clear target, and carefully aimed at him. With the moon highlighting the outlaw in a silhouette she fired once, twice three times, at the fast-approaching figure, and seconds later she heard a loud yelp, then Wilson fell off his saddle, as his empty horse galloped past her.

Kate came to a halt and slowly dismounting approached Wilson's body. Keeping her gun trained, she kicked the body once, with no movements. Keeling by the corpse, she saw where a bullet had plowed through his throat.

On the other side of the trail and far away from the stagecoach, Tucker, back on his feet, came up shooting just as Slade drew to a stop and dismounted. Slowly Slade walked toward Tucker, not taking any cover since there was none, and steadily fired his gun.

Tucker's rounds landed wide of Slade, too shaky to take careful aim when his gun clicked on empty. It was at that moment when two of Slade's rounds struck Tucker almost in the center of his chest that threw him back, dead before he hit the ground.

Later, Slade found Tucker's buckboard, and with the help of old man McCoy, they loaded the bodies. McCoy had only suffered a flesh wound and had stopped the bleeding. Back on the stage, he set off for Round Rock. On the buckboard, both Slade and Warne sat side by side, with Slade on the reins they set off after the stage.

# CHAPTER 9

# MAJOR JOHN SALMON FORD
# NICKNAME *"RIP"*

*Slade Ranch, Blanco, Texas,*
*Mid-November 1859*

Larry Slade and his wife Martha leaned on the corral fencing, watching their now fifteen-year-old son John try to break in a fresh horse. Twice he was bucked off, and twice he got back on. In the past, Larry was the one to bronco the horses, breaking them in to sell to the U.S. Calvary. But now those duties were turned over to his six-foot-tall son, with a few other ranch hands.

*Fifteen,* he remembered, as his mind traveled back when he, at the same age as John, marched off to fight in the Texas Revolution or as some would later call the War of Texas Independence. It was in September 1835 when he set off and served until the war's end in 1836.

He vividly remembered hearing stories from other Texans about Stephen Austin, who in 1826 led a militia in aiding the Mexican military in suppressing the Fredonian Rebellion group in an attempt at securing independence from Mexico by settlers around Nacogdoches, and he always wanted to get involved with the adventure and the rebellion.

When Santa Anna, the dictator of Mexico, along with his Army of Operations, began to reassert central control over Texas, Santa Anna, Larry sent in three to five hundred troops to San Antonio.

Slade reminisced as he traveled back in time and smiled, for he remembered the first of several battles he joined that would lead to the full-scale rebellion on the part of the Texan revolutionaries.

His first involved skirmish came in October 1835, when Mexican soldiers moved on Gonzales to take possession of one cannon offered previously to the town, by Mexico. He along with eighteen Texan forces halted the Mexican advance at the Guadalupe River.

When the Texanican forces out-numbered the Mexican troops he, and the rest of Texanican militiamen attacked the Mexicans with a cry that echoed through their ranks of "come and take it!" forcing the Mexican army back to San Antonio. However, the rebellious Texans pressed their attack and soon captured San Antonio.

If that doesn't beat all, he remembered saying, all for a damn cannon!

His memories rambled on as he stood there, paying no heed to anyone around him, as if he was the only person there, with no ambient sounds to distract him.

In mid-October 1835, when Austin began the siege of San Antonio, he was pulled into that as well. He remembered the battle over a mule train where he was wounded, as two bullets struck his chest, and one caught his right leg. He was hospitalized for over a month, missing out on the taking of San Antonio.

During the first part of 1836, right after he was pronounced fit for duty again, Slade was asked to join a band of Texas Rangers to patrol along the Rio Grande River and the town of Victoria.

Once again, he was wounded in the battle at San Patricio. And soon thereafter, he along with the other Rangers heard of the fall of the valiant defenders at the Alamo in the siege by the Mexicans where 200 Texans, along with Colonel William Travis, Davey Crockett, and Jim Bowie met their deaths.

Besides the war, in 1858 he recalled sitting in a restaurant in San Antonio, reading a newspaper article about a certain young lady named Kate Warne that caught his eye and smiled. According to the article, The Pinkerton Detective Agency assigned Warne to the Adams Express Company in an embezzlement case.

During her subsequent investigation, she was successful in gaining valuable evidence against a Mr. Maroney who stole fifty-thousand dollars. With Warne's help, thirty-nine thousand dollars were recovered.

Shaking off the memories, he gazed over at his wife and smiled. Martha gazed at her husband standing by her side and saw that faraway look he usually had when his mind would drift back to his war days and his time as a Texas Ranger.

Her husband, now thirty-eight, was retired and building up their ranch. Her greatest fear she maintained, was the possibility Larry would yet again volunteer as a Texas Ranger.

Martha read the newspaper headlines and stories relating to tension between the slave and the Free States in the Union, as they were attempting to maintain the balance between the opposing viewpoints. She knew Texas was admitted to the United States as a slave state, and fear of civil war hung in the balance. She knew Larry was concerned about it too. They would sit and talk about it later. Her one hope was that he wouldn't pack up and leave at the mention of a potential war.

With a sigh, however, she acknowledged to herself that for the moment they were safe. She knew of course, that at any moment everything could change at the drop of a hat.

Now that his son had finished two other horses, it was time for a trail drive to Galveston to sell them to the U.S. Calvary. However, a series of events would curtail his plans, for little did he know, he would shortly be commissioned again to the Texas Rangers.

The sun was up over the horizon and with the Texan fall being short and sweet, it brought crisp cool winds that caressed their faces while Larry read a newspaper and Martha Slade sat knitting on the veranda. Their conversation turned toward the civil unrest and a war that could pit the North and the South against each other over the matter of slavery.

"I don't think Texas will join in the fight, but times are a changing, Martha. I just don't know if war is the answer."

It was a question she'd put to her husband earlier in their conversation. "I do believe Texas will be put to the test," Martha responded, "and eventually, she'll join in if it comes to war."

"I think you may be right, honey."

Young John walked onto the porch and into the middle of his parent's conversation. Having fixed some sandwiches for himself, he leaned up against the porch railing, and munching on a sandwich, he said, "If it comes to war, I think I'll do my duty and join, Dad, Mom."

"There won't be any time for that, John," Larry said. "We need you here at the ranch. Soon, you're going to take over for me, and I can't afford you going off to a war that won't last but a month of Sundays."

Larry understood his son's eagerness to set off on his own. The sense of adventure was already calling out to him, as it did to him so many years ago.

Then he turned his head and stared hard out over the horizon. Something caught his attention. With a keen sense of hearing, he heard the faint galloping horses' hooves far in the distance. And then, with the sun behind them, he saw just over the horizon dust sweeping across the dry trail that led to the ranch.

John's eyes flashed toward his father. "I hear it too, Dad. Sounds like one rider."

Suddenly, as Larry's gaze lingered on the rider fast approaching the house, gradually, the man came into full view. Both John and his father relaxed, recognizing who it was. It was Pete Jenkins, one of his ranch hands he'd placed out beyond the spread to warn off strangers or Indians that might be approaching.

Without turning toward his son, the father said, "John, go fetch my guns, wear yours as well. If I'm not mistaken, we may have visitors before too long."

A few minutes later, the rider reined up. Jenkins climbed down out of the saddle, removed his hat, and dusted the trail dust off his rawhide chaps and shirt. Stepping onto the veranda, and addressing his boss, Jenkins said, "Sir, two riders are approaching."

"Did you recognize them, Pete?" Slade asked.

"No, sir, I can't say that I have," Jenkins replied. "But I could be mistaken."

"Good, Pete, thank you. On second thought, grab two ranch hands and have 'em close to the house, in case of trouble."

Jenkins nodded and walked away to the bunk house.

The two riders came into view just as they topped the crest of the hill overlooking the ranch less than a quarter-mile away. Larry and John were still seated on the veranda, while Martha went to prepare a fresh pot of coffee.

They rode high in the saddle, Larry observed, and at a slow and steady gait, down the dust-laden path. Larry was feeling a familiar itch in the back of his neck, for he thought he may know one of the riders.

Moments later, with Larry standing on the veranda, John instinctively positioned himself by his father's side and slightly to his right rear with his gun hand clear for a quick draw in the event of trouble.

The two riders came to a stop in front of the house. The tall, six-foot man on his right with penetrating black eyes stared down at Larry and his son with a semblance of a smile. With a long thick mustache dropping past his chin, with flakes of graying long hair that draped his shoulder, Slade knew the man, and he too smiled.

Slade immediately recognized the tall man having served with William G.Tobin, for a spell in 1855 and '56, ranging down in San Antonio, chasing after Mexican bandits. But after a long conversation with Tobin, he told Slade that he was quitting the Rangers as a position as city marshal in San Antonio had opened up. That was the last he'd seen of him until today.

"Bill Tobin, as I live and breathe," Larry said. "Get down the both of you and let's get some coffee and apple pie in ya before you say what ya came to say."

Off his horse, Tobin approached Slade. He removed his sweat-stained hat and greeted the ex-Texas Ranger with a solid handgrip while looking Slade square in the eyes. "You're a hard man to find, Larry."

"Apparently not hard enough," Slade said smiling.

"Reckon so, my sidekick is Lieutenant Richard McAdams," Tobin said, "We've come a long way to see ya."

"Lieutenant, glad to meet you," Slade said, glancing over at McAdams.

"My pleasure sir," McAdams said, "heard a lot about you."

"Well, let's get inside," Slade told them. "John here, is my son. John, please take their horses into the barn."

Handing their horses' reins to the boy, they followed Slade into the house. As they entered, Tobin's mentioned the resemblance between father and son.

Slade replied with a grin, "Yeah, we get that a lot."

With his second cup of coffee and a second serving of Martha's apple pie, they sat around the dining table; Tobin on the left and McAdams on the right. Slade faced Tobin with John on his left, facing them across the table. Martha, her hair done up in a knot, sat in a corner knitting but paid close attention to what they would say. Her eyes roamed from Tobin to her husband, then John, in anticipation.

It was Tobin who broke the momentary silence.

"Larry, I'm a Texas Ranger once again. I hold the rank of Captain. Our fifty-three State troops of Texas Rangers are commanded by Captain John S. Ford."

Here he paused.

Slade's eyes widened, nodding.

Slade remembered Captain Ford who enlisted in John Coffee Hay's regiment of Texas Mounted Rifles, where he made the rank of lieutenant, and served, just like him, in the Mexican War between the United States and Mexico from 1846 to '48. Slade heard that Ford and Robert Neighbors later began exploring the country between San Antonio and El Paso, which later became known as the Ford and Neighbors Trail. And he knew how Ford got the nickname of 'Rip.'

Slade nodded. "The one called Rip. I've heard of him."

In her corner, Martha did not turn from her knitting, but Larry saw her shoulders lower slightly with an audible sigh, maybe in disappointment, for she immediately knew they wanted her husband back in service. And if that was the case, nothing she would say would make him change his mind. He would be leaving with them.

Tobin continued. "That's him, all right. He's the Senior Captain in the State troops. On command from Governor Runnel, the Rangers have been sent to the Rio Grande where we joined operations with Captain George Stoneman of the 2nd Cavalry in quelling and removing a Mexican named Juan Cortina." Here he paused once again.

Larry Slade squinted and licked his lips. He stared at his wife and son and saw the disapproval glances they sent his way. Deep down in his soul, Slade knew he couldn't and wouldn't say no, and his family knew that from the get-go.

"Why is he called Rip?" John asked.

Larry turned to his son. "During the Mexican War, Ford received the nickname RIP for his peculiarity of including the words 'Rest In Peace,' after every name when he composed his company's casualty list."

Captain Tobin reached into his jacket and came away with a sealed envelope. "This is from Captain Ford," he said, handing it across the dining table.

With the envelope in hand, Slade broke the wax seal, opened it, and extracted a one-page letter. He scanned it briefly. And then he scratched his chin and read the letter word for word. After a minute, Slade shook his head and let the letter drop on the table.

Glancing at Tobin, Slade said, "I'm gonna have to think about this."

"From my understanding, Larry," Tobin said in a hushed voice. "It isn't an invitation."

"I gathered that from the letter," Slade said, staring at Tobin. "*Commanded* is the right word. He's given me the rank of captain and a six-man team of Rangers. I'll have my orders the moment I report in for duty."

Slade paused and then said, "You'll find sleeping accommodations over at the bunkhouse.

The next morning, Larry Slade woke out of a nightmarish sleep.

Slade saw himself dying at the hands of a pack of Mexicans and Indians. Both groups wanting his scalp as they tied him spread eagle on the ground, and his body was on fire! Then he realized where he was. From the perch on the edge of his bed, he heard Martha waking.

Martha Slade woke suddenly by his side. It was dark in the bedroom. She then blinked and turned to her husband.

"Your dreams are going to be the death of you, dear."

"I reckon, honey."

Getting his clothes on, he slipped into his boots and headed to the kitchen to put on a fresh pot of coffee.

Twenty minutes later, with the sun rising, he packed his bedroll and headed to the stables. He was met by his son, who had saddled his father's horse.

"Y'all up and bright and early this morning son. I see you couldn't sleep either."

"To be honest, Father," the young Slade said, "I haven't slept since you decided to leave with the Rangers. I was hoping maybe I could come with you."

The father shrugged. "Where I go son, I can't take you with me, besides I need you here with your mother and the ranch. You're the boss now, at least until I return."

"And how long will that be?" the young man asked.

"I don't know. A few weeks or two months, but I will return."

"I'll hold you to that, Dad!"

After a hearty breakfast, and kissing his wife goodbye, the three gradually disappeared over the horizon.

# CHAPTER 10

## JUAN (CHENO) CORTINA
## THE MEXICAN BANDIT

On the afternoon of their sixth day of travel, the three horsemen coming in from the north topped a hill overlooking the Rio Grande River and Fort Brown just on the outskirts of the Texas town of Matamoros, as the slow-moving waterway meandered around curves from side to side.

They halted, as Larry Slade glanced past the town onto the river, and into the Mexican city of Matamoros, on the opposite shore.

Slade glanced to his left. Out in the near distance he saw a huge, enclosed fortress. Turning to Tobin, he asked, "Is that an Army post?"

"Yes, that's Fort Brown," Tobin said. "It's commanded by Major Samuel Heintzelman who rode in from San Antonio to take command of troops from George Stoneman of the 2nd U.S. Cavalry Brigade. He coordinated all armed groups, and his orders were to put an end to the Cortina threat. With Major Ford's Texas Rangers of fifty-three ... ah, correction, fifty-four with you ... we aim to do just that."

Slade wasn't that interested in who commanded what, if he was given clear orders regarding what was expected of him. "The Fort doesn't look old," Slade said, more curious about its origin than anything else. "What can you tell me about it?"

Dismounting, Lieutenant Richard McAdams along with Slade and Tobin took some time to rest and dismounted. Pulling their canteens from their saddle-horns, they flushed the trail dust off their faces and gave their horses water which they poured into their hats.

Moments later, Captain Tobin replied to Slade's query. "From little that I've gathered, it was named Fort Texas when the U.S. Forces of Occupation arrived on the Rio Grande in '46. Originally, the earthen star fort was constructed on an 800-yard perimeter, with six bastions, a wall more than nine feet high, and surrounded by a ditch as you can see; fifteen feet deep and twenty feet wide. It was later named Fort Brown, when the commander, Major Jacob Brown died and was buried on the premises."

Slade, casting his gaze at the fort's construction marveled at the engineers who had the foresight to create such a bastion of protection. "I see a brick wall."

"That was built back in '48," Tobin replied, "and was called the Quarter Master's Fence, which as you can see from up here, several quarters for officers and enlisted men were constructed."

"And what of the town of Matamoros ... something we should be worried about?" Slade asked.

"It's just a sleepy little border town," Tobin replied, "with white tents and not much else. However, on the other side of the Rio Grande, the city of Matamoros has a population of roughly thirty thousand Mexicans, with a standing Army. The town is a boat transport hub."

"Interesting," Slade commented. Most of the U.S. Army forts he'd encountered through the years weren't nearly as solidly built as Fort Brown, he mused.

"Well, gents, let's mount up, we don't have that far to ride," Tobin said.

With the sun setting in the west, with an orange ball hanging low in the sky, they were sitting on the open porch of Major John (RIP) Ford's cabin office. Slade was with Major Ford, along with Captain

William Tobin, after enjoying a steak dinner with baked beans and corn muffins.

After finishing their late evening meal in the major's sumptuous dining room, they parted for the porch to discuss their upcoming battle plans, as all three held onto mugs of steaming hot coffee.

Once they were seated, they lit their cigars and enjoyed the cool night breeze. Major Ford frowned. "You arrived just in time, Captain Slade. But before I proceed as to why you're here, I'd like to give you a little background on Major Heintzelman. I was ordered by Governor Hardin Runnels to report here and combine my Rangers with that of Heintzelman's forces."

Ford paused to inhale his cigar smoke, and exhaling, he continued. "There is a history between him and a bandit named Cortina. When Heintzelman moved the garrison from Fort Ringgold from Rio Grande City, it prompted Juan Chena Cortina, with a band of 450 Mexicans to attack Rio Grande City and all along the Rio Grande Valley from Laredo to the Gulf of Mexico."

Slade was astonished to learn that no troops were left behind to safeguard Fort Ringgold. "So, there was no army left at Fort Ringgold to stop them?"

"None," Ford replied. "Along the fifty-mile march from Fort Ringgold, we encountered many acts of vandalism ... houses had been robbed and torched, fences burned, and its inhabitants fled for their lives. Cortina had committed these outrageous acts, and he wasn't going to get away with it."

After a brief pause, Ford continued. "Yesterday, the 25th of December, we got word that Cortina was camped on the main street of Rio Grande City. Heintzelman plans on marching against Cortina and we have orders to leave this evening. Mount-up time is nine, o'clock."

"So, I don't have too much time to get acquainted with my six-man team of Rangers," Larry Slade said stubbing out his cigar. "What's the order of battle?"

Major Ford glanced at the two men, and in a somber tone of voice replied, "My Rangers are to left flank Cortina's forward forces from a hill overlooking the city of Rio Grande, while Major Heintzelman would approach with artillery pieces at dawn tomorrow on Cortina's right flank. Hopefully, we can drive Cortina and his men back into Mexico."

"And what part do my Rangers and I play?" Slade asked.

Ford cleared his throat. "I was getting to that. You're to conduct a reconnoitering party, meet and attack Cortina's advance force denying them access to the battlefield before they try to gain ground in front of the Rangers and Heitzelman's position. We need someone with your battle expertise and courage under fire to accomplish this task ... that's why I chose you. I saw first-hand what you're capable of Larry, and you're the sort of man and leader I need."

Slade studied him intently for a moment. It took a lot to shock Slade at this point in his life. He'd been involved in several battles and came out with his life, along with a few wounds here and there.

Then he said, "So, I have no choice in the matter."

"Oh, my friend, yes you do," Ford replied. "You can go on home and be with your family, but damn it man, I need you here and so does Texas."

"Fair enough, major," Slade pronounced. "I'll stay ... for now. But I need to ask, what prompted Cortina to attack Rio Grande City in the first place?"

"I'll let McAdams answer that, Larry."

They both turned toward the lieutenant, who was sipping on his coffee.

"Last week," McAdams began, "I went to the town of Brownsville and came up with an interesting bit of information. I reported this to Major Heintzelman. In my report, I found that on July 13th, the Brownsville town marshal Robert Shears was shot in the arm by Juan Cortina for brutalizing his former sixty-year ranch hand, who was reportedly drunk and causing a scene in some coffee shop. According to the marshal, Cortina just happened to pass by and asked if he could handle the situation. The marshal said, in no uncertain terms, *"What is it to you, you damned Mexican?"*

A brief pause, as the lieutenant sipped his coffee again.

"Here it gets sticky in the telling," McAdams continued. "According to the Marshal, Cortina drew and fired a warning shot high above them. It was at this point, that the witnesses differ in the telling. Marshal Shears did not stop brutalizing the ranch hand and Cortina shot Shears in the arm. Cortina grabbed his ranch hand and once he had him in the saddle, they both rode hard and fast out of town."

Here Captain Ford interjected. "With tensions increasing between Cortina and the town's authorities, on September 28th, Cortina raided and occupied the town with a band of between forty to eighty men. Once he occupied Brownsville, Cortina issued a proclamation. I secured a copy and you can read it at your leisure. Cortina retained control over Brownsville until the 30th of September, when the Brownsville townsfolk formed a twenty-man group to fight Cortina's force."

There came a brief pause as if Ford was searching for just the right words.

"They were called the Brownsville Tigers," he continued. "Once the Tigers learned that Cortina would be staying at his mother's ranch in the nearby town of Santa Rita, they set about to attack him there. But the fight was one-sided and unfortunately for the Tigers they fled in retreat from Cortina's forces. As a matter of fact, the Tigers will be under my command tomorrow. They want to get their pound of flesh."

"Sounds like a dangerous hombre to me," Slade said. "It's always good to know the enemy you're about to do battle with. Thank you for the update."

Larry Slade had no time for a bunk to catch some sleep, and after the long ride here, he was still exhausted.

And the funny part about it was, Slade thought, shaking his head, he wasn't given a room or a tent to ready himself for the fifty-mile ride to Brownsville. After leaving Ford's place, he saddled up and sought out his team of Rangers.

The wind was light and the night clear and chilly, as he set out for the Ranger encampment.

He found them, all six of them around a large campfire, situated by the side of a small creek. They had a pot of coffee on, as they sat around the fire, eating their dinner of hot beans and bacon. They had their horses tied to a picket line, and to this Slade led his horse.

Dismounting with his back to the group, he unhitched the straps to the saddle and removing it placed it on the ground next to him. As he grabbed a small brush from his saddle bags, he began brushing the dirt off his horse.

From the campfire, the six Rangers looked curiously on, wondering who the hell asked the stranger to park his horse with the rest of them.

"Stranger," one of the Rangers spoke up, "Who and what do you think you're doing?"

Not turning around, still brushing his horse, Slade asked. "You six Rangers ... waiting on your commander?"

"Yes, that's right. But ..." a short stubby Ranger began.

Turning slowly around Slade interrupted the Ranger. "I'm Captain Slade, your commander."

Another of the Rangers, a tall, dark-skinned, bearded fellow with a long thick mustache, wearing a dirty white shirt over a tan vest, red bandana around his neck, tan trousers and boots, and a high holstered gun, rose and approached Slade. Wearing a frown, he asked, "Are you ... Larry Slade, the famous Indian fighter back in '36 ridden with the Cherokee Rangers? I've heard stories about ya, sir."

Approaching the Ranger, Slade stopped as the other men, all similarly dressed, rose and came to see their new commander. The bearded Ranger stopped in front of his Captain and extended his hand. "It's an honor meeting you, Captain Slade. I'm Sergeant Frank Hammer, ranking enlisted, and these behind me are the handpicked Rangers assigned to you by Captain Tobin."

The two men, followed by the other Rangers, walked back to the campfire. Once Slade and the rest sat by the fire, Slade said, "Yeah, well, Sergeant Hammer, I hope those stories you've heard weren't too exaggerated."

"Don't rightly know, sir," Hammer said with a slight grin. "Read them in the newspapers. But they sure caught my fancy."

Slade laughed and refrained from asking questions and wondered about the stories written about him, and who did the telling. "I see, so it would seem that I've made the papers."

Captain Slade caught them staring at him. All probably imagining what they were going to do in the next day or so.

Slade closed his eyes, and let his body relax for a moment. Opening them he said, "On the trail, I hope to get better acquainted with you Rangers. But for now, I need to know if anyone here has any knowledge of the terrain around Rio Grande City, I need a forward man for the job."

"We all do, sir. We hunt in the woods and fish in the river."

Slade paused. "Can I get a small stick?"

Once a stick was given to him, Slade said, "All right, gather closer, gents, and I'll illustrate our battle formation."

Raising his head, Slade gazed at each one of his men. With the stick, he drew a circle on the ground. "According to Major Ford, his Rangers will turn on Cortina's left flank, here." Slade picked up a small pebble and placed it where he struck the stick in.

Slade looked up and stared at the team making sure they understood. "Major Heintzelman with the US Army behind him would approach with his 40 pounders at dawn, here, on the right flank."

Again, Slade poked the stick in the ground on his right side and placed another pebble on the spot.

Captain Slade continued. "Their objective is to corral the Mexican force and wipe them out. But I see a flaw in the plan—the Rio Grande—we have no force there to stop them from fleeing across the river back into Mexico. If they flee into the river, we will chase and kill as many as we can."

Sergeant Hammer raised his hand, stroking his beard, and asked the most pressing question. "What of us, Captain? What are we to do?"

Slade blinked. He was waiting for that question to pop up. "We are ordered to conduct a reconnoitering force on the right flank. Stop and attack any force trying to gain ground behind our forces, here." Once again with the stick, he stuck it into the ground on his right side just by Ford's position.

A cough from one of the Rangers filled the empty silence.

That seemed to get a reaction from Sergeant Hammer who stood and paced a moment. "Captain, if I may be so bold, all seven of us?" Hammer asked slightly perplexed. "That's a mighty tall order, I dare say, Captain."

Slade rose, turned facing toward his horse, and turned back around. "No doubt it's fraught with danger and we could lose one or two Rangers. However, we're here to settle this once and for all. I for one don't want to come back here anytime soon."

When Slade was finished all stood and without a word from their Captain, they began to clear the camp and prepared for the long march to Brownsville.

# CHAPTER 11

# BATTLE
# OF
# RIO GRANDE CITY

*Rio Grande City, Texas*
*December 27, 1859*

The long march was uneventful, but during that time Larry Slade became acquainted with his six Rangers. He found that all were accomplished woodsmen, effective sharpshooters and Indian fighters. Captain Tobin, Slade realized, had chosen well. His six Rangers were to branch off toward the river and move forward into Cortina's force on their arrival.

Just before dawn, the standing force of U.S. Army regulars, supported by the Texas Rangers, totaling three-hundred-forty-eight men, joined by the twenty-man Brownsville Tigers, had reached a hill overlooking Rio Grande City. Major Heintzelman with his forty-pounders immediately broke away from the main force and moved toward the right flank, leaving Ford's Rangers to attack at daylight.

Major Ford glanced up to the skies and was aware of the weather holding. No bitter snow or winter's cold winds would affect the forthcoming battle, but a heavy fog was beginning to roll in that could be troubling. The Major waited until Heintzelman's artillery was set up and eagerly anticipated the first signs of daylight.

Twenty minutes later, an advance scout from Major Heintzelman's regulars, rode hard and fast into Major Ford's Texas Rangers position on the hill.

At full gallop, the trooper dismounted on the fly, came to a halt besides some Rangers and asked for Major Ford.

Larry Slade and the Texas Rangers along with some of the Brownsville Tigers swarmed around the trooper.

Breaking through the gathered Rangers, Major Ford came striding through and stopped in front of the newcomer. Ford cocked an eyebrow and said wryly, "I'm Major Ford, trooper, what do you have for me?"

"Sir, I'm Corporal Miller," he said as he looked at Major Ford, "I was ordered by Major Heintzelman to scout ahead and find Cortina's camp. The Major wanted me to pass on the information onto you, sir."

Slade, the closest to Miller, a small man with a broken nose, long flowing dirty blond hair under his hat, overheard his statement and waited for the Major's reply.

Ford cocked his head to one side and said, "What's the information?"

Stifling a yawn, Miller gazed at those around him, saying, "Sorry, sir. I've been up most of the night."

Major Ford placed one hand on Miller's shoulder. "Take your time son, but make it quick, the sun is about to rise."

When Miller spoke, his voice was low. "Yes, sir, I found out that Cortina is camped on the main street of Rio Grande City." Here he paused for a moment. "He has a huge number of Mexicans in his force. I found his artillery pieces on the Roma Road, and under a cloud of thick fog. Major Heintzelman ordered Lieutenant Fry and his detachment of Army regulars to silence them. Ringgold Barracks has a small contingent of Mexicans as well."

Ford glanced at his men; he had a sense of foreboding. They weren't expecting a huge Mexican force. Things had changed for the worst. "I see, do you know about how many are in the enemy's force?"

"Just a guess, sir, I'd say five, six hundred," Miller replied.

There were murmurings around the cluster of men, with uncharacteristically restless nods. Slade was among those, but outwardly he showed no signs of distress. He'd been in battles with overwhelming odds and had come up the victor.

"Do you have anything else to add, Corporal?" Ford asked.

"No, sir."

"Head on back to your company, we'll take it from here."

Corporal Miller grabbed the reins of his horse, jumped on the saddle, turned his horse back around and galloped away.

Ford glanced around him. "Are Captain Tobin and Captain Slade here?" Ford asked.

Moments later, both Slade and Tobin broke from the crowd and stood in front of the Major.

"Gents, nothing's changed," Ford began, his voice confident, self-assured that things will turn out in their favor. He reached for the brim of his hat, removed it, and continued. "I'll start the attack down from this hill and drive Cortina's forces to the left to the Rio Grande. You're with me, Captain Tobin, along with the Tigers. Captain Slade, the moment I start the attack, move your Rangers to the right, stop and drive away any enemy reconnoitering party. Together we have to drive them into the river."

Slade and Tobin stared at each other for a moment and flicked the brim of their hats as if to say good luck or goodbye.

Ten minutes later, Slade and his six Rangers, mounted up and set off down the hill, while Ford and Tobin waited for the first signs of daylight.

Just as he finished organizing his force, Major Ford sat in his saddle watching the orange, yellows, and purple watercolors, as the sun crept through the first shades of daylight. He hoped this wouldn't be the last sunrise he was to ever witness. To his men, he said, in a loud even commanding voice, "Let's ride, men!"

This was the start of the battle!

Armed with their sidearms, they rode at full gallop down the hill. While out in the near distance, cannon fire was heard, as Major

Heintzelman's artillery began their bombardment on the Mexican force and into Fort Ringgold. Minutes later, out by Roma Road, an answering volley of cannon shot was heard loud and clear, as Cortina's big guns opened up on Ford's Rangers.

The enemy cannons laid out a deadly barrage of fire that instantly killed several Rangers to the rear of his force. But that didn't stop Ford's advance, as he drove through toward Cortina's picket.

Moments later Cortina's cavalry charged Ford's Rangers!

Two miles from Ford's position, out on Roma Road, Lieutenant Fry's troopers gained sight of Cortina's cannons through the forest of tall trees and heavy fog. There were three forty-pounders each with four men operating them, with a small guard of five Mexicans keeping watch behind them.

Suddenly, thunder roared, and they saw two of the cannons open fire, as a thick wall of white smoke hung in the air.

Fry knew there was no way he could attack them without losing several troopers in the clash. Assessing his situation, he ordered his men to ride around and come up behind them. It was a much better plan than attacking straight on.

They rode slowly through the thick forest of trees as the dense fog prevented fast riding when finally, they came around to the Mexicans' rear. Way out in front of Fry and his men was a four-foot-tall barricade. They drew their guns and in a column of two's they galloped hard, and just before reaching the wall their horses jumped the barricade. With Fly and his top sergeant first over the imposing obstacle, the sergeant was shot off his horse. Fry taking a quick glance behind, saw the sergeant get back on his feet.

Straight through the guards they charged, one, two, and three Mexicans fell to the onslaught of fire from the Army regulars, and then they aimed their fire on those working the cannons. At the first sight of the American force, the Mexican soldiers ran away, as Fry's troopers gave chase. They heard them yelling out, *"No me mates, no me mates!"* Don't kill me!

All were killed, effectively silencing their cannons.

Fry's top sergeant located a horse, stripped the dead horse of his saddle, bags, and rifle, saddled the mount, and was back with Fry's troopers.

With the fight over, Fry and his regulars not suffering any casualties galloped hard and fast toward Major Heintzelman's forces.

Larry Slade, tall, strong, and riding high in the saddle kept his eyes ever forward. They rode slowly and silently through the forest line. The fog was thickening as he and his Texas Rangers called a halt.

Out on the battlefield, they heard continuous cannon and small arms fire, but suddenly, the cannon fire ceased, though the gunfire remained steady.

Moments later from the fog bank toward his left, Slade heard the faint sounds of a horse moving steadily toward their position. With him being on the frontline of his Rangers, he drew his gun, ordered his men to arms and watched for an attack to come through the fog.

A minute later, a bird whistle sounded through the murkiness. It was the signal of Slade's advance scout. A return call sounded from the ranks of the Rangers, the okay signal.

Then, emerging through the fog rode his scout as Slade and his Rangers holstered their guns.

Coming to halt beside his Captain, Ranger Ira Wilson gave his observations. "Sir, Cortina's forces are stopped a quarter of a mile up the road. I counted about forty to fifty men."

"Reckon there's more than enough for us Rangers," Slade said as a grin creased his lips.

Dismounting Slade rallied his troops around him. Picking up a small stick, he said, "This is how I plan to attack, men. We'll form a Vwedge formation, which I will lead. Let's keep the wedge fairly wide and will cut 'em down before they know death is upon 'em!"

A moment of silence passed through them and then they nodded their acknowledgment.

"Check your loads, men," Slade ordered, "we may not get a chance later."

One at a time, Slade drew all three of his 1851 Colt single action revolvers, spun the cylinders making sure they were fully loaded and returned them to their holsters.

"Let's mount up, we may have the advantage here," Slade said in a low voice and added, "We do the devil's work this morning, men."

They moved at a steady gait, guns drawn in Slade's wedge formation and the leading Rangers made out the Mexicans sitting on the ground.

Suddenly, Captain Slade yelled, "Charge!" and at full gallop they rushed straight into the Mexicans.

Slowly, a forward lead Mexican sounded the alarm, but too late, the Americans were already breathing right down their necks.

The bloodletting had begun!

# CHAPTER 12

# BATTLE
# AFTERMATH

The fog was thinning; daylight was creeping through the overcast skies as down the hill at a full gallop rode the three-hundred-forty-eight-man force of Major Ford and Captain Tobin's Texas Rangers and the Brownsville Tigers! Most drew their sidearms while others their rifles as they spurred on their mounts, firing their weapons without the advantage of aiming first.

Up the hill to meet them head-on, at a steady gait, rode Cortina's four hundred plus cavalrymen. Moments later, Cortina himself, riding at the head of his force, ordered his forward cavalrymen to dismount and from a distance of six hundred yards, they unleashed a barrage of rifle fire into the advancing American force. However, most of the volley whizzed over the Rangers' heads.

From atop his horse, Cortina spurring on his force shouted, "Mueran los gringos!" as he ordered his force to charge. With wild shouts and war whoops the Mexicans advanced on the American forces.

Out on the frontline, Ford spurring his horse over the crackle of gunfire made out the Mexicans' cry of Death to the Americans! *Yeah, we'll see about that*, he thought. With two or three of Ford's Rangers falling off their mounts from the hail of bullets, the undaunted Texans continued the advance.

Captain Tobin riding just behind Ford suddenly felt a bullet graze his forehead, eliciting a scream as moments later blood seeped down the side of his head and his eye, while another round tore into his right shoulder, nearly pulling him off his saddle.

Suddenly, both forces met head-on!

Many Mexicans and Americans fell dead onto the battlefield; mixed with the dead lay the dead or dying horses, while valuable equipment and weapons lay strewn all over the ground. The haunting moans of the dying were heard throughout. The charge took a heavy toll on the Mexicans as Cortina, knowing the American forces had turned the tide against him, ordered a retreat.

Those of Cortina's cavalrymen still mounted, turned their horses and headed down the hill. A few on foot stopped to reload, which was a mistake as one, then several other Mexicans fell to the bullets of the Texas Rangers.

Ford knew a quarter of a mile separated the Mexicans from the Rio Grande, towards which they were hard riding. *Damn*, he thought, *I need to cut down his force before they reach the river.* Then riding hell-bent for leather, he shouted, "On men, time to teach these Mexicans a lesson!"

Onward Ford edged, when on his left, he spied Mexican soldiers, some on horseback and others on foot, hastily retreating under fire from Larry Slade and his Rangers. Once Ford and Slade were together, they forced the Mexicans toward the border.

Slade, hearing the gun battle on his right flank, knew instinctively that the Mexican forces were fleeing. He spurred his horse on faster when he felt a bullet lodge in his left shoulder; thankfully it missed his bone. Disregarding the pain and the flow of blood down his arm, and with both his guns out of ammo, he reached behind his back, drew his Colt, and kept firing at the Mexicans.

In a cloud of dust from Ford's right flank rode Major Heintzelman's regular Army troopers, and those of Fry's small recon team. Also teamed up with Major Heintzelman's force were Ford's and

Slade's Rangers, as they pursued and cut down the fleeing Mexican soldiers before they reached the Rio Grande.

Now Captain Slade had run out of ammo. Slowing his mount to a gait, he reloaded his Colts. Once done, he put spurs to his horse and joined the frontline of his Rangers.

Through the thin fog and the wooded plane, they pushed Cortina's forces as the gunfire never ceased. Many a Mexican horse galloped off, carrying an empty saddle. Cortina's cavalrymen left on the ground met their deaths by the guns of the advancing American force.

Minutes later, at the river, the Mexicans tried to flee from the onslaught of gunfire from the Texas Rangers, the regular Army force, and the Brownsville Tigers, as one by one they were cut down before some could reach the other end of the riverbank. The river ran red with Mexican blood! The dead flowed on the river and the wounded gave up the fight and were swept downriver.

On the bank, the Rangers shouted and yelled. Major Ford called for a ceasefire from his force, as Major Heintzelman's Army also stopped their firing.

Larry Slade, once at the river, did not join in the slaughter, instead, he found a tree far from the gunfire and mended his wounds. He wasn't of a mind to take part in what he was witnessing; shaking his head, he turned his face away from it all.

At one o'clock in the afternoon, Ford, Tobin, and Slade, having been tended to by a doctor, sat and met with Major Heintzelman in his office in Ringgold Barracks to discuss the result of Cortina's hostilities and the battle of Rio Grande City. After lighting up cigars and enjoying several shots of whiskey, they settled down to get an after-battle report.

Puffing on his cigar, Major Heintzelman opened the briefing. "Major Ford's just finished his assessment on the enemy. He is reporting that Cortina suffered over two hundred killed. Our forces only sustained sixty-three wounded, some severe, while others reported as minor, with no deaths. We were lucky in that respect, gentlemen."

Downing his whiskey, Major Ford said, "Luck had nothing to do with it Major, our training was the factor here this morning."

With nods all around, a brief silence ensued.

Captain Slade knew training and knowledge of military tactics most often wins battles, but he had only one concern that kept running through his mind. "What of Cortina, sir? Have we found his body?"

"I can answer that, Captain Slade," Captain Tobin broke in. "My scouts reported that Cortina, along with the rest of his force, retreated into Mexico near the cities of Guerrero and Mier."

"I fear gentlemen," Slade said in a cold hard tone, "that we may not have heard the last of Cortina."

By 4:00 p.m. Larry Slade, under a breezy wintery afternoon having resigned from further command, battle-weary and wanting to get back home to his wife and child, said his farewells to Major Ford and Captain Tobin.

The three men met at the stables, just as Slade was finishing loading his packhorse.

"It's time I headed on home Rip," Larry said, taking time from his packhorse. "I have a lot of work that needs doing back home."

"We could use your gun here for a few months' more, Larry," Ford said with a grin.

"I appreciate that," Slade replied, "but, to tell the truth, I'm a lot too old to be doing this anymore. Let the youngsters like Tobin take command."

Tobin standing behind Ford stared at the two men. One of whom he'd heard stories told of his adventures and unbelievable tales of gunfights and the other his commander.

Major Ford sighed and with a smile said, "I believe I know what you mean. I'm getting up on age myself."

Seconds passed as a solemn silence fell between the three Rangers.

Ford withdrew an envelope from his pocket. "Larry, take this with our appreciation. It's not much, but you'll receive full payment in a few months. It will help you on your trail."

Taking the envelope, Slade opened it and saw a fair amount of cash.

"I can't take this Rip," Slade said, handing back the envelope. "Use it for your child," Ford replied. With a sigh and a nod, Slade pocketed the envelope, mounted his horse and with a tip of his hat, rode away from what was to become his last battle in service with the Texas rangers.

# CHAPTER 13

# THE CAPTIVES

It was mid-afternoon, that time before sunset, of his fifth day of travel that found Larry Slade deep inside Comanche territory.

Riding low in the saddle, the air was cold, with brutal icy headwinds. Wearing his gloves, he held the reins tight up against his chest. He rode with his jacket collar up and around his neck, while his leather chaps kept his legs warm; his gun belt carried his twin 1851 Colt Navy .36 caliber revolvers, but he kept his third Colt and extra cylinders in his saddlebags. And across his lap he cradled his Slant-Breach Sharps carbine rifle. Behind him, bringing up the rear was his packhorse.

Slade reined his horse to a stop and stared out into the snow filled wilderness. He turned around in the saddle as if expecting trouble from that quarter. Finding none, he turned forward and looked about in awe at the breathtaking beauty and utter calm of the open country and forest lines around him; the snow covered everything.

*It's like riding through a magical dream world*, he mused.

"It sure is pleasantly quiet, horse, and so serene," Slade said as he rubbed the side of his horse's neck. "Hope it stays this way to the ranch."

He still felt the achiness in his left shoulder where a bullet sizzled clear through the muscle; even though the doctor did a great job patching it up, some pain persisted. As if on impulse, he instinctively placed his hand to the shoulder and stroked the bullet's point of entrance, but a few seconds later he ignored the aching throb.

With a slight smile, he nudged his horse and began traveling once again.

At least two feet of snow covered the landscape, as his horses plowed through slowly, making their way to a wide river a quarter mile ahead. With his hat drawn tight around his forehead and his bandana wrapped around his face, he tried to stay as warm as possible.

Fifteen minutes later, as he approached the riverbank, the quietness that he felt earlier shattered as he heard the screams of what he believed was that of a woman, seemingly crying out for help!

Just as he reined his horse to a stop before reaching the riverbank, suddenly, through the forest of tall oak trees covered in layers of snow and tall bushes, a woman wearing a thin flimsy blouse and ankle length skirt, her long dark hair flying behind her, her arms bare and thin, popped out of the bushes running low and fast.

Within seconds, at the edge of the bank, and without the slightest hesitation, she jumped into the river which came up to her hips, ran, and pushed her way through the fast-moving frigid cold water straight at Slade, just as two screeching hostiles came running through the bushes shooting at her.

Not halfway across the river, the woman glanced up and saw someone on the opposite bank. It was still too far for her to make out what or who it was. Now, with danger to her rear and possibly to her front, she had no alternative but to stop and decide what to do.

Hesitating a few seconds, she was about to change directions, when Slade seeing her uncertainty shouted, "Come on over, you'll be safe with me. But make it quick."

Still on his horse, Slade stood straight up on his stirrups, raised his Sharps rifle, cocked back the hammer, and taking deadly careful aim at the hostiles behind her, pulled the trigger.

The sharp crack of the rifle was loud, as seconds later the large-caliber bullet struck center-mass as it flung a hostile backward dead before he knew what had happened. Then, two more hostiles on bareback emerged from the forest and joined their comrade. As they stopped at the bank, they raised their handguns and unleashed a volley of hot lead in Slade's direction, ignoring the woman for now.

The bullets whizzed over and around Slade as he jumped out of the saddle. With no time to pull a bullet from his saddlebags and armed the single-shot weapon, he dropped his rifle, and lightning quick drew his two Colts as he watched the two hostiles on horseback plunge into the river.

In a matter of seconds, he cocked both firearms, took careful aim, and pulled the triggers. Walking forward a few steps he saw one, then the other hostile drop dead. He stopped at the riverbank, and just as fast, Slade aimed at the remaining Indian and fired but missed as he dashed back into the woods. Slade watched as the dead hostile bodies were washed away by the fast- moving waters.

He holstered his gun and made his way to the riverbank where he helped the woman out of the icy waters. She was breathless, and her panting bosom showed she had fought every inch of the way to freedom. Lifting her eyes to the stranger, she said, "Please, they have another girl tied up back there. Please help me, she's my sister!"

Slade gave her one of his Colts. "Take this," he said, "and find some cover, I'll see what I can do. You do know how to use it, don't you?"

"I'm fourteen, sir, my Pa taught me well."

"What's your name?"

"Beth, and Julie's my younger sister."

With a smile on his lips, Slade handed over his Colt.

The girl easily cocked her head, took a deep breath, and looked up at the man. "Thank you, whoever you are."

Slade, untying the packhorse from his saddle grabbed the reins of his horse and jumped up onto the saddle, goosed the horse into a steady gait, and plunged into the river.

Once on the other side of the riverbank, Slade dismounted, opened his saddlebags, and pulled out the extra cylinders for his Colts. He quickly exchanged them and pulled out his third Colt.

　　　　TWO GUNS ACROSS TEXAS　　　　ALVAREZ

From around the tall oak trees, he heard yells and curses in Comanche up ahead. Gradually, he crept forward and from around a bend, he stopped, knelt, and hid among the tall bushes, unseen by the hostiles.

He saw her then, the captive sister, not much older than eight, as keeping a sharp eye on the hostiles he saw just the two Comanche warriors, but he waited a short moment to make sure no others showed up on the scene.

Slade watched as a Comanche shoved the small female child to the side of his horse several feet away. The child had her hands tied behind her back, her clothing in tatters, torn and ragged, gagged and blindfolded while another hostile kept guard.

Twice the child fell into the snow, and twice she was grabbed by her hair and yanked to her feet and struck across her face while the Comanche yelled throughout.

Now, forty feet from the scene, Slade rose, lifted his two Colts waist level and without aiming he gazed at the back of the hostile keeping guard as he knelt. Walking unhurriedly as he approached behind the watching hostile, and before anyone knew death was upon them, Slade cut loose with two shots at the back of the Comanche and lightning-quick, he turned his guns on the last Indian.

However, just as suddenly, as with the crack of the intruder's guns, the hostile dropped the child, and with a knife in hand ran to attack the Whiteman. The hostile was agile as he was fast on his feet. Still running the hostile threw the knife into the air aimed at the intruder and kept running toward Slade.

But Slade was ready.

With years of action against hostiles, Slade was well aware of their tactics.

Sidestepping the path of the knife, he felt it as it whizzed by his shoulder, and cocking both his Colts he shot the Indian as he leaped into the air to grab at him. The hostile was long dead before he hit the hard-packed snow not two feet from Slade's boots. Holstering his Colts, he glanced down at the girl.

Suddenly, Slade heard a loud yell behind him, without a second to spare he dropped to a knee, pivoted around, and in the same motion drew his handgun just as the hostile was upon him. With his gun on his side, he fired a shot that impacted the hostile in his neck. Quickly back on his feet, Slade cocked back the hammer and fired a second-round into the hostile's chest before he hit the ground.

Holstering his Colt, Slade walked toward the girl lying on the snow unmoving, as he heard her sobs through her gag.

"It's okay little one," Slade said, in a gentle reassuring voice, "I'm going to cut your binds. Your sister is safe on the other side of the river and she's waiting for you."

In the shadow of death, the howling of wolves in the distance came to his ears. "That's not a good sign," he muttered. With the child free, he picked her up, cradled her in his arms and she stared at the stranger with soft sobs and tear-filled eyes, as he ran toward his horse.

If the wolves caught the scent of death, they would surely be coming for a look, and if that happened Slade knew he needed to be as far away from them as possible.

As they rode double, Slade galloped over to the riverbank and plunged into the icy waters. He kept it slow not hurrying his horse. Out in the near distance, he heard the howling of the wolves.

*Damn, they're getting closer, I need to find shelter and start a fire,* Slade thought.

The older of the two sisters, upon hearing the gunfire on the other side of the river feared the worst. The stranger must be dead, and my little sister gone, were the thoughts that raced through her mind, as she started to cry.

Her mind wandered back to the day they were stolen from their home. Her parents were on the other side of the ranch rounding up stray cattle. Five hostiles burst through the front door. She didn't have time to pick up the shotgun to shoot them and give a warning to her parents.

She bowed her head and prayed the stranger had saved her sister, Julie.

What must have seemed an eternity later, she heard the stranger calling out to her, getting to her feet, from around some bushes she spied the stranger from a distance, riding up to her, with her sister.

"I'm here, I'm here!" she yelled out to Slade while waving her hand in the air.

Halting beside the girl, Slade dismounted and helped the other sister off his horse. "We don't have too much time; we may have visitors in the form of wolves soon."

"We were—" the older sister started to say.

"No time for that now, we have to find shelter soon," Slade interrupted her.

Slade removed his blanket tied from behind his saddle, and another from his packhorse and handed them to the girls who draped the blankets around their shoulders. Gazing at the older sister, he said, "Climb up on the saddle, and I'll get your sister up on the packhorse. Quickly now, we don't have much time."

Just as he said that the howling grew much closer.

Grabbing the reins to his horse, Slade walked on the horse's left-hand side and led the big animal forward. He hoped they would soon make it far away enough from the killing field. But if the wolves caught their scent, he would have to be prepared for them one way or another.

After covering a few miles, a thick heavy snow was beginning to fall, the sun was slowly setting, and as darkness descended, Slade came upon a cliff in a snow-covered wooded area, about a three-minute ride.

If it wasn't for the remaining sunlight, he would've missed it. He could barely discern the outline of a dark cave. To this, he led them. He hoped he could find some shelter there from the weather and from the wolves that wouldn't seem to leave them alone.

Slade trudged through the snow, pulling his horse behind himself and the two girls, who were now covered in a blanket of bright white snow. Arriving at what he made out to be the cave's entrance, he halted. The cave possibly a hundred feet in diameter and nine or ten feet in height showed promise. Brushing away layers of snow, he drew his Colt, cocked the hammer, and proceeded slowly into the cave's mouth.

It was dark inside, but after a few steps, he gratefully confirmed it would indeed accommodate the three of them along with his horses. It had a smooth well-worn floor, and evidence of animal habitation, as he found small animal bones.

Slade walked back to the two girls who were sitting on the ground watching his every move. He rummaged through his saddlebag, found his matches, and proceeded to build a torch, with his old shirt and a branch.

Once lit, he glanced down at the girls and said, "It'll be a few minutes until I get a fire started inside." Turning his back to them, he went back into the cave.

At the entrance, he saw light at the end of the cave. He carefully made his way and once there saw the end of the cave and a cliff that dropped several feet. At least no one was coming through that, he thought.

Minutes later he had a fair size fire going.

The girls were now in the cave. He unsaddled his horse and removed the burden bundle from his packhorse. He had to get them to lie on their side. Moments later he had a pot of coffee brewing.

Slade knew the wolves may have caught their scent and knew exactly where they were. He began to reload his Colts. With his saddlebag next to him, he grabbed gunpower, ball and patches. It was a process that took several minutes to accomplish. Then he loaded his Sharps rifle and propped it by his side.

Suddenly, he heard the howling of wolves getting too close for comfort, maybe a few hundred feet from the cave. Thinking quickly, he had Beth position herself to his left side with a Colt and Julie behind her. He drew his gun, cocked the hammer, and said, "Beth, aim and fire and keep firing. Don't let them come close to you or your sister. I'll keep us covered way before they enter."

Two wolves ran into the cave and were stopped by Slade's Colts almost firing in unison to each other, both wolves dead as two more ran in but halted growling. The gunshots were deafening in the confines of the small cave. Beth opened fire shooting two-handed and shot one in the head, as Slade fired into the side of the second wolf.

That may have stopped their charge ... but Slade wasn't taking any chances!

He cocked his Colts, and unhurriedly strolled into the open, just as three wolves slowly advanced on him. He just stood his ground and fired at one, then at the rest, until the three lay dead or dying. Slade cocked his guns and fired again just in case, but the hammer fell on empty cylinders.

Holstering his guns, he didn't hear nor see any more wolves and hoped that was the end of them.

Back in the cave he found more dry wood and moved them to the front of the cave and started a second fire, hoping to keep any stray animals away.

With his guns armed once again, he made sure the girls were fast asleep and laid down on his saddle with a Colt on his chest.

"Hope I get some sleep tonight, but I doubt it," Slade muttered.

## CHAPTER 14

# THE TRAIL HOME

The next day before sunup, Larry Slade woke.

He turned toward the girls, still fast asleep on a far corner, wrapped up together in their blankets. He hated to wake them, considering the hardships they'd experienced being held captives to a bunch of Comanches. So, he set up building a small campfire, and with snow for water, he brewed a pot of coffee.

The fire at the cave's entrance now covered by a foot of snow had gone out completely during the night. It took him just a moment to scrape all the white stuff away. Stepping outside, the skies were clear with at least three feet of snow on the ground. It was sunny but with cold, gusty winds.

With a mug of hot coffee warming his innards, Slade, one by one, led his horses out of the cave. He saddled his and loaded up the packhorse. It was time to get back on the trail.

He didn't know which direction home was for the girls, but reckoned he'd find out soon enough.

While working on his horses, Slade's thoughts drifted to his wife and son. It was a pleasant memory of their conversation he'd recalled with his family. He remembered he'd said this would be his last trail ride with the Rangers. His wife and son smiled, knowing if called again he would go. They'd said so, and all he did was smile. Now, he needed to get back to them, but his priority was getting the girls safely back to their parents.

Walking back to the cave, he noticed the girls warming by the fire and sipping on his cup of coffee.

Good, he thought. He had questions for Beth, the oldest one.

Stepping over to the fire, Slade asked, "You girls ready to ride home?"

Coughing, after taking another sip of the hot brew, Beth, the closest to Slade, raised her head to the person who saved their lives.

"Yes sir, we are," she whispered, staring at Slade, and asked, "Who are you?"

Slade ignored the question for a moment. "Can't fix breakfast, I don't want to stay here any longer than necessary. Wolves may come looking for the pack we killed." He didn't mention the Comanches. He knew he was in the Quahadis territory, one of the most ruthless of the Comanches. It wouldn't be long before they came looking for their warriors.

Then, crouching by the fire, Slade smiled as the young girl had beaten him to the questioning. "My name's Slade, but you can call me Larry."

Beth and Julie smiled as they fixed their eyes on him. "We know of you, Mr. Slade," Beth said with wide, knowing eyes. "We heard my father say you were a Texas Ranger and that you have a ranch not forty miles from our home."

Julie with a wide grin just nodded.

Slade cocked his head and gave her a faint smile. "Well, well," Slade said, "I didn't know there were settlers out past my ranch. So, we travel the same trail home."

A brief silence as the girls passed the coffee cup to each other and sipped on it.

Slade frowned. "I'm curious, though, how did you two happen to be with the Comanches?"

There was the faintest of hesitation, as Beth looked away frowning, almost not wanting to bring up the memory of that day; as tears rolled down her face, she wiped the wetness from her eyes as she responded. "It happened when our parents were away from the house.

Two Comanches came through the front door, while two more came through the back. We were taken completely by surprise, and I didn't even make it to the shotgun by the front door when they jumped us. I tried to fight them off, but there were too many."

Julie, crying said, "They beat us and kicked us, and I cried and cried yelling for my Pa."

Slade swallowed, knowing the pain and anguish these two had experienced. And coming out of it alive, their lives had changed dramatically; a mark that will last them the rest of their lives. He knew the girls would be married off to young warriors or sold across the border to the highest bidders.

"How did you escape from them, Beth?"

Again, Beth looked away, and then fixed Slade with a serious gaze, but this time without tears and explained how she'd escaped. "They didn't tie my hands behind my back tight," she began. "So, I worked them until I got free. It wasn't until I got them loose enough that I waited for the right time when they weren't paying attention to us. When I did, I undid the ropes around my feet and ran, praying I get to someone to rescue my sister. God sent us you. The rest, you know. I'm so happy you came along."

"I don't know about God, but it was providence that I came along. You don't need to cry, you're safe now; I won't let anything happen to you two. And *I will* get you home."

Slade rose, his aching legs asking for relief. "Can I have my cup back?"

Once Beth handed him the cup, he poured the rest of the coffee from the pot and sipped on the warm liquid as he contemplated the long trail ride.

By his reckoning, they should arrive late morning of the second day. Once he'd finished his coffee, he tossed the rest of the liquid onto the fire. He kicked some rocks and dirt onto what remained of the flames, grabbed the coffeepot, and said, "Let's go, girls. We have a long ride ahead of us."

By the early morning of the second day, they'd traveled through the Brazos River without mishap.

The girls were almost jubilant knowing they were almost home.

Coming to a halt, he gave the girls a chance to stretch their legs. Coming around to the packhorse, Slade rummaged through some bags and pulled out some hard biscuits, hard-tack, and offered them to the girls. Feeding his horse's carrots, he poured water into his hat and let them drink.

Turning to Beth, he asked, "Which way, Beth?"

"North, sir, about twenty miles, I've been around here with my father hunting several times."

"North it is, then."

It had been a week since their two girls went missing, and it had taken them this long to put together a search party from other ranchers and townspeople.

Money and time were the two most determining factors for those helping. They believed Comanches may have taken them, and if that was the case, Jed knew they may already be too late to save them.

Another reason they had not started on the trial was they didn't have an experienced tracker to work with; that alone was the key factor. They just didn't know the country that well.

Jed and Cora would not give up. They'd heard of a tracker, a mountain man that knew the trails, who could help. But once offered the job, the tracker wanted more than what they had.

This had been just yesterday.

Today, with the sun setting low on the horizon, Jed was not sure what to do next. Sitting next to his wife Cora, she gazed at her defeated husband, and felt the stress he was under. It pained her heart in seeing him this way, and it turned her own life upside down, not knowing what they would do without their girls.

"Is there anything else we may not have thought of Jed?" Cora asked.

Nodding his head, he replied, "I've been thinking honey. Tomorrow I'll set off by myself and see if I can pick up their trail."

"I'm coming with you; I'll not stay here alone."

Suddenly, they heard their horses out by the corral snorting loudly. "Wait here Cora, grab my rifle and stay by the window. Something or someone is coming." Removing his gun from its holster, Jed opened the front door, stepped outside onto the porch, and saw a man leading two horses approaching the house.

"Stop right there, hombre!" Jed yelled, pointing his gun at the stranger. "Who are you, and what do you want?"

"Daddy, Daddy, it's us, Beth and Julie." The girls jumped off the horses and ran straight into their father's open arms. Cora ran out of the house and joined them in a big hug.

Slade watched them for a few moments. The happiness washed all over them.

Pulling himself away from his family, Jed approached the stranger. "I'm Jed Coleman, sir. I can't thank you enough for saving my girls. God bless you."

"Glad to help," Slade said. "I best be going on. I have a forty-mile ride to my ranch."

"Who are you, sir?"

"Name's Slade, Larry Slade."

"Why don't you come in, Mr. Slade, and have a hot cup of coffee and tell us how you saved my girls?"

"Thank you, sir, but I need to be getting on, wife and son waiting. Besides, Beth can tell it better than me."

"I understand, maybe we can get together sometime."

"I reckon we can."

Tipping his hat, he saw the girls staring and smiling at him. Turning his horse around, he jumped onto the saddle and spurred the animal into a slow gait.

It was late evening when he topped the ridge overlooking his ranch. The lookout, Flint Adams recognized the rider immediately.

Riding out to meet him, Adams yelled to his boss not to shoot him. "Welcome home, boss!"

Slade already had drawn his Colt and cocked it just in case. "Who is that?"

"It's me, Flint, sir."

"Come on ahead, Flint."

"Great having you home again, sir."

"Glad to be back," Slade responded, holstering his gun.

"You want me to ride in with you, boss?"

"Nah, stay at your post, we'll get together later."

"Yes, sir, will do."

Ten minutes later, as young John Slade stepped onto the porch after having his dinner, he saw a rider coming toward the house and peered into the darkness, but instinctively he knew it was his father. Stepping back into the house he yelled out for his mother. "Mom, Pa's back!"

Seconds later, John heard the opening and slamming of the door behind him as he stepped off the porch onto the dirt-packed ground. He knew his mother was on the porch watching the rider approach, and he smiled.

His father was back!

# CHAPTER 15

# TRAGEDY STRIKES

*Two Years Later*

On the morning of January 11, 1861, Larry Slade and his son were preparing to set off on the hunt for wild game. The Texas morning was clear without a cloud in sight as they packed their gear onto the packhorse, when suddenly, Larry bent over coughing as blood dripped down his mouth.

John, now seventeen, grabbed his father before he fell onto the ground and yelled out for his mother.

Larry immediately caught himself, wiped the blood from about his mouth, stood up straight on his own feet, pointed his hand out to his son and said, "I'm alright, John, just a little dizzy. Help me back into the house."

Running out of the house, Martha went straight to her husband. "What happened, John?"

"Mom, he started coughing blood again," John responded.

Once in the house, Larry laid on the bed, as Martha administered the medicine prescribed by the town doctor. His body ached and he had an overwhelming sense of fatigue. Martha was concerned; Larry hadn't had a fit of coughing for the last several weeks. She knew it was getting worse; something the doctor said it would.

She remembered the doctor's words.

"He has consumption, Mrs. Slade. It's going to get worse as time goes by. There is no cure, you must prepare for the worst."

Then she asked the one question she dreaded, "How long does he have?"

"It's hard to tell, months, a year, maybe two."

Now all she could do was give him the laudanum and see if he gets better. After two spoons of the brownish liquid, she pulled the sheets up around his shoulders and turned to John, who was hovering over the bed.

"He's getting worse, John."

"I'll be fine Martha," Larry said in a low tone of voice. "Just need to rest awhile. I'll be ready tomorrow, John."

"No Pa, I'll take care of the hunting, you just rest and get better."

Slowly, Larry Slade slipped into a deep sleep.

Early that evening, just before dusk, John Slade, riding his father's pinto and packhorse, set out to hunt for much-needed game. He preferred to do the hunting himself, instead of sending out one or two cowhands.

While his parents slept, he left the ranch to their four hired hands that would protect the premises without question.

John went well-armed. With his new Spencer lever-action repeating rifle, purchased just a few months ago and two new Colt model 1861 Army revolvers, one holstered down his right leg and the other in the reverse grip holster on his left, he would keep an eagle eye out for danger along the trail.

Mounting the pinto, he started heading south instead of north. He knew the south had more plentiful game, but it was a long way from the ranch. If he got lucky, he should make it home before breakfast the following day.

The ranch was still fast asleep, the hired hands still locked up in the bunkhouse, as their day wouldn't start for several hours.

Martha and Larry, sound asleep, were unaware that two new candles she had left next to a set of closed curtains were still burning. The flames were high when a steady cool light breeze came through the open bedroom door. The flames flickered and sparks caught the curtain behind it. Slowly at first, the flames touched the flammable material and caught fire.

In seconds, the curtains now in flames spread onto the wooden desk. Flames fell onto the wooden floor and caught fire. The fire spread to one side of the house engulfing it in flames as they shot up to the ceiling and ignited other furnishings.

Slowly the flames caught the edge of the bed and immediately the flames spread. Within moments, the bed and the entire bedroom were a raging inferno.

Martha was the only one that woke to yell out for help, but before anyone came to her rescue, her body was instantly ablaze.

Some half-hour later found John in very familiar surroundings. Places he and his father had roamed together four years ago. He was much surprised to note that it had overgrown the area with bushes more than he cared to remember.

Danger lurked everywhere, he surmised... *Best be careful*, he told himself.

John wasn't given to needless worry. He tried to convince himself that his father would pull out of what he had, or he wouldn't. So, he busied himself with the prospects of catching the spoor of either an antelope or deer; he wasn't picky.

Since entering the edge of Indian Territory, his hopes were not too tangled up with hostile Indians. "Don't become careless, John," he muttered. Not as experienced at fighting Indians as his father, he would argue, but he could take care of himself in a fight.

John was very familiar with the country. Shortly, he was following a well-beaten game trail that led to higher ground and a range of mountains that dropped into a valley. All that morning, he caught not a glimpse of game.

Late night shadows were forming as Slade reached the comparatively level ground and he urged the pony into a canter and proceeded through lush green foliage of trees. Here were old and fresh animal tracks; just what he needed to see.

Finding just the right place to make camp, Slade led his pinto to the spot, drew rein, and dismounted. He tied his packhorse to a tree, mounted the pony, and with the Spencer rifle on his lap, he set down the well-worn-out trail.

It wasn't long until he caught the strong scent of antelopes up range of him, not more than a few hundred yards on his left. As quietly as he could, he dismounted, found a spot to tie his horse, cocked back the hammer on his rifle, and stepped toward his left.

Through the moonlight, John followed the trail for perhaps a hundred yards. A sharp turn to his left brought him to a small watering hole. He decided to wait it out here, so he laid out on the grass floor, brought his Spencer to his shoulder, and waited.

Slade didn't have long to wait when through the bushes a pronghorn-buck antelope appeared. He quickly guessed it weighed about one-hundred pounds. It was a fine specimen. Aiming, he waited until it showed his side. He finally saw his opportunity and as the animal turned, he squeezed the trigger.

An hour later, once he'd dressed and skinned the buck, he draped it over the packhorse.

Not wanting to wait until morning to depart, young John headed back home.

By the time John reached the boundary of the ranch, at the far end of the valley, he knew something was wrong at home. As the wintry winds drifted up to him, he smelled what he believed was a pungent, foul smell of fire. Out in the distance, he could make out white smoke drifting over the treetops.

Forgetting the packhorse, he barreled forward. He didn't know the course or where the fire started. He hoped all was well with his parents.

As John rounded a corner, he galloped through the small river … then he caught sight of the ranch house that was still smoldering, the smoke drifting up into the night sky.

"No, no, oh my God, fire at the main house!" he yelled, putting spurs to the pony.

Around the house, Slade saw the cowhands who were trying to put out the fire that still lingered and burned at places.

Dismounting on the fly, Slade pulled up in front of them. He tried to dash into the still-burning house but was stopped by two of the hired hands. "It's no use, John," the ranch wrangler, Jim Watts said, "You'll get caught in the smoke and fire. Your parents didn't get out. We're so sorry, John."

John dropped to his knees as tears flowed down his cheeks.

Two days later, standing above his parents' grave, John Slade, hat in hand, said his last goodbyes.

Earlier, once it was safe to enter what was left of the house, he'd found his father's letters and written accounts of his life in a bound notebook under the floorboards of their bedroom. There also, he found his father's two guns still intact.

After selling his ranch to the cowhands, Slade with a packhorse and his steed slowly rode away from the ranch. At the river, he stopped, turned in the saddle, stared back at the house, and sighed.

Seventeen and not knowing where he was going for the time being, John Slade turned back, gritted his teeth, and spurred his horse forward.

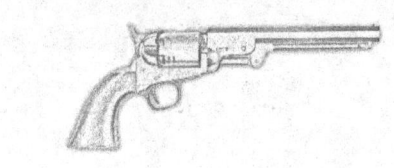

## PART TWO

# LIFE AND TIMES
# OF
# JOHN SLADE

# CHAPTER 16

# THE LONELY TRAIL

*San Antonio, Texas*
*Mid-April 1861*

After the death of his parents, John Slade roamed the ranches in central Texas. With odd jobs and a cattle drive, he made fair enough wages.

However, he soon learned it was a lonely experience, often broken by drinking and gambling with a bevy of loose women in one town or another. Most times getting involved in gunfights or back-alley fistfights: most not of his doing.

Throughout those towns, he kept hearing that war between the North and the South was inevitable. He hoped to avoid getting involved with it. He didn't want to take sides in a war that was all about slavery, and partially about states' rights and westward expansion of which he'd read in local newspapers.

His father, Larry Slade, never entertained the idea of slaves working the ranch; always paying fair wages to those that came looking for work. Like his father, he didn't particularly condemn nor condone slavery. But one way or another, the issue would be settled with blood on the battlefield, he was sure of it.

After a final successful cattle drive, he rode through the Brazos River, heading to San Antonio. Cattle drives had stopped because of possible war brewing with the Southern states needing all the beef for the cause.

He'd read somewhere that Texas had been admitted to the Confederate States of America, with Austin its capital, and volunteers were needed.

Arriving in San Antonio almost penniless—part of the money spent on much needed supplies for his travels—he came looking for work. Riding through town all he heard about were men being arrested for the crime of being Union sympathizers, chiefly among the German Texan population.

To his left was the Alamo Chapel, now being used by Confederate Army soldiers as a supply storage facility. What a difference it represented now. A small cadre of brave men died at that venerable bastion defending liberty and freedom, facing impossible odds against hundreds of Mexican soldiers.

This was young Slade's first visit to San Antonio. What amazed him was the jumble of races, costumes, and buildings, some three, four stories high, on either side of the main thorough fare.

Those streets were packed with many types of wagons moving here and there. Some loaded down with goods and supplies, others with families, while a heavy swell of pedestrian traffic kept the noise level high.

Moments later toward his right just outside a saloon, two men Slade figured were mountain men or trappers, faced each other in a heated argument. One drew his weapon, the other followed suit as two shots rang out above the din. When the smoke cleared, one lay dead in the dirt, and one was left standing, bleeding from his left arm. Both shots spooked his horse as it reared up.

With his steed back under control, Slade rode down the dusty streets and soon spied another saloon on his left. Several men were standing around watching the crowds. Four were sitting on chairs on the porch, armed to the teeth. Two of those men kept staring at him as he passed them. He cautiously kept his hand on the butt of his weapon, hammer cocked.

One of those four, a tall, stocky, broad-shouldered man named Jett Miles, wearing buckskins, from out of the corner of his mouth, posed the question, "What about that one riding by?"

"He looks promising," Ellis Miles, his brother replied, rubbing his black and grey beard. "Then again, he looks too young for our business."

"Yeah but look at how he strapped on his guns."

Ellis shrugged and nodded.

"I'll follow and see what he's made of," Jett said.

"Good idea. We could use a fresh gun," Ellis acknowledged, shaking his head ever so. "We lost two on our last job."

"Yeah, and you almost lost me there too."

"Quit your griping you're here now, right?"

Standing, about to follow, Jett Miles, replied, "No thanks to you brother."

Toward the end of town, Slade caught sight of a hotel that advertised a hot bath, shave, and wash of clothes, reasonably priced. It was exactly what he needed. Past the hotel he led his horse to the town stables.

With his saddlebags draped over his shoulder, his rifle carried in his left hand, Slade ambled over to the hotel.

The bath as promised was hot. It was a welcome change to not having bathed in several days.

Now with a room, with an old man pouring water into the tub, Slade was enjoying the comfort it brought to his weary young body. He decided to strike up a conversation with the old-timer.

Just as he was about to leave, Slade asked, "Would you know of any work to be done in town?"

The man stopped and turned to face him. It had been that kind of day he reflected. This young man wasn't the first or the last to ask that same question. "The only work you'll find around here is with the Army young man." He turned to leave, and then stopped again. "Unless you hitch up with some bounty hunters on the other side of town, they're always looking for one more gun hand."

"Don't reckon I'll be doing either of those," Slade said. "Thank you for the advice."

Once showered, Slade studied his reflection above the washbasin mirror through his squinting grey eyes that stared back at him. He was just over six-feet-one, broad-shouldered as his father had been, with thick dark flowing hair that reached his shoulders. He kept wondering what his future held in store for him. It was a reoccurring nagging question now that his parents had passed.

After his shave and a change of clothing, he strapped on his guns, grabbed his hat off the bed and left the room. What he needed now was coffee and some grub. Coming into town, he'd noticed a café across from the hotel.

Stepping out onto the hotel's porch, Slade glanced around the crowded street and putting his hat on, he stopped and stared at a tall thin man, wearing a tan hat, dirty looking white bandanna around his neck, white shirt with a dark vest, with a long tan trail duster and low-slung gun belt.

Slade was sure he'd seen him before. Then he placed him. Earlier on a saloon porch: bounty hunters. He was being followed. "What's this about?" He muttered.

*Probably nothing,* Slade said to himself, shrugging, *but I'll keep an eye out just the same.*

Crossing the street, Slade approached the entrance to the café and momentarily stopped, turned, and not catching sight of the bounty hunter, smiled.

Entering the café, he noticed a bar set off to a corner just at the entrance and ambled over to an empty table. Removing his hat, he placed it on an empty chair, sat at a table and glanced around the filled room.

Sitting at two packed tables were six Confederate soldiers having their meals and conversing in low tones. One soldier referred to an elderly soldier across from him by the name and rank of Colonel Ford.

At the mention of the name, Slade's ears perked up. Could this be the same Ford his father fought alongside back in '59 he wondered.

Should he interrupt the soldier's meal and ask, or should he postpone it for a later time, maybe once the Colonel was by himself? In any case, it would have to wait; first things first—he needed to get a good hot meal under him.

Most guests were leaving while more than half were entering the café. It would seem this was a very popular diner. Slade took notice of one man in particular. The man hesitated by the door and glanced around and stopped once they locked eyes on each other.

He was the same one young Slade felt was following him: the bounty hunter!

Dropping his eyes from him, Slade felt the man staring at him from across the room. Turning his gaze on him once again, he saw the man smiling as he worked his way through customers toward him.

Halting in front of Slade, Jett Miles stooped low and still smiling showing some missing front teeth, asked, "Would like a word with you stranger. My name's Miles, Jett Miles."

John Slade turned with a blank expression to the man standing in front of him and took a deep breath, guessing what the man already wanted. "Oh ... what about?"

"Can I sit down?" Miles asked, as he reached for a chair, already feeling slightly impatient with the young man as he took his hat off.

Slade decided to handle it as quietly as he could. "Depends ... on what you want."

Releasing his hold on the chair, Miles replied, his smile gone, "A proposition and a job."

"You one of those bounty hunters I saw riding into town?"

Miles shrugged at his question. "Reckon I am."

Staring up at the stranger, Slade said, "Then, I'll say this once, leave now. I don't need that kind of work."

Putting his hat back on and exposing his gun, Miles didn't need to take this crap from anyone. Hell, he thought, he'd killed for far less. It's hard enough taking it from his brother. He didn't have to stand here and take it from this stupid kid. He was going to teach him a hard lesson.

Miles shrugged and asked, "You any good with those guns of yours, youngster?"

This was not good, not in town long, and already in trouble. This would not end well, he thought, and said, "Mister ..." Slade paused. "You don't need to do this."

Miles straightened and noticed the room had quieted around them, as if expecting a gunfight inside the café. From across the room, the soldiers stood, expecting gunfire. One called Ford stared hard at the young man as if he'd seen him before.

Taking four steps back from the table, Miles angrily said, "Stand up, let's see what you're made of sonny, unless of course, you're a yellow livered coward!" This last he said through gritted teeth.

It was at that same moment, Ellis Miles, strode into the café and stopped at the edge of the bar, as he watched his younger brother and the young stranger, fully knowing the outcome.

# CHAPTER 17

# INCIDENT AT THE CAFÉ

John Slade pushed the chair back and rose, careful to keep his gun hand close to the butt of his cross holstered Colt.

Tense seconds passed. No one moved in the café, nor was a word spoken as both men faced each from only nine feet apart, waiting for the other to clear their holster.

Slade sighed audibly. "You should stand down, mister... you might live a little longer."

The next few seconds were the longest Slade ever had.

Shaking his head, Jett Miles shrugged. "You should worry about your own life, youngster."

Ellis Miles stared at the two. He was going to let this play out, knowing how fast his brother was with his Colts when out of the corner of his eye he caught the barkeep raising a shotgun.

Quick on the draw, Ellis pulled, cocked the hammer, and covered the barkeep behind the bar. "Let's keep this fair. Put that scatter gun away, mister."

The barkeep, who was also the owner, grimaced, but with the man's gun leveled at his chest, he had no choice but to do as he said. Replacing the shotgun back under the bar, he stared at the two men facing each other from across the room.

From his right, Slade saw the action behind Jett Miles right shoulder. Just as Slade's eyes returned to the bounty hunter, Miles saw his chance. Fast as lightning, his hand went for his gun, and before he raised it level with his opponent, Slade drew fanning off two quick shots.

The gunfire boomed inside the café.

Jett Miles was driven back a step, the slugs impacting his chest, gun clattering onto the hardwood floor, a surprised look on his face. One word escaped his lips, "Shit," and as blood dripped down from his mouth, his knees gave way as gravity did the rest.

One soldier standing with an unobstructed view of the kid immediately commented to the group, "Good Lord! Did you guys see that? I didn't even see the kid clear his gun. Damn, that was fast!"

From across the café, Ellis Miles yelled out for this brother. His gun flew to his hand aiming at his brother's killer. Suddenly, from the standing soldiers, someone shouted, "Look out, kid!"

With his Colt still in hand, Slade pivoted the barrel toward the danger, and as fast as his left hand fanned the Colt's hammer, two shots struck the bounty hunter about his chest driving him backward as his body slammed into the café door. He slumped to the floor, dead. But not before Miles had triggered his gun, sending a slug toward Slade that grazed his left shoulder.

Not giving his shoulder the slightest concern, young John Slade pulled his other gun and fanned the barrels left and right on the customers.

"Anyone else care to die today?" he said, his tone firm, filled with malice. He'd killed two today, for no apparent reason, and it didn't sit well with him.

Through the café doors, strode the city Marshal, a haggard whiskey-filled lawman and his two deputies, shotgun pointing at Slade. "Drop 'em irons, boy!" he yelled.

Instead, Slade holstered his Colts and stared at the lawman. "It was self-defense. Justified as it was. They drew first, Marshal."

Aiming his shotgun at the kid and stepping over the corpse with his two deputies behind him, the Marshal said. "Tell that to the judge. Let's git."

Suddenly, all the customers, man after man, sided with the youth. One soldier in particular, the Colonel, pointed out, "They came looking for it, Marshal. The kid had no choice. Two against one wasn't quite fair to begin with."

After they cleared the bodies from the café, and with the Marshal, satisfied with the overall claim of self-defense, Colonel Ford reached out to the kid. "Let me buy you a drink young man. I seem to have seen you someplace before."

Once at the bar with two whiskey glasses in front of them, Slade said, "And I seem to recognize your name, sir."

"Oh?"

"You by chance have a nickname of Rip?"

Nodding, Ford responded, "That would be my nickname, how do you know that name?"

John felt relaxed in front of Ford, breaking into a smile. "My father rode with ya and the Texas Rangers."

"I see. What's your name, son?"

"Slade, John Slade."

*Son of a bitch*, Ford thought. It can't be. But the resemblance was uncanny. "Is your father...Larry Slade?"

"Yes, sir."

"You're the spitting image of your father, youngster."

Downing his drink, Slade shrugged. "Yes, sir, most say so."

"And you're as fast as Larry, I give you that," Colonel Ford said, downing his drink too and smiling.

For the briefest moment, Slade went quiet, remembering the day he buried his parents. "He was a great teacher."

"How is your father these days ... John? Mind if I call you John?" Ford asked.

"I don't mind, sir. My Pa died in a house fire along with my Ma."

"Sorry to hear that, I could've used him in our fight against the Northern aggressors."

A brief silence as the barkeep refilled their glasses.

"So, what on earth brings you to San Antone?"

"Came looking for work."

"You're not going to find it here," Colonel Ford said. "Most young men are volunteering for the Confederacy. The war will be starting soon."

"So I heard, sir."

"Are you interested in joining up with us?"

"No sir, I'll be moving on first light."

"Fair enough," Ford said. "If you change your mind John, I'll be at the Menger Hotel. I have command of the Rio Grande Military District. I could use you son. Seems there is trouble coming from Zapata County. I can promise you fair wages, a horse, and whatever you may need. If you change your mind that's where I'll be."

"I'll keep that in mind, sir."

With March drawing to a close, it saw young John Slade, still without employment and his funds whittled down to almost nothing.

In early April, he'd heard of a ranch hiring wranglers out by the Red River in the town of Eustace Texas. Just after breakfast he loaded up his saddlebags with provisions and rode out of San Antonio.

Slade was determined to work his way on some ranch, instead of fighting in a war he had no interest in joining or becoming a bounty hunter, which was no life at all. Without cattle drives, all he could hope for was a meager wage and an honest day's work. His father had taught him well; it would not be hard showcasing his life experiences on a ranch.

He spent nearly a year on the Red River ranch, until one day early in 1862, they let him go. The family was moving back East. No other ranches in the area were hiring, and the war was crawling slowly into Texas. There weren't any other means of support except to join in the fighting.

After fine-tuning his quick draw with both of his Colts over the year he'd spent on the ranch, maybe Colonel Ford could have use of them, he thought. And he figured he could use the experience one gets of being a soldier.

But what was to come? If he lived through the war, what was next for the son of a Texas Ranger, Larry Slade?

The gust of the night wind in its rustle to and fro in the branches of the pecan
during midnight.

"There was no one alive" he voiced. "Other things had arisen, while the fury
and the chaos," he explained sadly. "The..." [illegible]

# CHAPTER 18

# THE RECONNAISSANCE MISSION

*San Antonio, Texas,*
*May 1862*

"So, John, you decided to join us after all."

John Slade hesitated, and then shook his head. "It left me without
a choice, either this or bounty hunting. And I'm plum broke."

Colonel Ford grimaced. Reaching into his shirt pocket, he pulled
out a stogie and with a match from the same pocket, lit it and inhaled
its sweet aroma. Glancing at the young man across from him and
blowing the smoke out to one side, he replied, "Times are rough all
over, John."

The two men sat across from each other in Colonel Ford's makeshift office, which the Menger Hotel owner set aside for the Colonel
and his soldiers. Ford was a tall, lean man, with black eyes, a clean-
shaven face, and hair cut short. He wore grey buckskins, with his
double Colt handguns lying on top of the table by his right hand.

Ford's build contrasted with Slade's, which was over six feet tall, a
physique of solid thick muscular build—built by years of hard work
on a cattle and horse ranch.

Back from the border with Mexico, Ford had commanded his
troops, the 2nd Texas Cavalry based in the Rio Grande in the defense
of Zapata County. The invaders, led by a Mexican renegade named
Juan Cortina, had entered the Zapata County courthouse and hanged

the court judge. During the battle, they killed several of the invaders, with Cortina retreating into Mexico. This minor skirmish of the war occurred two weeks before the bloodless Battle of Fort Sumter, in Charleston South Carolina, which marked the beginning of the Civil War.

Now tasked to run the Bureau of Conscription for the State of Texas in San Antonio, Ford had his hands full. The laws were a series of measures taken by the Confederate Army to produce manpower to fight the war. He was also in charge of border operations protecting the Confederate-Mexican trade.

Ford had the Mexican border area in mind for Slade. He sensed Slade was a man of courage and versatility and could handle himself in any fight. And if he was half the man his father was, he would be a definite asset in that region. Fingering the stogie, Ford pulled out handwritten notes, dipped a quill pen into an inkwell, and signed his name to both slips of paper.

Handing over one of the notes, Ford said, "Here, take this note to the quartermaster, he'll assign a horse and whatever else you'll need." Ford paused as he grasped the second note, handing it to Slade. "Take this second note to the paymaster. You'll receive three months' pay in advance."

Standing, Slade grasped the notes and was about to leave, when Ford said, "When you're finished, come on back and I'll have your first assignment."

"Yes, sir."

It didn't take Slade long before he was in possession of a new saddle, saddlebags, and a new horse's bridle. After receiving thirty-three dollars in advance pay, more than he currently had, he saddled his horse and rode back to Colonel Ford's office.

He had no inkling of the assignment "RIP" Ford had for him but was prepared for any the colonel ordered.

Once seated across Colonel Ford's desk, Slade leaned back and waited as the older man signed his name to several documents in front of him while keeping a lit stogie clenched tightly between his teeth. Another officer stood by waiting to receive the signed documents. Once the officer, a major, had them in hand, he left the office.

Glancing at Slade, Colonel Ford said, "What I have in mind, John is for you to join my officers of the 2nd Texas Cavalry to head off would be Mexican and Indian attacks on the Rio Grande and protect our trade with Mexico."

"I'll do what I can, sir."

For the next two years Slade, working with the Confederate officers of the 2nd Texas Cavalry, engaged in several running battles and skirmishes. In six different battles he was wounded twice and lost twenty soldiers, but the Mexican bandits suffered heavily under the Cavalry and his guns.

On 25 July 1864, as Slade lay in the hospital having his wounds tended to, a courier arrived with orders from Colonel Ford addressed to him.

Opening the message, he read:

*John, report back to San Antonio, as soon as you can.*

Slade smiled as he ripped the message up, throwing it on the ground, laid back on his chair, and let the doctor continue sewing him up. The message was short and direct. Ford, because of security, did not mention *why* he was needed, nor the mission. It was another mission, no doubt. So, for the time being, he'd just have to wait it out. He would have liked some clarification, but that's the military; secrets to be kept close until they were ready to be divulged.

Glancing at the doctor, he asked, "How soon before I can ride, Doc?"

"Just as soon as I'm finished, young man," the doctor replied in a low voice.

*Now that was great news* he thought, shrugging, the act not lost on the doctor. Nothing major physically to preclude his starting for San Antonio at first light.

"Keep still, soldier," the doctor rudely said, "I may do more damage than good here."

Slade took a deep breath and reluctantly sat back and rested his head as he smiled once again.

Some hours after nightfall of the second day, Slade crested a small hill overlooking the outskirts of San Antonio. The night air was hot as it gently blew on his face. Lights from the town were visible from his vantage point. Coffee and a bath were the only thoughts that swirled through his mind before he sat with Ford.

Riding down the main street there were people about, two drunks passed out just outside a saloon door, while others were heading to their rooms for the night. Slade stopped in front of the livery stable and bed his horse for the night. With saddlebags draped over his shoulder, rifle in hand, he proceeded to the Menger Hotel.

Walking by a restaurant he overheard birthday wishes being sung. Stopping just long enough to peek through a window, he saw a mixed crowd of people standing around a table but couldn't make out who the lucky person was.

He stayed glued to the window, thinking of his youth as he remembered his birthday. He pondered this for a moment. "Now that I've turned twenty," he said to himself, "it reminds me of my parents and all the fun we had on my birthdays."

He turned twenty at the height of battle and it just came to mind peeking through the window. Thinking of his parents, he sighed as a tear rolled down his cheek. Feeling the presence of people moving around him, he walked away from the window.

Tired and aching from the patchwork the doctor did to his wounds, the long ride, and after signing for a room in the hotel, he sat in the restaurant for a hot meal. Afterward, he walked down the lobby to the last room on his left. He unlocked it and turned the knob. Pushing it open, he saw his bath had already been prepared.

Once out of his bath, and shirtless, Slade felt more human now and was toweling his hair, when a soft knock sounded at his door, catching his attention.

*Now who the hell could that be,* he thought.

Another knock!

Grabbing a gun off the bed, he wrapped the towel around his neck and approached the door.

"Whoever you are, you've come at a bad time," Slade said through gritted teeth.

"John, it's Colonel Ford, we need to talk son. It can't wait."

They sat six feet from each other as Slade waited for the other man to continue.

Slade slouched on the edge of the bed, still drying his long hair, set back from the window of the second-floor bedroom of the Menger Hotel. Seated to his right on the only chair in the bedroom sat Colonel RIP Ford, who lit a cigar and crossed a leg over the other. Ford, according to Slade, held a certain degree of military seriousness about him indicating the serious nature of his visit.

At that same moment, Slade dropped the towel on the bed, and lifted his gaze at the colonel, as he was slowly enjoying his cigar. He rose, walked over to the side of the washbasin, removed his shirt from a hook, and donned it. Tucking it into his pants, he walked back to the bed and sat.

Slade thought for a moment. "Right nice neighborly of you to come calling instead of the other way around, Colonel."

The colonel was decked out in buckskins, his grey Army cap laying on the table next to him. He had a cultivated two days' growth of beard, and a pair of rimless thin glasses perched on his nose. His hair was streaked with gray. "As I was saying John, I have assembled a thirteen-hundred-man force, the newspapers are calling it *The Cavalry of the West*, it has a nice ring to it, with the objective of capturing Fort

Brown. Currently the fort is occupied by Union soldiers under the command of General Nathaniel Banks, with a large body of soldiers under his command. General James Slaughter and I will lead the attack at daybreak on the 30th."

Ford paused a second time, exhaling cigar smoke, as he removed his glasses, cleaning the lenses with a handkerchief pulled from his jacket pocket he kept there for such occasions.

Slade pursed his lips for a second. The 30th was just two days away. With a sigh, he asked, "What is it you want me to do, Colonel?"

"I'm getting to that, don't rush me, son."

This time Ford rose to his feet, clasped his hands behind him and walked up and down the bedroom floor for a few moments, cigar gripped tightly in his jaw.

Here the colonel stopped pacing, adjusted his glasses, and stared at the young man. "We want you to lead a small five-man team, who are well trained, well-armed and will be well led by Lieutenant Jacob Rose and yourself into Brownsville to gather intelligence for our forces. You are to assist Lieutenant Rose in this matter."

Slade didn't look too happy about the mission. Although he'd led men into battle, he wasn't sure he could pull off what the colonel wanted. One burning question kept repeating itself in his consciousness. He cleared his throat and asked, "Why me, I don't think I have enough command time, Colonel?"

Colonel Ford frowned. "According to your men, they describe you as a fearless fighter and skilled leader and your bravery under fire is beyond reproach. You have made a name of yourself with those quick guns during the last two years son. An admirable trait if I may say. You're the right person for his mission, John. You'd make your father proud."

Slade's face was impassive. He stared hard at Ford, then nodded. "Alright then, my next question is … when do I start?"

Ford picked up his hat and started walking to the door, stopped, and with his hand on the knob, turned to face Slade. "Tonight. You're to meet up with your team at the livery stables and leave immediately thereafter."

Once Ford had left, Slade strapped on his gun belt, donned his hat, grabbed his saddlebags, draped them over his shoulder, lifted his rifle from the bed, and with that, he stepped out of his room.

"Doesn't leave much time for anything else," he muttered.

# CHAPTER 19

# FORT BROWN AND
# THE SOFT PROBE

It was around midnight as he made his slow way to the livery stables.

With his saddlebags draped over his left shoulder, rifle in hand, John Slade wasn't too happy about riding in the depth of night. Besides, he hadn't slept in the last eighteen hours. However, with this new mission, he was too excited to close his eyes. Sleep would have to be taken in the saddle.

With the night air cool and crisp on his face, cool enough that he almost needed to break out his duster, he spotted the stable on the other end of town. Down the middle of the street, he made his way and just before he stepped up to the stables entrance he stopped as he heard hushed talking and saw the glow of cigarettes from inside.

*Seems someone else wasn't sleeping tonight.*

He continued on his way.

Arriving at the open doors, he glimpsed shadows of a group of men sitting on the wooden floor in a dark corner, speaking in low tones. Just as he stepped in, a shadow appeared to his left.

The voices abruptly stopped.

"You want something stranger?" the shadow asked. Just as Slade turned toward the sound of the voice, he heard the unmistakable ratchet of a gun's hammer being cocked.

Slade couldn't see the man behind the shadow. These were well-trained soldiers; They had posted a lookout. "Looking for Jacob Rose," Slade answered.

"Who's doing the lookin'?" a soft-spoken Southern drawl asked from somewhere in the shadows.

"The names Slade, John Slade."

A figure loomed up in the darkness and approached the young, physically imposing six-footer. "So, you're Slade. Been expecting you."

It was the voice with the Southern drawl. "I'm Lieutenant Rose," he said, slowly making his way toward Slade through the near darkness.

As Jacob Rose stepped out of the gloom, someone lit a lantern in a far corner, illuminating the lieutenant and Slade in its glow. Out of the edge of his left eye, Slade spied four men rising from their positions, all wearing the Confederate States of America uniforms.

Gazing back at Rose, he let his eyes linger on the man as he came to a halt a few feet in front of him. Rose was short, not over five feet nine, and skinny, with long black hair just touching his shoulders. He sported a half-grown beard and mustache, and he too wore the Confederate uniform. His face was the color of burnt leather, with wrinkles and dark bags under his eyes which were a clear ocean blue as he squinted at Slade.

Glancing furtively around the stables, Slade quickly saw his horse, and made sure no one else was with them. Placing his saddlebags down and laying his rifle on them, they smiled and shook hands.

Rose motioned Slade toward the back of the stables. "Come on over and let me introduce you to the rest of the men: on your left is Sergeant Dan Shipley. On his left is Regis Greene, and Wilfredo Valdez alongside Doug Johnson."

Without a word, the four men came forward and shook hands all around.

Rose faced Slade. "To be frank with you, Slade," Rose said. "We hadn't expected to be back in San Antonio so soon."

Slade raised his eyebrows. "From where y'all coming from?"

"We're from the Texas Brigade," Rose replied in his drawl. "I, and my men received new orders to report to Colonel Ford here in San Antonio and to meet up with you. We've been waiting since late this morning. The Colonel said you were to fill us in on our mission."

Slade gave a brusque nod. "Yeah, Ford also ordered me here. I just arrived two hours ago."

Rose raised an eyebrow. "Ah."

John Slade remained silent for a moment. So, Ford had left it up to him to read out the mission parameters. He felt rather uncomfortable in that respect. He was no officer but held the rank of sergeant. Why these men? Couldn't Ford have simply called up soldiers much closer than the Texas Brigade out of the Eastern Theater? He'd heard of them of course. Some considered them the shock troops of the Confederacy. Still, why them?

"Let's all sit together, and I'll explain our mission," Slade finally said.

There were no chairs in the stables, so they sat on the hard-wood floor in a circle. Slade leaned slightly forward and took a deep breath. "Under normal circumstances," he began, "the lieutenant would be in charge of this mission. However, Colonel Ford felt that both of us should work together and get the information he needs."

"And what is that, exactly?" Rose interjected.

"We're heading to Brownsville and Fort Brown, to conduct a reconnaissance operation," Slade explained.

"That's my home, Brownsville, or just outside the town," Rose said.

"That's my home too," Valdez, said.

Slade looked around at the men for a moment. He now knew why Rose and Valdez were chosen—they knew intimately the area they would work in. Further, Slade surmised, Ford couldn't use any soldiers close by fearful of spies in their midst.

"What kind of information will we be looking for?" Sergeant Shipley asked.

"First, let me ask this question," Slade said. "How many of you have taken part in anything of this nature?"

No one spoke up.

"Slade," Rose said in a low voice. "We're only soldiers, told to fight wherever they need us. This is all new, even for me."

Slade shrugged. "Okay then, let me explain." Slade removed his hat and wiped the sweat from his hair with his palm. "We are going into enemy territory. There we'll scout the area and gain as much information as we can about the enemy's activities, their strengths, and weaknesses. We need to figure out their weak and strong fortifications, cannon placements and troop positions. Colonel Ford is preparing to attack the Fort and drive out the Union from Brownsville."

"So ... you have experience in this sort of thing?" Rose asked.

Slade nodded.

"How do you propose to accomplish all this?" Rose sniffed.

Slade went still and didn't answer the question.

They all waited on him.

"First," Slade said, finally breaking silence, "I need all of you to strip off your uniforms and don civilian clothing. If you don't have any, someone needs to break into the merchandise store and steal some. We'll go in as civilians and not soldiers. We leave within the hour."

"Slade," Rose said, staring at him. "Again, I ask, how are we going to pull this off?"

Again, Slade waited until he was sure no further questions were forthcoming. "I have a plan."

An hour later, the six rode out of San Antonio.

# CHAPTER 20

# FORT BROWN

*Brownsville, Texas*
*27 July 1864*

Two days later, Slade and his team arrived at the outskirts of Brownsville.

Having slept on the trail, the scouting party drew rein, and through a cloudless and starry night sky, Slade eyed Fort Brown in the far distance, and the town of Brownsville, by the Rio Grande River.

The plan outlined by Slade was simple. On their arrival in Brownsville, Jacob Rose would lead them to his home, where they would coordinate the soft probe of Fort Brown, gathering all the information they could as he'd outlined prior to leaving San Antonio. The men would be split up into two-man teams, each with a designated area. Rose and Slade would enter the fort and conduct their observations.

But first they needed a clear picture of Fort Brown with points of ingress and egress in case of trouble. That would fall on Slade and Rose.

This was Slade's first time in Brownsville, so he needed a full description of the fort and the two people that would provide that information would be Rose and Valdez.

On Slade's instructions, Rose led the team in a wide berth of the town and the fort, in the event they came upon Union patrols.

Throughout their ride, Slade noticed something quite peculiar—the lack of Union patrols—and voiced his observations to Lieutenant Rose, who couldn't explain the absence either.

Once settled in at Rose's home, Rose's only living relative, his father, a short grizzled gray-haired old man, walking with the help of a long wooden stick, with a face wrinkled like an old pair of leather pants, welcomed them.

Later, they sat around the dining table enjoying supper of beef stew, baked beans, biscuits and coffee, prepared by Rose and his father, their first hot meal in days.

Sergeant Dan Shipley sat back in his chair staring at those around the dining table, having been the first to finish, and with his second cup of coffee in hand, for the briefest moment he shook his head.

Shipley, a soldier since volunteering for the Confederacy at the outset of the war had fought in numerous battles and one thing that stood out to him since arriving in Brownsville, was the lack of Union patrols in the area. They should have met one or two that close to the fort.

After finishing his coffee, Shipley set the cup down on the table and leaned back in his chair. He stared at Rose, then lingered on Slade. Ever since they'd met in the stables Shipley wondered if Slade was the same man he'd heard so much about, fast with his guns and fearless in the face of battle.

However, this was not the time to concern himself with that, his chief concern now was the lack of Union patrols. "I have a question, Lieutenant," he said, waiting for Rose's attention. Once Rose placed his coffee cup on the table, he turned toward his sergeant.

"What's the question, Sergeant?" Rose asked.

John Slade, half-sitting, was curious as he listened.

Slade wasn't the only one listening. The others perked up, waiting to hear what Sergeant Shipley had to say. They'd been with the sergeant for two years, and knew he was a man of few words, never questioning but at times giving of his opinion.

Sergeant Shipley sighed audibly. "Was I the only one to notice the lack of Union patrols through the area since our arrival, sir?"

Slade and Rose stared at one another and smiled.

"It has occurred to us as well, Sergeant," Rose answered.

"Why do you think it's so, sir?" Sergeant Shipley asked.

"We don't know," Rose answered.

After dinner, they sat around the dining table.

John Slade glanced around at the men, momentarily stopping on Rose and Valdez. "I need a full description of Fort Brown."

Getting up from his chair, Rose said, "Give me a second, Slade." Rose then headed to another room and from a writing table he came back with paper and pencil.

Standing around the men, Rose drew an outline of the fort. "They built the Fort in a six-sided star-shape fortification. From what I've learned of it, each face extends about 125 to 130 yards. The walls are about 9 to 15 feet high. There used to be a moat 20 feet wide and 8 feet deep. It doesn't exist anymore. That's all I know about it."

Valdez said, "The lieutenant knows more about it than I do."

"Here's my plan," Slade said, and for the next twenty minutes he outlined the plan. Once everyone was on board with it and team assignments announced they left Rose's cabin heading for Fort Brown.

Rose's cabin was on the northeast and about ten miles from the town of Brownsville. Heading east, then cutting south, they crossed the Hermila's River making good time. As they neared the high lands just west of the fort, Slade was mystified by the lack of Union barricades or patrols in the area. Why that was, he wondered; he would soon find out.

By the light of the stars and a half-moon, they rode single file. No one said a word, keeping silent as they neared Fort Brown. Slade was thoroughly alive in his element and alert as he rode behind Rose. At a prominent ridge, just half a mile from the fort, Slade called a halt.

Reaching across into his saddlebags, he pulled out a pair of double-lens brass binoculars. He put them to his eyes and began scanning the area. Still too far to make out any activity at the fort, he noticed something strange, no campfires anywhere around the structure.

Handing the binoculars to Rose, he said, "Tell me what you see, Lieutenant."

Rose scanned the fort but didn't see anything out of the ordinary. "The fort is completely asleep. You see anything different, Slade?"

"You would think, since it's fairly cold, there would be campfires or smoke from burning chimneys," Slade said taking the binoculars back.

"You're right. Something's going on," Rose said. "What do you think it might mean?"

"I don't want to guess, but we'll know soon."

Slade turned to his men. "We'll split up here. You all know what to do. Try to stay out of any shooting ruckus with the enemy. Report back here once you're finished. Okay, let's go."

Fifteen minutes later, not encountering any resistance from Union roadblocks, Slade and Rose rode side by side down the road leading to the main gate.

As they approached to within a few yards, they noticed the gate wide open and not one guard in sight. Riding through the gate, they stopped. Both men experienced the same eerie feeling.

The fort seemed deserted!

"What do you make of this?" Rose asked.

"I don't," Slade replied, "this would explain not encountering patrols, but let's look around and make sure no one was left behind."

Once they finished, and not finding any signs of life, they rode back to the ridge to meet up with the rest of the team.

At the ridge, Slade asked for a volunteer to ride back to Colonel Ford with his message. Slade knew Colonel Ford and his army would already be riding in force to Fort Brown for his planned attack.

However, Slade had "taken" the fort without a shot. In the meantime, the rest of the team stayed in wait for Colonel Ford's arrival as they made camp inside the abandoned fort.

On Ford's arrival, John Slade quit the Confederacy, and with a full packhorse, courtesy of RIP Ford, he set out for Austin, Texas.

# CHAPTER 21

# THE TEXAS RANGERS

*Travis County, Austin, Texas,*
*Mid-October 1865*

It was early evening, the skies were clear with a brisk cool breeze that wafted in from the west, as John Slade rode through a barren landscape. Out in the far distance, he heard the rustling of the San Jacinto River. Listening to it as he traveled, he guided his horse toward it.

The breeze abruptly shifted, sending a sudden gust of icy desert winds that caught Slade like a slap to the face, stopping him in his tracks. As the wind subsided, he continued on his way. He needed to make camp before total darkness shrouded the land, making it impossible to continue, and before the cold set in.

He was in central Texas, about forty miles northeast of Austin, his next destination. Setting up camp on the banks of the swift-running river, he brewed a pot of coffee and ate the last of his hard-tack and meat.

As he crouched by the campfire and sipping his last cup of coffee before bedding down, he took a piece of twig, set fire to the tip, and lit a stogie. His mind wandered back to the last conversation he had with his mother about his father's condition and the events soon thereafter of their deaths and all the misery and hardship he'd experienced along the way since that awful time.

Closing his eyes, he recalled her words etched forever in his mind...

*"He has consumption, John. It's going to get worse as time goes by. The doctor said there is no cure and to prepare for the worst."*

*Then he asked only one question. "Will he die from his condition?"*

*"Yes, maybe in a month, a year, maybe two."*

*Death is the one thing constant in my life.*

Opening his eyes, he pulled himself out of his musings and instead focused a moment on his parents...

His parents were all he ever knew, his father never spoke of his grandparents and whether they were still alive, or if he had other relatives elsewhere. Once he remembered when he was nine, asking his mother about her parents and if they were coming to visit someday. She explained her parents died when she was five years old from cholera, and without siblings, she was alone. An uncle raised her in Ireland, and at ten they moved to Texas. When she turned fifteen, the ranch the uncle had built came under attack by Comanche warriors. She was the sole survivor. Since then, she'd lived in a boarding house in Nacogdoches and worked as the local schoolteacher, until she met his father.

Would he too be alone forever, John wondered, or would he find his one genuine love as his parents did?

*Only time will tell*, he told himself.

In May 1865, at the end of the war of Northern Aggression and having left the Ranger service behind him, John Slade yet again, found himself roaming from one cattle ranch to another, and in several towns, he never met the *one* that could share his life with forever. He had affairs, but not a one that came close to winning his heart.

Not staying put in any one place, and after his last cattle drive, Slade once again found himself almost penniless. He would have to make a decision soon, either find permanent employment or return to the Texas Rangers. But he'd cross that bridge when he came to it.

With a pained sigh, Slade flipped his stogie, covered himself with his blanket, drew one of his guns, tucked it under the blanket and laid back on his saddle and tried to sleep as he wanted to arrive in Austin in the early morning.

With the early rising birds chirping and flying overhead, he gazed as the morning sun peeked from behind a tall building, a few trees, and felt the warmth of its rays warming his face. Mornings always felt as if they held the promise of a new beginning. With his horse at a slow lope, John Slade rode through Austin's main street.

He approached and passed two Texas Rangers whose metal badges* pinned to their vests gleamed off the sun's light as they sat behind a booth. A sign to one side read: *Volunteers needed for the Texas Rangers.*

---

*The first Texas Ranger badge was worn by Ranger Ira Aten in the 1880s. The first state-issued badge was introduced in the 1900s. The author used the badge much earlier than the 1880s for illustrated purposes only.

Slade, the son of a Ranger, upon seeing the sign, knew fate was leading him toward the life he knew too well. And he'd be following in his father's footsteps once again. But for now, he needed to find a restaurant and have breakfast.

As the sun emerged to all its glory, Slade spotted a café to his right. The two hitching posts in front of the establishment were almost full, but between a pinto and mustang he reined up his horse to a stop. Dismounting, he tied the reins and ambled onto the street, his metallic spurs jingling behind him.

At the café door, he entered and stopped at the threshold. The large room was full of patrons making it difficult in finding a lone table. He spotted one on the far corner, next to the kitchen doors.

*Too hot for most*, he thought.

Slade wove through the crowded restaurant and felt eyes on him. Shifting his gaze to the patrons, he couldn't see any signs of danger; yet his right hand gravitated naturally toward the butt of his gun.

Once he'd placed his order, he had that strange feeling again that someone was watching him. Slade gazed from one table to the next and stopped at two men dining. He stared briefly at one of the men, an old-looking large man, with shoulder-length long black graying hair, who dropped his eyes the moment Slade gazed at him, but not before offering a brief smile.

The man, Slade noticed, had a scar that started below his right eye and ended just touching his upper lip. He was wearing a dirty white shirt under a black leather wrinkled open short jacket and chaps. But the strange thing was, he was wearing the badge of the Texas Rangers.

Slade didn't perceive any danger from him and looked away as his breakfast was being placed in front of him.

Minutes later, he sat back on his chair and lifted his mug of lukewarm coffee to his lips and sipped. Setting his cup back on the table, he gazed at the Ranger once again. This time the older man raised his mug in a friendly salute.

Likewise, Slade returned the gesture.

A few minutes later, Slade noticed the Ranger walking toward his table with a full mug of steaming hot coffee in hand.

The first thought that crossed Slade's mind when watching him approach was *this could be trouble*. In one fluid motion, he gripped the butt of his gun, drew, cocked back the hammer, and placed it on his thigh.

Stopping in front of Slade, the man smiled. "Easy pard, you can holster your piece, I mean you no harm, unless of course there's a bounty out for you, which I doubt."

"What do you want?" Slade responded. Again, he sensed the Ranger was no trouble. He slipped his gun back into its holster and placed his hand on the table.

"Can I sit?"

Slade only nodded.

Once sitting facing Slade, the Ranger set his coffee mug to one side, reached into his vest pocket, and pulled out a piece of metal.

Palming it and with three fingers he slid it toward Slade and stopped it in front of him.

"What's this?" Slade asked, but he already knew what it was before the Ranger drew back his hand.

"Me and my partner," the Ranger began, "Saw you come in. I saw you stop at the door. Saw you as you scanned the room, looking for what? A table, my partner said. But no, I knew differently, you were scanning for danger, my young friend."

"And that concerns you, how?"

"And" not answering Slade's question, the Ranger shook his head, smiled, and not missing a beat, continued, "you gripped the butt of one of your guns as you passed by."

Then the Ranger drew back his hand and exposed the star of the Texas Rangers.

Slade eyed the badge but offered no signs he was picking it up. "What's this about?"

The Ranger grinned. "From the moment I saw you come in, I knew you could be a gunfighter, an ex-lawman, or a bounty hunter. Which one is it young man?"

There was a pause and the two men looked at each other.

"I'm only here looking for work," Slade said, glancing at the badge. "But not this."

"I know," the Ranger said, "I do. It ain't much of living, but its steady honest work, but it pays well too. You get a horse and three meals a day."

Slade breathed out. "Got a horse."

"Listen, what's your name? I'm Billy Silas."

"Slade, John Slade."

"So, John Slade, what say you?"

In answer, Slade gazed at Silas, lowered his head and slid the badge back to the Ranger.

Billy Silas waived a hand. "Well, if you change your mind we'll be across the street.

John Slade, for the better part of an hour, had visited one establishment after another seeking employment. And he knew the only option left open was the Rangers.

Sighing, he took stock of his circumstances. There was no way around it. He was down to his last dollar, no jobs anywhere and no one to turn to. Admittedly, he knew it was time to fill his father's shoes. He would try it for a month ... what did he stand to lose?

John Slade swallowed, climbed onto his saddle, and turned his horse's head toward the Rangers booth. A few minutes later he reined his horse in front of the Rangers. Standing there was Silas, along with two comrades, gazing up at the young man.

Dismounting, Slade turned toward Silas. "That badge still available?"

# CHAPTER 22

# CAPTAIN LEANDER McNELLY
# TEXAS RANGER

*Lost Valley Settlements, Young County, Texas,*
*June 1875*

Texas Ranger John Slade had seen the last nine years pass in the blink of an eye, with memories as fresh as yesterday. He reflected on its swiftness and of his time as a Ranger.

Slade served in B Company of the Frontier Battalion under Major John B. Jones and his seventy-five Texas Rangers. When Mexican bandits and Indians were threatening the frontiers, they'd tasked the battalion to solve the problem, along with the control of ordinary criminal elements and the defense against hostile Indian tribes of the Comanches, Kiowa, and the Apache nations.

The young Ranger soon learned that experience was indeed the teacher of all things—in the words of Julius Caesar—and had applied it to his way of thinking. Rising rapidly through the ranks, Slade ultimately made the rank of First Sergeant. He became famous for the lightning draw of his sidearms and without fail bringing to justice those they sent him after; always bringing them back alive. His comrades liked and admired him, as did all those that came to know him.

John Slade took part in his last major skirmish with Major Jones and twenty-six Rangers when they fought over fifty Kiowa warriors led by Chief Lone Wolf in Lost Valley. A rim of hills surrounded the valley, a twenty-square-mile region. Twenty miles west is the town of Jacksboro in western Jack County. The valley is major cattle ranching mecca.

In the fight, Slade sustained two non-life-threatening wounds and the company lost a Ranger shot dead from his horse. Slade underwent two surgeries to repair his left arm and thigh. By the time he returned to duty, the northwest frontier settlements were relatively safe from Comanche and Kiowa depredations. However, the Apaches still posed a problem.

Taking a respite from his everyday duties, Slade entered his tent and sat down on his bed. Suffering a massive headache, he rubbed his forehead. His thigh and left arm still ached, and he was bone tired.

With the day drawing to a close and staring around his tent, he gave a short, nasty laugh. "Ah hell," he muttered. There wasn't any more he could do. A good night's sleep is what he needed.

Lying on the bed, he closed his eyes briefly. He'd given them nine solid years and thought it was enough. Enough so that he needed a new direction in life besides that of a Ranger.

Slade opened his eyes and looked up at the top of the canvas tent and shrugged. A rancher like his father would be high on his list.

He'd saved enough to start his small spread.

But fate had other plans for the Texas Ranger.

Two hours later, just west of Lost Valley, in the town of Jacksboro, two Texas Rangers sat around a dining table in their hotel restaurant as a light rain fell. They faced two large glass picture windows a few feet from their table as they dined while conversing in low tones.

Major John B. Jones, a short stocky man with dark brooding eyes, neatly trimmed black hair, bushy eyebrows and a long handle-bar mustache stretching down past his lips, lifted a tall glass of white wine, sipped the liquid, returned the glass to the table, sat back on his chair and stared at the man sitting across from him, Captain Leander McNelly.

"How long you're in town for, Leander?" asked Major Jones, looking up at his friend.

Not staring at Major Jones, McNelly forked a mouthful and with a full mouth replied. "Just long enough to raise a few more men."

Captain McNelly, unlike Jones who wore a dark three-piece suit, was wearing tanned trousers, knee-high boots, with a white shirt over an open tanned cowhide vest with his pinned Texas Rangers badge on the left side. A large red bandana encircled his neck.

Pushing his plate away from him, Captain McNelly lifted his wineglass to his lips. A trickle of the clear liquid dripped down his thick black full goatee, streaked with gray that extended down below his chin and a dark bushy mustache.

Swiping a palm over his goatee, McNelly set the glass back on the table. "My friend, what's this meeting about and why were you asking about my next command?"

The night was hot and humid, but the rain shower held the promise of cool winds. However, their conversation came to an abrupt halt when the rain built up to a powerful thunderstorm with lightning flashing across the sky.

It was intense and sudden!

After dinner and undaunted by the sharp, loud cracking of lightning and the booming of thunder and heavy rainfall, they enjoyed their glasses of wine, which went well with their stewed fruit, soused calves' feet, cornbread, and some stewed oysters.

Major Jones leaned forward and placed his hand on the table. "I heard through the Governor's office that you've been tasked for work down at the Nueces Strip and have been recruiting men to assist you."

"You hear well my friend."

"I try to make it my business to keep up with the politics of information, Leander. And I heard you were headed this way."

"I see. So yes, I've been ordered to organize a small band of Rangers." McNelly paused, raised his glass and downed the last of the wine, then continued in a quiet voice. "My orders are to assemble men to put an end to several Mexican outlaw gangs and a Texan outlaw and gunman named King Fisher."

Jones nodded. He took a sip of his wine and considered what he wanted to say.

"How many men have you recruited so far?" he asked.

"Thirty-eight. I would have more, but I've limited the recruits. I've rejected most native Texans who had applied. I didn't want them to fight their friends or relatives."

"You have a set number of men for your command?" Jones asked.

"Forty, forty-five, no more than that."

This was encouraging. Major Jones glanced off to the side, trying to choose his next words wisely. Then he stared at Captain Leander. "My friend, we go back away's. I have a request to make of you."

A tentative nod from McNelly.

"I have a Ranger in my command that could prove beneficial to your operations," Jones said. "He is one of the fastest guns I've ever seen, and his father was a famous Ranger. Strong, courageous and honest."

Another nod.

Silence fell.

McNelly said nothing.

Jones couldn't read his friend's tanned face.

Leander thought for a moment. "Major, I'm not here by chance," he began. "I've heard stories of a Ranger with a fast draw and I'm hoping to recruit him. I heard he was somewhere down in Lost Valley. Maybe he's the same person you're recommending. His name is Slade, John Slade ... Have you heard of him?"

Major Jones laughed. "We're talking about the same man here, Leander. Slade is recuperating from his wounds but is available to ride."

McNelly frowned. "Is he as fast as they say he is?"

Jones considered his next words. "John is a prodigy son. Larry Slade, his father, served in the Texas Revolution and became one of the first Texas Rangers. He, too, had one of the fastest cross-gun draws in the Rangers. There are stories told of John's father, some a little hard to swallow. But it's said he let his guns speak for him. And the apple doesn't fall far from the tree."

McNelly stared at Jones with faint amusement. "Of course, I've heard of Larry Slade and his exploits, I just didn't put two and two together. There wasn't any mention of a son that I knew of."

Major Jones shrugged. "Then you'll accept Slade into your company?"

"Quite so. When can you have him report to me? I'll only be in town for a day or two."

"I'll have my adjutant send a telegram and have him report to you tomorrow afternoon."

Then, lifting his glass slightly above his head, he said, "Now, how about another glass of that delicious wine?"

One and a half hours later, a young soldier stepped up to a canvas tent.

The name above the door read: *First Sergeant Slade.*

It was dark, and the soldier had to light a match to make sure he was at the right one. "Sergeant Slade," the soldier called out, repeating the name when he received no answer. He would've had called out again, but he finally heard someone from inside.

"This had better be good, whoever you are out there," Slade yelled out. "Or there'll be hell to pay." After being woken from his sleep, John Slade roused himself from his bed. "Hang on out there while I light a lamp."

A short moment later, with the soldier gone, Slade stared at the unopened telegraph and had an uncanny sensation of being ordered to his next objective. He always knew being a Ranger meant he was told where to go and what to do. But damn, all he wanted now was to quit the Rangers and start a spread of his own. His heart quickened at the mere thought of another battle looming in his future.

What he should've done before this was quit. Now, it may be too late.

Shrugging off his misgivings, Slade, with a twinge of annoyance opened the telegraph.

The message was short and to the point. He was being ordered to meet up with a Captain Leander McNelly in Jacksboro tomorrow afternoon for his next assignment.

Slade let that sink in.

He was well familiar with Captain McNelly, whose exploits during the War of Northern Aggression while serving in the Confederate Army were legendary. His battles at Valverde, Galveston and Louisiana made front-page headlines in the newspapers and gained him notoriety as a somewhat unstoppable force to be reckoned with. And at the battle of Mansfield, along with Hempstead, he rounded up deserters.

Slade had also heard McNelly was organizing a troop of Rangers to fight Mexican bandits. How true his information might be was anyone's guess? Were these his orders, to team up with the Captain and fight the Mexican bandits? He'd know tomorrow afternoon.

As he lay on his bed he thought of the force or forces keeping him a Ranger. Someone or something was dictating his life as if he wasn't in control of it. It was a terrible feeling. Slade had always thought he'd been in control, but now he wasn't so sure.

He didn't feel the slightest drowsiness or sleep but closed his eyes, nevertheless. At last, sleep overtook him as he turned his head to one side of his pillow.

## CHAPTER 23

# THE MISSION

It was a hot dry morning without a cloud in sight, nor rain to cool the desert landscape, only the hot drifting winds shearing through his eyes to keep him company.

John Slade had been riding since the crack of dawn. And it wasn't until late that same morning that the Texas Ranger crossed the banks of Lost Creek, with the town unseen through the haze of the shimmering sun's rays just a mile or two in the far distance.

Crossing the creek, he rode through several hills when he spied an old worn-out wooden sign on the side of the dirt path proclaiming *Jacksboro* town limits straight ahead.

Halting, his throat and mouth were parched. His hatband was soaked with sweat stains. And as the beads of perspiration slowly dripped down his body, he lifted his canteen, satisfied his thirst and splashed water onto his face. Then, after his horse had its fill of the creek water, he put spurs to his horse and rode on.

Finally entering the town, Slade made his way down Jacksboro's Belknap Street. For a small place the streets were congested as he passed small-time business storefronts. The town, along the banks of Lost Creek and the waters of West Fork and Keechi Creek and south of Mineral Wells and northwest to Wichita Falls, was a no-man's-land until they constructed Fort Richardson in 1870. But it was in 1871 when the fort gained national attention when two Kiowa chiefs, Satanta and Big Tree, were tried for murder.

According to the rest of his message, it was at Fort Richardson where Slade was to meet up with Captain McNelly.

Riding slow and easy through the bustling town, Slade observed the Butterfield Overland Stage and Mail pulling away from its depot as a small group of bystanders waved their goodbyes to those on the stage. A normal life, he kept repeating over in his mind—was what he yearned for. He hoped this would be his last posting, for he was willing to quit right after.

As the stage went by, Slade pulled up rein for a moment, removed his hat and wiped his brow with his bandana. As he sat in his saddle, he gazed warily up and down the long curving street and behind him, squinting in the hot rays of the sun, it was as if someone was trying to outflank him; he was ever cautious of his surroundings. It's how he'd stayed alive this long.

Riding through town he was looking for a café. Finally, rounding a short curve built around a small hilltop, he spotted one further up on the sunbaked sandy street on the right side. He was hungry and a bit saddle weary. He rubbed his arm, feeling the slight ache from his gunshot wound.

Seeing no signs of danger, Slade tied his bandana around his neck. Setting his hat back on he continued down the street as riders and several buckboards made their way up and down the crowded main street, loaded with supplies; yet some were empty and others were packed with families. Slowly he rode until he came to the restaurant, set back a piece from the rest of the buildings. The boardwalk with three steps onto it was crowded with what he supposed were waiting patrons.

He couldn't wait.

Slade rode past the restaurant, heading to a corner saloon. The name above the establishment read *J.B. Jarvis Saloon*. A billboard to one side said *hot meals served*. And it had no waiting lines; all to his liking.

With a red-striped canvas awning overhanging the boardwalk and two hitching posts in front and three horses tied, Slade dismounted, tied his horse, and ambled through the open doors. It had a few patrons, all cowhands from local ranches he assumed. A sign over the bar suggested ordering meals at the bar, which he did. Twenty minutes later he was enjoying steak and potatoes with a cup of coffee.

By the time he'd finished his meal it was time to meet Captain McNelly at Fort Richardson. Back in the saddle again, he rode to the far southern part of the town for about a twelve-minute ride.

Texas Ranger Sergeant Major John Barclay Armstrong, a rather impressive six-foot-tall man with a thick bull neck and shoulders as wide as the door he'd walked through seconds before, possessed a thick black heavy and bushy handlebar mustache, streaked with gray, that adorned his dark tanned face paused at the center of the room. Removing his hat, he swept off the dust and sand from about his pants.

Armstrong wore black trousers, boots, a tanned vest under a white sweat-stained shirt, cross holstered gun on his left side and another down his right leg. He kept his long shirt sleeves from slipping below his hands with elastic arm garters. He'd been nicknamed *"McNelly's Bulldog"* by his men because of his size and formidable qualities that gained respect and fear at the same time.

McNelly's Sergeant Major looked tired and in a foul mood, not having made time for his lunch after having interviewed several prospective hombres for the job as Rangers. Out of twenty he'd screened—following his captain's guidelines—he chose only two.

Sergeant Major Armstrong had to make his report to the captain before he even thought of sitting down to lunch.

He was at Captain McNelly's temporary quarters on the far right of the fort's Battalion Commander's quarters in Fort Richardson.

With a deep breath, he continued into the room. He heard Captain McNelly, sitting in an armchair with his back to him, stir and asked, "How many did you enlist, John?"

Coming around to an empty chair, Armstrong sat facing his captain, who was smoking a pipe. Suddenly, McNelly leaned forward of his chair covered his mouth with a palm and began coughing hard. Armstrong saw blood dripping down from his lips.

McNelly grasped a handkerchief from his breast shirt pocket and wiped the blood and sat back as if nothing had happened with his pipe in hand.

Armstrong knew better than to ask of his condition, knowing full well his captain's health was deteriorating as he suffered from tuberculosis.

Settling back on his seat, Armstrong lit a cigar and stared at his commander, "Ah, sir—" the Sergeant Major referred to McNelly with either sir or Captain, never with his given or surname, "I hadn't had the time to ask, sir, but did you ever find Ranger John Slade?"

McNelly glanced at Armstrong. Although the Sergeant Major volunteered just a short a month ago, he respected and admired the sacrifice and dedication of the man. And his fearlessness under fire. Armstrong served as a lawman in Austin Texas before joining McNelly's newly created military branch of the Texas Rangers. He knew how to keep his men in check.

McNelly couldn't put a finger on it, but someone—he suspected Armstrong—had nicknamed his force the *Little McNelly's*. He didn't care, all he wanted was to have a cohesive force willing to follow his orders.

Neither man spoke. McNelly gathered himself up.

"Yes, I have. He's due in sometime this afternoon," McNelly said.

"This afternoon?" The Sergeant murmured, frowning.

McNelly hesitated for a moment. "I would like you to be here when he arrives. Also, I want to see how fast he is with his guns. We'll set up a quick draw exhibition between you and Slade. I know you're fast also. So, let's see if what they say about him is true."

"And if he isn't, what then?"

"In that case," McNelly said, almost to himself, "I won't be needing him."

A few minutes later, John Slade rode into Fort Richardson.

Off to his right stood the headquarters building. And, ten minutes later he knew from the officer on duty where Captain McNelly was quartered.

Moments later, having tied his horse to the hitching post, Slade stood in front of a one-story stone structure that housed the quarters of Captain McNelly. With his spurs jingling softly behind him, he climbed the two steps onto the boardwalk. Then, under the wooden awning, he stopped at the solid wooden door left ajar. He knocked once politely and a voice from within said, "Come in."

Removing his hat, he nuzzled the door in, entered and stopped at the threshold. He found himself in a spacious living room with a fireplace on the left. Two curtained windows were open lighting the interior. Three armchairs spread around a decorative carpeted floor. A huge mirror was hung over the fireplace. A short oaken dining table with four chairs adorned the other side of the room. And a table with bottles of liquor was set off to a corner up against the wall with an assortment of glasses.

In two of the armchairs sat two men who stared up at him.

"Ranger Slade?" Captain McNelly asked as he stood with an outstretched hand. "I'm McNelly and this is Sergeant Major John Armstrong."

"Heard a lot about you, Sergeant Slade," Armstrong said, not bothering to stand.

"I hope all good," Slade replied.

Taking the proffered hand and staring into McNelly's eyes, Slade said, "I've heard and read a great deal about you, sir. I don't yet know what I can help you out with, but I guess you'll clue me in."

Taking his seat, McNelly said, "Pull up a chair and I'll explain the mission, and what role you'll have in it."

Slade seated himself in an armchair across from the two men.

And for a moment, McNelly didn't say anything as he pulled a handkerchief from his shirt pocket and coughed into it.

Then McNelly leaned toward Slade, while Armstrong lit a cigar, sat back, crossing one leg over the other and listened to what he had already known of the task.

"The newly elected Governor," McNelly began, "Richard Coke, ordered me to create a special force of Texas Rangers and I to command it. With you, we have forty-one men. Enough to get the job done. The job calls for bringing law and order to the Nueces Strip. The strip, or Wild Horse Desert, is an area of South Texas between the Nueces River and the Rio Grande and is a hotbed of cattle thievery and banditry. A Mexican bandit named Juan Nepomuceno Cortina, also known as the Rio Grande Robin Hood on the other side of the border, conducts guerilla-like operations against the local ranchers."

"I know of Cortina and the strip," Slade said, "my father was involved with fighting off his bandits several years ago."

"A fine job they did too," McNelly responded, "but it wasn't complete. Cortina still operates with impunity on the Strip."

A brief pause as McNelly lit his pipe. Inhaling the sweet aroma of the tobacco and blowing it to his side, he continued. "Cortina has a long history of banditry, as we well know, raiding Brownsville and retreating across the border. He has a force of about sixty men. Besides that, there is an American bandit and gunman named King Fisher and his band of outlaws we are tasked to put down."

"What do we know of King Fisher and his band?" Slade asked, glancing at one, then at the other Ranger. Slade was more curious about Fisher than he was about Cortina. Fisher could prove the more formidable foe.

"I'll let Sergeant Armstrong answer that," Captain McNelly responded. "He was the one that secured the information for us."

Sergeant Armstrong leaned forward. "Oh, there's not a great deal about Fisher that I could find, but what I did is this ... Fisher served four months in a Goliad prison for breaking into a house. From there he put together a small band of bandits and moved to Dimmit County. Through their property records, I found out that he'd established a ranch in and around where cattle rustling was rampant. He put himself right in the middle of it and by witnesses' accounts, he even rode with Mexican rustlers, making off with a hundred head of cattle. His activities led to violence. It's reported, but not substantiated, that he killed several Mexicans and Americans gaining a reputation as a skilled gunfighter."

Slade shrugged. He was beginning to see what McNelly wanted of him. The captain may have thought that if they came gun to gun with Fisher, his fast guns would be their ace in the hole. But he kept his thoughts to himself, for now.

"How do I play into all this?" Slade asked.

McNelly stared at Slade. "I'm coming to that... first, we'll need a demonstration of your fast draw. And what I have in mind for your assignment, you'll probably gun down some very dangerous bandits before we finish with this mission."

Sergeant Armstrong stared at Slade, and there was a hint of a smile that played across his face.

The smile wasn't lost to Slade's keen eyes. Armstrong's dead cold eyes said little, but Slade gathered the man was having some fun with him. Slade also figured, the sergeant had the face of a man that had seen his share of violence and death; better to keep him on his good side, Slade said to himself.

"Let's head outside," Captain McNelly said, rising from his chair, "and you can show us your quick draw skills." Staring down at Sergeant Armstrong, he said, "You too, Sergeant Major."

It was a typically quiet, hot and humid afternoon, with no clouds in sight. Yet as they stepped down from the boardwalk a slight breeze from the south blew onto their faces. Slade, Armstrong and Captain McNelly set their hats down lower over their brows, shielding from the scorching sun.

Along that part of the fort, soldiers and civilians alike went about their business. Wagons crept up and down the street far away from the three men.

McNelly led Slade and Armstrong a few paces from his bungalow. McNelly told them, "I'm going to tack two pieces of paper with a circle drawn in them up against that shed yonder. On the count of three I want you both to draw at the same time and see who gets closest to the center of the circle."

A small crowd gathered behind them, mostly soldiers. More onlookers came to see the shooting match between Sergeant Armstrong and the tall, dark stranger. Bets were made who would be closer to the center of the circle.

Armstrong untied the leather strap to his cross-holstered gun. Drawing it, he checked the loads and made sure the hammer rested on an empty chamber. Holstering the gun, he said, "I'm ready sir." Slade did the same.

"On my count of three."

Slade watched the expression on Armstrong's face. It was impassive, without the slightest edge of excitement on it.

"One..."

Slowly, both men slid their hand to the butt of their guns.

"Two..."

"Three..."

Both men drew and fired their guns at the same time.

Again, Captain McNelly walked to the shed. "Well, I'll be damned, Slade is dead center, and Armstrong is at the inside edge."

As they heard a small shout from the crowd, money quickly exchanged hands. News of the match spread rampantly through the fort and the small crowd grew. No one had ever heard of Slade, but Armstrong's reputation with a fast gun was well known.

"I'm impressed, Slade," Captain McNelly said, "that is some fine shooting. However, just another match if you don't mind."

"Suits me, if it's okay with the Sergeant Major," Slade responded.

With the sweat dripping down his face, Armstrong dragged his cuff across his forehead, trying to keep it out of his eyes. "Fine by me."

"Someone get me a can," the Captain said to no one in particular.

Moments later, with a can in hand, McNelly threw it on the ground. "You'll both draw and shoot, the first one that hits the can wins."

Now, this was more to Slade's liking, he'd played around with this sort of thing with his father. And each time he'd won. Removing his bandana and hat, he dried off the sweat from his brow preventing it from possibly stinging his eyes. With his hat back on, he waited for the Captain.

The crowd was excited. Again, bets were placed and now that they had seen Slade's gun come alive, the bets were two to one, against Armstrong.

"Please stand side to side," Armstrong said, "at the crack of my gun, draw and fire."

Both Rangers waited, each of their hands already close to their guns in anticipation of the sound of McNelly's gun being fired.

Suddenly, McNelly squeezed the trigger and like lightning, Slade's hand was once again a blur of motion as he drew his gun and holding it down his side fired two shots both hitting the can even before Armstrong let off a shot of his own!

The crowd shouted the winner's name, "Slade," as money was exchanged once again.

Captain McNelly shouted at the crowd to disperse. Then, turning to Slade, he said, "The stories they tell about your speed and accuracy with your guns are all true, Sergeant Slade. Welcome to McNelly's Rangers."

Sergeant Armstrong approached the two men and extended his hand towards Slade. "You are fast youngster, the only other person I've seen faster was James Hickock. You'll do well with what we've set out to do at the Strip."

"Let's get back in the house," Captain McNelly said, "and drink to our mission."

# CHAPTER 24

# THE GUNFIGHT AND SKIRMISH

*Fort Richardson, Jackson County Texas*
*June 1875*

"Slade, before you joined up with Captain McNelly, we were given our orders."

Sergeant Major John Armstrong sat in an armchair in Slade's temporary quarters, a neat two-bedroom bungalow on the other side of Fort Richardson and across from the post headquarters. He'd come with a bottle of Old Crow whiskey to celebrate Slade's fast draw win.

Slade accepted the offered bottle, then poured two half-full glasses of the whiskey and sat back on his armchair across from the first sergeant. After a sip of the warm liquid, Slade said, "I heard about the orders from some Rangers. I also heard you had a run-in with some Mexican bandits. Can you tell me what happened?"

"Well, to begin with and as you may know or not," Sergeant Armstrong replied, "The Nueces strip between Corpus Christi and the Rio Grande is a dangerous place and one that Captain McNelly and our Rangers were ordered to subdue. The reports from the Governor's office and those of local law enforcement were that they were being overrun with violent Mexicans who were stealing, killing and raping along the Strip."

Armstrong paused and took a big gulp from his glass, and after wiping his mouth with the sleeve of his shirt, he cleared his throat and continued. "It was up the river and north of Brownsville where we had our first fight with a Mexican gang led by a man named Juan Flores Salinas...

"...Mind you, he didn't have the manpower of Cortina's band, but they put up a good fight. The gang was headquartered at Camargo Mexico, and directly across the border from the US Cavalry outpost of Ringgold Barracks near Rio Grande City. We didn't lose one Ranger and we sure gave 'em what for."

This bit of storytelling Slade absorbed in silence, as he exchanged a glance with Armstrong. *I can guess there is more to it than that*, he wondered. But he kept it to himself.

"Where do you think we'll go from here?" Slade asked.

"We'll be heading out for Palo Alto in the morning," the sergeant said. "Make sure you pack enough ammo. We may have to fight it out with Cortina's gang. With the help of merchants and ranchers in the area, they chipped in to outfit our Rangers and also provided us with single-shot, 50 caliber Sharps rifles for long-range shooting with an ample supply of ammo."

The evening was fast approaching when Sergeant Armstrong left Slade's bungalow. He left Slade with more questions and no answers. Tactics are what he wanted to discuss with Armstrong, but each time Slade brought it up, Armstrong would simply brush it aside. So, that was going to wait until the morning.

After breakfast, Sergeant Armstrong, along with Slade and their commander, Captain McNelly, sat around the dying embers of their campfire, sipping on their warm cups of coffee. In the far distance, a coyote's single lone howl signaled he was looking for his pack. A mountain lion's growl and hiss sounds resounded from far away. They thought the unsuspecting traveler was on the prowl for food.

With the sun slowly rising, those sounds didn't bother the forty-one Texas Rangers who were packing up the campsite, ready for their destiny with Cortina's band of Mexican outlaws.

Captain McNelly was the first of the three to finish breakfast and his coffee. He rose from his chair without a word, rubbed his chin and stared down at Sergeant's Armstrong and Slade. Then, equally wordlessly, the two Texas Rangers rose and came around to their commander's side.

"We ride to Palo Alto, gentlemen!" Captain McNelly commanded.

With his forty-one Texas Rangers, led by Captain Leander H. McNelly, Sergeant Major Armstrong and First Sergeant Slade, each commanding a troop of men, the first major gunfight between the Mexican bandits and the Rangers occurred in mid-June 1875.

Acting on information from a captured Cortina's bandit, it was learned that three hundred head of cattle would be driven to the Rio Grande and then onto a steamer bound for Cuba by Cortina's hand-picked men, who boasted they could cope with any Rangers or vigilantes that came their way

McNeely planned to take them by surprise!

Once on his saddle, Captain McNelly's orders to his Rangers were clear and concise. "Don't shoot to the left or right. Shoot straight ahead. And don't shoot until you've got your target good in your sights. Don't walk upon a wounded man and pay no attention to a white flag. And don't touch a dead man."

John Slade instinctively knew this was going to be a long day and a long gunfight ahead of them. His questions on strategy were finally answered.

Slowly, the Texas Rangers came upon the bandit's trail, which wasn't that hard to follow, what with the cattle noises, trail dust and the yelling of the bandits. Following the trail, they soon reached the outlaws.

Minutes later, the bandits spied the Texas Rangers behind them. The Mexicans took flight. Shooting into the air, they ran the herd into a frenzied pace, until they reached a little island in the middle of a salt marsh.

Knowing the Rangers were almost upon them, the bandits halted the advance of the cattle, turned, and waited for the pursuers to cross the shallow, muddy lagoon.

With Armstrong and Slade to either side of McNelly, it was Armstrong who first spotted the trap. "Seems they set up a little ambush for us, sir."

"I see that as well," Slade said. "We could be in for a long fight."

Coming to a halt, Captain McNelly called his men around him. "Rangers, across the muddy lagoon are some bandits that claim they're bigger than Texas law. This won't be a standoff or a dogfight. We'll either win completely, or we'll lose completely."

As the cool morning desert winds blew through the prairie, Captain McNelly ordered his men to attack. Halting just at the lagoon entrance, McNeely waited for the bandits to show their hand. And then, just as the outlaws started their frontal attack, the Texas Rangers moved in as both forces clashed head-on.

The battle fiercely surged back and forth all day in a succession of single-hand fights and close quarter gunfights.

Slade, with bandits all around him and his Rangers, dismounted on the fly, and once on his feet, he met three bandits that aimed right at him. Fanning his Colt, Slade shot and killed two, while the third got off several shots of his own, striking the Ranger.

Slade sustained gunshots to his left arm, right shoulder, and left leg, dropping him to his knees while his gun slipped through his hand. Just as the bandit was reloading, Slade drew his second Colt and shot him between the eyes.

Losing blood at a fast pace, Slade whistled out for his horse, and moments later the horse halted his approach to his master. He quickly jumped into the saddle and at full gallop headed to the rear for the medical tent. Halting at the makeshift hospital, he fell off his horse unconscious as the two medical aidmen rushed to his side.

The battle at Palo Alto ranged on throughout the late afternoon!

---

References: Leander H. McNelly (March 12, 1844–September 4, 1877. The Nueces Strip. The Battle at Palo Alto, from the Handbook of Texas Online. *Legendary Texians*, Volume 11, Austin TX: Eakin Press.

# CHAPTER 25

# EMILY

*General Hospital, Brownsville, Texas*
*November 1875*

A doctor in a wrinkled and bloody white medical coat over a dark shirt, trousers and boots stepped into a room in the recovery section of the hospital and saw his patient wide awake. "Good morning, Ranger Slade. This is your second day back from a month-long coma. It's been my experience that patients this long in a coma don't make it out and die. You're a very lucky man. How do you feel?"

Slade was staring out a window on the far side of the room, as light freezing rain was falling. Soon the snow would fall, with Christmas just around the corner. He had no recollection of how he arrived at the hospital or by whom. It was an eerie feeling.

"Hi, doctor," Slade replied as he turned to meet the man. "I feel weak and tired with some minor pain that keeps shooting up my leg. But other than that, when will you be releasing me?"

"Not for a while I'm afraid, Ranger. We need to get you back walking and get your arm back in complete circulation and pain-free. And that will start this morning. I have assigned a volunteer nurse to help with your recovery."

"Thanks, doc. I can't wait."

"In the meantime, I left word at the ranger station that you were awake. There are two Rangers outside the clinic that have been waiting. Should I call them in?"

Slade was sitting up in bed when Captain McNelly stepped into the room, followed by Sergeant Major Armstrong. McNelly and Armstrong found two empty chairs and pulled them closer to Slade's bed.

Both Texas Rangers were wearing long black heavy coats, with dark trousers and rawhide chaps, with white shirts and a dark vest over the shirts. Slade could make out their guns sticking out over their coats.

Once seated, McNeely noticed how pale-skinned Slade appeared and thought he'd be unable to mount soon. It was a pity. He could've used him on the next mission.

"Good morning, Sergeant Slade," McNelly said, laying a deck of cards on the desk by his bed. "Just in case you get bored. We were concerned you weren't going to make it. When I received word that you pulled through from your coma, we got here at first light today."

"I'm much obliged, Captain," Slade murmured. "Sergeant Armstrong."

The two men nodded their acknowledgment.

Curious as to the outcome of the mission at Palo Alto, Slade asked. "Tell me, Captain, did we win?"

"Completely!" Captain McNelly replied, taking a deep breath. "All the Mexican bandits driving that herd met their end. Two hundred and sixty-five heads of stock were rounded up. We drove them to the King Ranch. And we also recovered several saddles stolen from a raid in Nuecestown three months earlier. We didn't lose any Rangers."

Sergeant Armstrong tuned around and faced McNelly. "Except for one, sir," Armstrong corrected. "It was a seventeen-year-old Ranger. And due to his dark skin, he was believed to have been Mexican. Someone identified him as Ranger Berry Smith who got too close to a wounded bandit. Killed before he knew what happened."

Captain McNelly stared over at his Sergeant Major. "I wasn't made aware of that."

"Sorry sir, just didn't want to burden you anymore."

"I guess he didn't heed my warnings," Captain McNelly said in low tones.

"What's your next mission, Captain?" Slade asked.

"We received word that a Mexican leader, General Juan Salinas, was keeping in his stronghold at the Rincon de Cucharas or 'Spoon Corner' four-hundred head of cattle stolen and penned in Camargo Mexico. We aim to bring them back to Texas."

A slow nod from Slade.

Moments later, Slade heard a slight shuffling of feet outside his room and then the room curtain was dragged back halfway.

A female voice spoke out. "Hello, Mr. Slade, I'm your nurse for the duration of your convalesces. Can I come in?"

"Please come in nurse," Slade replied. "My visitors were just leaving."

"Slade," McNelly said, donning his hat. "We'll return to check up on you once we get back from our mission."

A quietness descended as a young, very attractive nurse stepped into the room. Both McNelly and Armstrong smiled at the young lady with a quick grin at Slade. Ah, to be this lucky, Armstrong thought, Slade is lucky in so many ways.

John Slade turned his whole attention on the young lady, with hazel eyes, soft-looking mid-level brunette hair and a richly tanned face, who possessed an almost hourglass figure and smiled.

*The Past – 1875-1882*

In 1875, John and Emily Slade were married after a courtship began in that hospital where Emily nursed John back to health.

The story tells of John Slade's incredible journey through the Old West and the gunfights and war he endured just to survive, and of famous gunslingers he'd met along the way. Death seemed to follow him. With parents that perished in a house fire; his first wife murdered before his own eyes, with himself left for dead, and his wife's sister and husband killed as well. For a while, with an unquenchable trail of vengeance, he found those responsible for their deaths and ended their reign of terror.

Now that the Hatcher brothers and their gang of desperados were dead and buried, he had no worries, except those of running a Ranger headquarters. There were a lot of things he'd had to learn on the fly now that he was the second in command.

But what John Slade didn't know was that a third Hatcher brother was coming out of El Paso Texas. And that shortly he will be ordered to track down and arrest a dangerous gunslinger and outlaw named Ben Collins.

John Slade first met the notorious Ben Collins in 1882, and he would ultimately play a crucial part in Slade's survival and the ultimate battle involving the last surviving Hatcher brother and his outlaw gang.

This is the continuing saga of Texas Ranger John Slade.

# CHAPTER 26

# HATCHER AND COLLINS

*The Present*
*El Paso, Texas*
*1882*

With the arrival of the railroads in 1881, El Paso transformed itself from a sleepy, dusty little adobe village of several hundred inhabitants into a flourishing community. The quintessential boomtown, it also became a Sin City, where scores of saloons, dance halls, gambling establishments and brothels lined the main streets.

Its city jail was usually packed with all types of desperados, murderers and horse thieves. Chief among those was James Wesley Hatcher, a notorious killer and stagecoach and bank robber wanted for those and other nefarious crimes; he and his gang had been terrorizing the area for several months. Now Hatcher faced the charge of murder, along with a stack of others.

Hatcher and his cousin Charlie Edwards sat inside one of the town's jail cells. Edwards rose and stood by the cell's barred door, as Hatcher, a tall, muscular man, with a week's growth of beard, stared up at the open barred window of the cell, deep in thought.

The two had been arrested the night before for shooting and killing two local cowhands in a card game. Hatcher had caught one man palming several cards and when he called him on it, the card cheat and his partner jumped out of their seat and before they drew their guns, Hatcher and Edwards drew shot and killed the pair.

A deputy in the saloon, having witnessed the killing, approached the shooters and arrested them with the help of some local ranchers.

Now awaiting a traveling circuit judge to make his appearance, Edwards turned to his boss. "What the hell do we do now?"

"We just have to wait for Slim and the rest of the boys to get here. They're supposed to be here later today. Just have to wait."

"How's about the bank?" Edwards asked. "Still going to make our move on it?"

"No, it'll wait for another day. Our main concern now is to get out of this cell."

Edwards just nodded.

Edwards, a stocky, five-foot seven-man, sporting a full beard, long handle-bar mustache curled at the tips, with long light-brown hair falling over his shoulders, heard someone at the front entrance and noticed the marshal and his deputy entering the jail.

"Hey Marshal," he yelled out, "got anything to read, pass the time while we wait for your judge?"

Marshal Hank O'Hanlon glanced over at his deputy, Earl Dunn and smiled. "Hell, man, didn't know you fellers could read."

"I like looking at the pictures," Edwards said, snickering.

"Well, the only thing with pictures is the newspaper."

Marshal O'Hanlon walked around his desk and pulled a few old newspapers from the center drawer. Then the marshal slowly approached the far wall, grabbed, and pulled a set of keys hanging on the wall, inserted a key into the locked door leading into the cell proper and approached Edwards.

Edwards watched the marshal approach with a slight grin. "Why thank you, Marshal."

Without a word, Marshal O'Hanlon stopped in front of the barred jail door and shoved the newspaper through the bars as Edwards reached in to grab it. The lawman then turned and walked out of the cell, closing, and locking the jail door behind him.

Opening the newspaper, Edwards walked over to the cell bunk bed, sat on its edge, and read through the headlines. "Ah hell, look at this," he said to Hatcher, as in disbelief. "Your two brothers got themselves killed by the Texas Rangers."

"What?"

"Say so right here," Edwards said, slapping the paper once.

"Give that to me," Hatcher growled, grabbing it away from Edward's hand.

Opening the paper to the headlines, Hatcher read through the article and stopped when he came to the name of John Slade, Texas Ranger.

"Ever heard of a Ranger named John Slade?"

Edwards shrugged. "Yeah, I think I have," he said, stroking his beard. "If he's the same one I think he is, the man is a legend down in South Texas. Fast on the draw. What of him?"

Hatcher's face reddened as a low growl escaped his lips. "Says here, he *killed* both of my brothers and joined in the gang's killing too."

"Sorry, boss."

"Not as sorry as that Ranger be when I tangle with him!"

"Yeah, well nothing you can do about it from here."

Ignoring Edwards, Hatcher only nodded and looked around the cell. All he could do for the time being was wait for the arrival of his men. And when he was free, he'd have to kill Slade.

With the sun setting over the Franklin Mountains to the west, two gunmen rode into the town of El Paso.

Riding past one of several saloons, they noticed their boss's horse, along with their buddy Edwards' mount, tied out in front of 'The Last Chance Saloon and Hotel,' a three-story building that housed a café. They weren't surprised, since they were supposed to meet up with their boss this evening.

"Reckon this saloon was better than any other," one man mused.

Pulling alongside the horses, they dismounted.

Slim Evers cautiously looked up and down the street for lawmen but saw none. Evers being the older of the two outlaws, with jet black hair down to his shoulders, with a two weeks' growth of beard, wearing buckskin britches, brown vest over a dark shirt, with his Winchester tied behind his back and high-rise holster that nestled a Colt .44 and standing six-foot, was an imposing figure.

Evers turned to face his partner, Jerry Miles, who was much younger and said in a deep baritone Southern drawl, "Jerry, stay here with the horses, I'll go inside."

In the saloon, Evers learned that his boss and Edwards had been arrested for killing two men and were being held at the Marshal's jailhouse. Now, Evers needed to know which cell they were being held in. He had the making of a plan to get them out. To do that, he needed to get into jail. So, thinking, he left the saloon and along with Miles walked toward the marshal's office.

Slim Evers' plan was simple. Once inside the jail, they would surprise the marshal and free his boss. It was an audacious and daring plan, but he saw no other way around it.

But once at the jailhouse, he noticed there were several people, including a few deputies hanging around outside—entirely too many with which to tangle.

Left with no further choice, Slim Evers and Charlie Edwards walked up on the boardwalk, stopped at the Marshal's office and strolled in.

Inside, they were met by two more deputies holding shotguns, sitting in the far corner, smoking and watching as they approached the marshal.

"Evening Marshal," Evers said.

"You two gents want something?" Marshal Hank O'Hanlon asked, looking up from writing his report about the killing at the saloon earlier.

"It's about your prisoners," Evers said. "Like to talk to one of 'em, if it ain't too much bother."

"And what business may I ask, do you have with 'em?"

"We're just concerned friends, seeing to if they need whatever."

"I don't see any objections," O'Hanlon said. "Leave your guns with the deputies there and I'll take you to them."

The visit was short; Slim Evers was to return after the sun set with two guns for their escape.

Slim Evers made his way down the darkened alleyway, package in hand. Halfway to his destination he paused, listening for anyone to his front or rear. Then he looked all about into the darkness. Nothing moved and he didn't sense anyone else with him along the alleyway. Still, he waited more than just a few moments and then continued. When he finally reached several windows with bars he knew he'd arrived.

The outlaw scooped up a few pebbles with loose sand and just as he leaned on the wall above the window, he reached up to the window ledge and released them into the cell where he knew his boss was locked up. It was the only cell with a light streaming out into the alleyway.

Hatcher was the first to make out the pebbles that seemed to fly into the cell and fall on his bed that, he could only guess, had come through the window. Edwards slowly made his way to the window's ledge, just as Hatcher was already standing on the bed gazing out when he heard a faint voice calling out his name from directly outside.

"Is that you, Slim?" Hatcher quietly asked. "It's 'bout time you boys came back."

"Yeah boss, it's me," Slim replied in an equally low voice, "got two guns for you. Your horses will be ready for you and Charlie by the side of the jail. The rest of the boys are waiting on the outskirts of town."

After Slim slipped the wrapped guns through the window, Hatcher removed the wrapping and gave one to Edwards, who immediately shoved it in his front pants pocket. Hatcher tucked his gun behind his back and waited until the evening meal was brought in to start their escape.

They didn't have long to wait, when they heard keys rattling behind the cellblock door, as Deputy George Kirkman, a blue-eyed dark tanned man with a thick black mustache drooping down his lower lip and wearing vest, white shirt and dark britches walked through with a basket of food in one hand and the other holding the cell keys.

Hatcher glanced at Edwards and motioned him to stand by the side of the cell door. He knew exactly what his boss wanted him to do, so walking just to the right side of the cell door he waited for Deputy Kirkman to insert the key, turning it and unlocking the barred cell door.

"Evening gents," Kirkman said as he slowly opened their cell door. "Got your evening meal."

Edwards waited for his chance.

Just as Kirkman pulled open the cell door, Edwards jumped into action. Then, in one swift motion, Edwards drew his gun.

"What the—!" But Kirkman didn't finish his sentence as Edwards cocked the hammer and pulled the trigger.

The slug tore into Kirkman's forehead, pushing through and exploding out the back of his head. It took blood, brain and bone that flew and ultimately, with a noticeable *thump*, splattering on the far wall, leaving a trail of blood on the floor of the jail.

Hatcher then leaped up and taking two quick steps was out of his cell stepping over the deputy's body with Edwards right behind him. They headed for the jail door and stopped; Hatcher quickly glanced in and noticed they were all alone.

Once inside, they found their gun belts in the marshal's desk and strapped them on, Hatcher went to the window, scanning left and right. Not seeing anyone who may have been alerted by the gunshot, he approached the front door. Then, pulling it halfway, they moved as one toward the side of the jail and their waiting horses. Quickly mounting, they spurred their mounts into a full gallop.

In the grainy evening darkness, on the outskirts of town, Hatcher and Edwards reined in their horses and stopped in front of the rest of his gang.

"Where to now, boss?" Edwards asked, as he turned in the saddle and gazed over at Hatcher.

"Back to the hideout," Hatcher said. "Then we ride out for Austin. Got some *business* needs looking into. Let's ride!"

# CHAPTER 27

## THE TRACKER

*Bastrop, Texas*

Ben Collins could feel someone dogging his trail, but try as he might, he'd seen no sign of anyone tracking him. He tried backtracking once but still didn't catch anyone.

*This tracker is good at his craft*, he thought.

Collins was not a large man, barely of medium height, but solidly built, with long black hair streaked with gray at the temples that hung slightly over his shoulders. He wore a thick black handlebar mustache, curled up at the tips. His face was hard and darkly tanned, with coal thin black eyes. The years had not been good to him.

Years on the run had kept him, now at thirty-seven, a little leery, highly alert, and somewhat paranoid. But it was a life he took upon himself to live, though there had been little choice since two killings back in '76 when he was a marshal in the city of Austin. Both were men that needed killing. And for that, he was made to turn in his badge. He'd escaped apprehension after a murder indictment was handed down; fleeing his deputies, the former lawman had not stopped running ever since.

From that Christmas Day back in 1876 on, he hardly entered any town during daylight hours, not willing to chance being recognized.

Collins reined in his horse just as he topped a low rise. Gazing about, he still could make no one behind him. His senses ever on the alert still.

It was a mild evening in mid-June as Ben Collins cast his eyes on the slowly setting sun draping its shadows over the sweeping landscape as he searched for a small ghost town. He knew the town was just due west of his location, but with nightfall and no moon yet to guide his way, he was biding his time.

John Slade finally received some much-needed information—at least now he knew the general direction his prey was traveling. But what he didn't understand was why the gunfighter had shown himself on a small cattle ranch, knowing he'd probably be recognized.

But stranger things had happened to Ben Collins during so many years. Things John Slade had read about in his reports on the man.

Slade had learned that gunfighters, the likes of Bat Masterson, John Wesley Hardin along and James Butler Hickok, were considered his very good friends. Interestingly enough, Collins was born an Englishman and at eight, his family moved and settled in Austin, Texas. Then, in 1861, he enlisted in the Confederate Army, where he was seriously wounded, spending weeks in a military hospital. And in later years Collins had served under Emperor Maximilian in Mexico. He was a slick one alright, he'd give him that, very smart and highly dangerous.

Now knowing the direction in which Collins was headed, Slade made his way over several mountain ranges in central Texas. It wasn't until just about evening with the sun slowly setting that he reined his mount and came to a halt. For just over a low rise, he could dimly make out a rider silhouetted in almost total darkness about half a mile ahead.

"I think we have him now, horse," he said, leaning slightly forward and rubbing his mount's neck. "Yep, I reckon we do."

Slade had traveled this way frequently and knew of an old, deserted silver mining town nestled just by Dry Branch Creek and south of Bastrop, about twenty miles further on. So, he knew he was between Austin and Bastrop.

"That could be where he be headed for," he muttered.

He dismounted, reached into one of his saddlebags and pulled out his binoculars. He placed them up to his eyes and he scanned over to the shadow of Ben Collins and his horse. His mother always said that patience was a virtue. So, he waited for Collins to make his next move.

Ben Collins looked down from his position. He knew the old town was about a mile or so toward his left, along a creek, just over the next rise. He should be able, with the help of the moon's silvery glow, to see the trail leading down. Soon after that he should see the rooftops of the abandoned structures and of a hotel where he could lay his bedroll once he topped the next high rise, which shouldn't take him much longer.

He turned on his saddle, gazing out behind him. He still had the odd feeling someone was coming up behind him but remained unable to catch sight of whoever it was.

The land he was traveling through was plagued with horse thieves, cattle rustlers, and murdering bushwhackers out to collect anything of value they could lay hands on. In the distance, with the moon making its way gently into the sky, stretched a line of low-lying hills, barren wasteland of rock, brush, and cactus. Great ambush spots from which he could be waylaid.

Turning back around, he shoved his hat down firmly on his head and nudged his horse forward.

# CHAPTER 28

# HATCHER AND HIS OUTLAW GANG

It was the last train to Austin.

The seven o'clock from El Paso was just under ten minutes late. With its one light glowing through the darkness it sounded its bells and with white smoke billowing from its stack and white steam escaping its sides, the locomotive chugged into the red-colored depot station. The train cast dark shadows over those waiting to greet the passengers. Then, with a loud hiss of stream, it drew to a stop.

Several minutes later, with the twilight setting of the sun, nine gunmen piled out of the first passenger car and stepped onto the depot platform.

They were grim, determined, silent and compact in their movements. Although they'd traveled a long distance, they were fully alert for any signs of trouble.

With their boss James Wesley Hatcher, his cousins Charlie Edwards and Slim Evers, they made it to Austin in the coolness of dusk.

These were hard dangerous men, outlaws all, wanted fugitives with a price on their heads. The Hatcher gang, comprised of the Stiles brothers, Sam and Rube, old by anyone's standards well into their late fifties; with a bounty of a thousand apiece, they had collected Indian scalps of men and women of well over sixty they'd killed in a year. Selling them for two-hundred dollars apiece—the going price for scalps during the Indian wars; also killing a deputy US Marshal with two other lawmen who tried to arrest them for robbery and murder, in San Antonio, back in '81.

And: William "Bill" Daly, out of South Dakota, a heavy-set, short man in his late forties, with a scar that ran from his right eye down to his lower lip. Some said it was his late wife that put it there. With a five-hundred-dollar price on his head, he was wanted for robbing the Deadwood stage several times. On one of those occasions in the winter of '79, he killed the stage driver who refused to surrender a small iron box full of gold bullion. When two local lawmen trailed and cornered Bill at the entrance to an old silver mine, a short gun battle erupted. Bill escaped with a shoulder wound, while the lawmen were shot to death by Bill and another desperado who suffered a mortal wound to his stomach.

And: Johnny McCloud, a tall lanky half-breed, a mixture of white and Mexican parents was wanted for train robbery in Tucson Arizona, with a bounty of one-thousand dollars. In late June 1879, he, along with his gang of four, made their way to an isolated train station by the Verde River just north of the Superstition Mountains range. There, they captured the station master and forced him to flag down the east-bound train. Once aboard the train, they stole the mail safe with eight hundred dollars in coins and bills. But before departing, McCloud shot and killed the station master to avoid getting recognized. But someone did.

And: The sixth member was a man named Thomas "Tom" Steele, a short, stocky black-eyed desperado wanted as a bushwhacker, murderer and rapist, who terrorized the vicinity of Mexico Missouri in mid-1878 and subsequently when things got too hot for him— being chased and almost caught on two occasions, hightailed it out of Missouri and headed for Texas where he joined the Hatcher gang in El Paso. He was lightning fast with his two Colts and was nicknamed *Lightning*.

And: A dark as coal craggy-faced black outlaw named Ned Huddleston nicknamed *Isom Dart*. A man of medium height and piercing black eyes, born a US slave and a bronco-buster, wanted for cattle rustling throughout the state of Wyoming. His fame to glory was that he rode with Butch Cassidy's gang for a while until the gang members were all killed. During that gunfight, Huddleston jumped into a grave and played dead. Later, he nursed his wounds, stole a horse and made his way into Texas and the Hatcher gang.

They all crowded around Hatcher, waiting for his orders.

Hatcher reached into this vest pocket, pulled out an old stogie, followed by a match, which he then struck alongside his pants and lit it. Inhaling the sweet smoke, he exhaled and looked at his men.

"Boys," he said, "Let's get our horses and meet at the hotel for some grub and drinks. We have a lot of planning to do." As one, they all walked over toward the last boxcar and got their horses.

Two hours later, they mounted their steeds, and without a word, galloped hard, traveling east.

# CHAPTER 29

# SHOWDOWN

Slade, still keeping a close eye on his prey, noticed that Collins had just started down the rise, apparently making for the old mining town.

Stowing away his binoculars, Slade nudged his horse forward and started after Collins before he could make the town's outskirts. The Ranger planned to see where Collins would bed down for the night and then, come morning, he'd make his move.

But owing to the nature of his job plans hardly ever turned out the way he'd hoped. Just like tonight.

Now with the light of the silvery moon, Slade had to be extra careful not to expose himself to his quarry. Halfway into the town, he dismounted and walked his horse to an outcropping of bushes, hidden from view from the remaining structures and a rundown hotel directly to his front. Just as he lay to wait, he made out Collins heading for the hotel. He'd made good time.

Leaving his horse to graze, Slade removed his spurs, tied them together, placed them on the saddle horn and walked into the town, slowly making his way toward the structure, a mercantile store boarded up on the same side as the hotel. He went inside and prepared to wait until morning.

Ben Collins dismounted and tied his horse to the hitching post. He removed both saddlebags and his Winchester, then stepping onto the boardwalk, entered the hotel. There were no doors left on hinges to open as he strolled in. Dust floated everywhere, but he found a reasonably clean spot just behind the front desk where he could lie down.

After unrolling his bedspread, he heard loud hoofbeats coming from the opposite side of town and by the sounds of it, there were two riders.

"Reckon whoever was doing the tracking just found me," he muttered.

Slowly drawing his gun, Collins angled over toward the front facing the street. Then, standing by a window, he could make out the riders galloping into the center of town and reining in their horses in front of the hotel.

"They ain't lawmen, bounty hunters by the look of 'em," he guessed.

One rider, Kenneth Jones, dismounted and drew his gun, as he glanced over at the second rider Jonathan Snider, staying mounted, who drew his Winchester, levered a round, and fingered the trigger, ready to fire at a moment's notice.

"Collins, Ben Collins!" Jones yelled. "Been tracking ya going for a while now. There be two of us, so come out with your hands in the air."

"And if I don't?" Collins yelled out.

"Will shoot your horse first," Snider blurted out. "Then you and take ya back to Austin."

"Ya boys bounty hunters?" Collins asked already knowing the answer.

"That's right," said Snider, glancing up and down the dusty street as a pair of tumbleweeds blew gently across the dust-covered street.

"So come out peacefully," Snider said, chuckling under his breath.

But Collins had other plans. "Okay, I'm coming out," he said.

In the meantime, Slade edging forward cautiously had worked his way around the back alleyway before the first shot rang out. Drawing his only gun, as he stopped wearing the second Colt after his latest injury, he thumbed back the hammer and made it around the back of the hotel just as the first shot from Collins's gun split the quiet night.

Keeping himself in the shadows as best he could, Slade noticed the open back door. Taking full advantage, he stayed close to the door jamb; he made his way inside, just as a second gunshot rang out.

Slade just made out Collins's figure by the window slightly in the shadows but bolted for cover as shots hit left and right of him from the outside; then hearing the exchange between the two remaining men, Slade stood his ground and waited for the outcome.

Kenneth Jones felt it then and he swallowed hard. It *was do or die time* as he nervously thumbed over the hammer of his gun, checking up and down the street, watching and waiting as if expecting a crowd to gather.

Suddenly, a shot from Collins's gun resounded from inside the hotel, slamming Kenneth Jones backward and killing him before he hit the ground, as his gun flew from his hand. A second shot grazed Snider's hat as he fired slug after slug into the hotel while dismounting and running to the side of the building, discarding the rifle for his handgun.

"You're a dead man, Collins!" Snider shouted with his back up against the hotel wall.

Now Collins knew where the bounty hunter was by the sound of his voice and he figured he had a pretty good chance of taking him out.

"Where have I heard that before?" Collins muttered.

Suddenly, Collins ran out through the front of the hotel, jumped into the air headfirst and before he landed on the boardwalk planking and onto his side, squeezed off two shots in the general direction of his would-be killer.

Snider turned toward the hurtling human body and yelled, "What the fu..." Those were his last words.

It had been a bold stroke, but it paid off, for just before Snider knew what was happening, a round hit him almost center mass, inches away from his heart. He staggered once, falling to his knees, clutching his chest, as his gun dropped away from his dead fingers. The second shot grazed his forehead.

Ben Collins picked himself up, dusted his shirt and walked over to the bounty hunter's body while holstering his gun. He then sauntered back into the hotel.

Then, from inside the hotel door, Collins walked right straight into John Slade's gun pointed at his chest. Collins figured he only had one thing he could do—he raised his hands over his head.

"Slowly now," Slade said with an edge of menace to his voice. "Reach your gun and pull it out by the handle and drop it on the ground."

Collins smiled and studied the stranger's expression for just a moment, before slowly reaching down, pulling out his Colt and letting it drop to the ground with a thud.

"You're another bounty hunter?" Collins asked.

"If I was, you'd be dead. Nope, the name's Slade, John Slade, Texas Ranger."

"Well I'll be, think I've heard of you. You were in the battle of Nueces Strip?"

"Reckon that be me alright," Slade said. "Come on ahead. Nothing funny, mind you, wouldn't want to kill ya."

Slade slowly pulled off to his right, letting Collins walk forward, still with his gun trained on his prisoner.

"So, reckon you'd be taking me in," Collins said as he walked into the center of the hotel's lobby, stopped and turned facing the lawman.

Slade offered him a crooked smile. "Reckon so," he said. "You can drop your hands but keep 'em where I can see 'em."

"Thank you Ranger, now what?"

"Why don't you grab one of those overturned chairs, set it in front of me and have a seat," Slade commanded.

Collins obeyed.

Ben Collins moved to the chair lying over on its side in a corner by the front window. He blew the dust off it, set it up-right, brought it over and sat down with his hands in plain sight facing the Ranger.

"Okay, now what?" Collins snarled, glaring at his captor.

Slade sighed but said nothing.

Then, just as Ben Collins sat in his chair, John Slade cautiously moved a few steps to his rear. He slowly turned and pulled a chair directly from his rear right side. A few feet from Collins, he sat and leaned back in the hard chair, placing his gun on his lap, folding his arms, dropping his guard just a little.

"Well, now we have a quiet conversa—" But Slade didn't finish his sentence!

Collins's eyebrows went up slightly, seeing his chance—just a chance—to catch the Ranger off guard. He timed it just as Slade placed his gun on his lap, folding his arms.

Collins suddenly jumped to his feet, grabbed the chair and flung it at the Ranger.

But Slade saw movement from the moment he'd folded his arms about his chest. Bad move and he nearly paid the price for the dumb oversight.

"Oh, *shit!*" ... Slade breathed.

*Did Collins think he'd be still sitting?* The thought raced through his mind.

He was wrong.

Slade bound out of his seat and snatched his gun, but just at that same instant, the flung chair struck his gun hand, knocking it away from him.

Collins's timing was impeccable.

By that point, the fugitive was still moving, as he ran and jumped the Ranger. Slade attempted to spin away but was too late. They crashed onto the floor as dust swirled around them.

For eight noisy seconds, they rolled, each trying to gain the upper hand, both grunting as they elbowed each other about their bodies and faces.

With blood spurting from around his open mouth, Slade and his opponent finally got back onto their feet. Blood oozed out of Collins's mouth and eyes as he spit out a tooth, breathing hard.

Ben Collins looked over the floor, trying to find Slade's gun, but suddenly Slade, with knees bent, propelled himself at his foe, once again colliding and trading blows.

Amid the shattered tables and chairs, each giving and receiving hard felt blows—Collins receiving the worst of them—and steadily being driven back to the opposite wall.

But John Slade was tiring and Ben Collins saw his chance—he swung harder—but he too started wearing himself out with each blow he connected or Slade parried.

Then Slade finally seeing an opening struck Collins a hard blow that landed right between his eyes. Seeing Collins's face snap upward, he thrust an uppercut to his jaw, stopping him dead in his tracks as he was flung up against a wall, his useless arms dropping to his sides.

Slade stepped back a step or two and saw Collins's eyes rolled up into his head, wobbled on unsteady legs and crumpled to the hard wooden planks of the hotel lobby's floor, unconscious.

Slade swiped at his bloodied lips.

Breathing hard, he bent his knees, leaned over and placed his hands on them, trying to get his breathing under control. Once he'd regulated his breathing, he found his gun and then he walked outside to Collins's horse, pulled down his lasso and went back inside. Collins's body had rolled onto its left side, still out of it, as Slade tied his hands behind him and his legs together.

After a few minutes' rest, Slade went to find his horse and rode back to the hotel, tying it next to Collins's mount. He pulled his saddlebags and bedroll and walked back into the hotel for a good night's sleep.

Texas Ranger John Slade stood in the hotel's lobby for a long-time watching Ben Collins's inert body. Then slowly he walked to the opposite wall, feeling the pains of the hard blows he'd received; spreading out his bedroll, he laid his tired body and began contemplating Collins's next day or two as he rode back to Austin with his prisoner.

Outside the hotel, a thin mist enfolded, and light rain fell for several minutes. Then flashes of lightning could be seen over the mountains, followed by rolls of thunder cracking the still quiet darkness of the night.

It sent a portent to John Slade, of violent events that may soon await him.

A frown crossed the lawman's face. He shuddered. "If I didn't know any better, I'm sure someone just walked over my grave," Slade muttered.

# CHAPTER 30

# THE BUSHWACKERS

The sun was just glaring over the east through a cloudless blue and orange sky, already sending its warm waves to shimmer and dance on the far distant hills as it dried the ground underneath their feet, when John Slade and Ben Collins rode across the trackless land of sand, cactus and rocky hills.

It was a good day and a half ride to Austin, maybe sixty miles, if the rain didn't stop them on the trail. So, Slade decided not to cause too much undue strain on the horses and himself. They had plenty of time to get back. Considering the only thing Ben Collins had waiting for him was the end of a rope.

An hour ago, they'd led their horses toward a small stream to water and graze. Now once more on the trail, with his prisoner handcuffed and tied to his saddle, Slade riding just behind Ben Collins, shortened the horse's reins and gently squeezing his legs under him, allowed it to trot at an even pace.

The sun shone brightly overhead as a warm breeze blew on their faces when two outlaws reined in their horses over a small stream.

Manuelito Amate De Jesus, a short fat Mexican with a boxy chin and narrow deep-set eyes, dark tan, wearing a wide-brim straw *sombrero*, two Colts strapped cross wise on his hips, a big black flowing mustache and holding a Winchester, was one of the best trackers this side of San Antonio. Along with his partner, a gringo named Joshua Kidd, they'd been following two sets of horse tracks for the better part of an hour.

"Hey, *Mejicano*," Kidd said using the Spanish word for Mexican to his partner, "see anything?"

Joshua Williams Kidd, a five-foot-six, slender-built man, had a chiseled jaw, weathered skin and piercing gray eyes, with a week's growth of beard, wore dirty black trousers, a red vest over a white shirt, wide brim hat, dark duster, and red bandanna. His Colt peacemaker was slung low in its holster and tucked under his duster.

"Hey, *Pinche Cabron*," De Jesus said glaring over at Kidd. "How many times I say to you it's Manuelito, *pendejo*. Asshole."

"Easy there partner, no need to get nasty," Kidd said with a wide grin. "Well, see anything?"

De Jesus and Joshua Kidd were two wanted fugitives who'd been arrested for stagecoach robbery and murder down in San Antonio. Jailed and waiting for the hangman, they'd escaped. Joshua Kidd had maimed a deputy while De Jesus killed another in their bold night-time jailbreak.

Along the way they held up two stagecoaches and relieved passengers of over three hundred dollars as they made a clean getaway. Now strapped for cash, they figured the two they were following may have cash and other valuables worth taking.

The Mexican dismounted and strolled over to the tracks left by the side of the stream. They were fresh, maybe an hour old. "Si, two sets," the Mexican said. "Two horses, no packhorse."

Kidd thought for a moment. "Which way are they heading?"

"North."

"Okay," Joshua Kidd said nodding. "Let's head them off and circle 'em."

Mounting up, the Mexican said, "*Vamoose Pues, Cabron*. Let's ride." With the sun on their backs, they galloped hard in a northerly direction, hoping to overtake the two riders.

Halfway to a large boulder in the distance, Ben Collins turned on his saddle. "Ranger, my throat's dry. Sure, could drink some of that water you're holding."

John Slade was getting a bad feeling about what could be up ahead. His years of tracking outlaws had ingrained in him a sense of self-preservation with the uncanny ability to know danger before it happens. Which had served him well during the war and again now as a Ranger.

The area was ripe for ambushes and the large boulder he'd seen jutting sky-high could very well be concealing lurking desperados in waiting. One could never be over cautious or paranoid in the land they were traveling through—the so-called—badlands. He could go around it, but that would add at least one or two hours to his traveling time.

*Just have to take the chance,* he thought.

Hearing no response from the Ranger, Ben Collins tried it again. "Ranger, some water if you don't mind," he said rather loudly this time.

Finally getting his attention, Slade slowed, almost coming to a halt.

"I reckon we could rest for a while," Slade said. "Pull up then."

Drawing his horse toward Collins's left side, Slade halted. He pulled the canteen from around the saddle horn and extended it toward Collins. Warily, Collins took the offered canteen, took two long pulls as he noted the Ranger's gun hand automatically drew to the butt of the holstered gun.

"You're a careful *hombre*, Ranger," the gunslinger said. As once again, he took a short pull of the canteen.

Slade smiled. "Yeah, helps me live longer."

Collins nodded. "Reckon so, after all I've heard about ya."

"Oh, and what exactly have you heard?"

"Heard tell," Collins said after taking a long pull of the water, "you lost a wife to a couple of outlaws and your friend getting cut down in a saloon. That could cause a man to think of his priorities. Don't you think?"

Slade looked him coldly in the eyes. "What my priorities are and my past are my business, outlaw."

Slade then made a quick scan of the surrounding area as his gun hand gently touched the butt of his peacemaker.

Collins showed no reaction. "Hey, just being friendly."

"I ain't your friend," Slade said, turning his gaze once again on Collins, "or your partner. You're a dirty ex-lawman who has killed with a badge. So, I'm taking ya back in for your day in court."

"Still a long way off to Austin," Collins said with a grin. "Hell, anything could happen before then."

"You try anything and I'll just shoot you dead, save the court's money."

"Reckon you could at that."

A short silence came between them.

"You finished?" Slade said, breaking the silence.

Ben Collins handed back the canteen and then nudged his horse forward.

Fifteen minutes later, Joshua Kidd and De Jesus came to the side of a twelve-foot-high boulder. In the distance, the outlaw De Jesus saw their dust trail down in the valley.

"*Gringo*," the Mexican said as he stared out in the distance, "they look like maybe ten minutes or fewer and they are on us. No?"

"I reckon so, *Mejicano*," Kidd said, stroking his beard. "We made good time."

"How do you want to play this?" De Jesus asked.

Thoughtfully stroking his beard, Kidd said, "You take the top with your Winchester and I'll be just around the boulder to finish 'em off."

"*Muy sencillio, Cabron. Simple Plan,*" De Jesús acknowledged. "So, you want me to take the first shot, no?"

"*Si*, have at it."

"Bueno."

A minute later, the Mexican outlaw had made it up the side of the boulder and bellied down with his Winchester from where he could just make out the trail in front of him. While Joshua Kidd stayed in the shadows behind the boulder, drew his Colt, cocked back the hammer, and waited.

John Slade reined in his horse to a stop, way back before the road went into a bend in the trail. He was getting a much stronger feeling this time—the feeling that all was not right up ahead. It appeared to be a good place for an ambush, he told himself. Then he was slightly distracted as he stared momentarily up to the sky.

Overhead, a circling crow looked down on the scene as its cawing could be heard for miles.

*That could be a bad omen*, John Slade thought.

Drawing up by Collins's side, Slade couldn't shake the feeling. So, he dismounted, pulled out his knife and cut the rope fastening Collins's legs into his saddle and removed the handcuffs.

"What's wrong, Ranger?"

"Got a feeling, that's all. You make a run for it and I'll shoot you in the back. Got it?"

"Yeah, I got it, Ranger. You know, you could give me a gun."

As he spoke, Slade watched Collins's face carefully. All he saw was a wide grin. Not sure if he was serious about the comment.

"No, I don't think I'll be doing that."

The trail curved around the boulder in shadow and then after a few minutes had gone by, De Jesus made out the riders coming through the bend in single file. Then, having the first rider in his sights, he waited until they were much closer.

He noticed both riders glancing up the mountainside as if looking for an ambush. *Hell, they weren't far from getting into one*, he thought with a grin.

De Jesus blew a low whistle letting his partner know the riders were close at hand.

Manuelito Amate De Jesus was considered a good shot with a rifle by many of his friends. So, he was very confident he could kill the lead man and fire his second slug at the second man before the first dropped off his horse—leaving it all to him to kill them both, which appealed strongly to his murdering senses.

But what he didn't count on was the speed with which both riders would react.

# CHAPTER 31

## MISSION ACCOMPLISHED

"Hey, Ranger, I'm getting a bad feeling about what's up yonder," Ben Collins said, nodding up the trail.

But behind him, Slade, with a cool-headed demeanor, didn't say a word, because he'd been feeling the same.

Then suddenly, as they rode through the bend, two Winchester shots rang out loud, clear, and deadly. The first slug caught Ben Collins as it plowed through his left shoulder. As he groaned in pain, his spooked horse reared up and pitched Collins behind him to the ground. Quickly, Collins rolled over toward the edge of the boulder, seeking some cover, while holding onto his bloody shoulder, as slugs kicked the dust and pinged off the rock wall just inches from his moving form.

While Ben Collins sought cover, John Slade, at the first sounds of gunfire, jumped off his horse and bending low at the knees, quickly drew his Colt while thumbing back the hammer and pulling the trigger in rapid succession. Snapping off four shots up onto the boulder, Slade then turned toward his right as wild gunshots kicked up dust all around him, missing him so narrowly as a slug blew his hat clean off his head.

Slade spotted his adversary then, just by the side of the boulder, firing haphazardly. Slade unloaded on the outlaw, as one bullet after another found their mark throwing him hard to the ground, dead, just as Slade's Colt clicked on an empty chamber.

But as soon as the outlaw succumbed to the gunfire, Slade was hit once as a round grazed his left shoulder and another plowed and kicked dust close by his right boot.

Then in rapid succession, Slade holstered his right Colt. After the fight with Collins, he started wearing his second gun belt with his other Colt and drew it, and then turning back to the bushwhacker on the boulder, he quickly ran firing as he went, trying to come around the side of the rock, but seconds later he heard hoofbeats galloping away from behind the huge rock.

The booming of gunfire all around had spooked the horses as they galloped down the trail.

Then all was quiet.

Seconds later, Slade found his hat and noticed the bullet hole just center on the front, inches away from the top of his head. Tucking on his hat, he turned his attention toward Collins.

"Hey, I'm hit badly Ranger," Collins said in a strained, pain-filled voice.

"Hang on and don't go anywhere," Slade said in a hard, precise voice. "I'll get our horses."

"You're a funny man, Slade."

"Yeah, glad you like my sense of humor," Slade said with a tinge of menace in his voice. "You try to make a run for it, and the joke's on you!"

Slade lifted his head slightly and blew a low pitch whistle. A few minutes later, his horse came galloping from behind him, stopping in front of him in a swirl of dust, just as Slade finished reloading his guns.

Jumping in the saddle, Slade gazed at Ben Collins. "I'm serious, don't go anywhere."

"Christ, lawman," Collins said in honest indignation, "do I look like I'm going anywhere soon?"

"I'm going after your horse. When I get back, I'll look at your wound."

Ben Collins was slipping in and out of consciousness due to loss of blood when Slade rode back with his horse. It seemed to Collins that hours had passed since Slade left, but it had only been ten minutes.

Dismounting, Slade pulled down his saddlebags, walked over to Collins and kneeling he pulled Collins's hand away from his wounded arm.

"Yeah, you'll need some doctorin'," Slade said as he pulled out some bandages and medicine. "I need to stop the flow of blood, Collins. And the only way I can do that is to burn it shut. The bullet went clear through. That's the good news. The bad news is I have to burn the front and back of your arm. It's gonna hurt like hell."

Collins nodded and watched as Slade prepared to set his wound. "Got any whiskey?"

"Yeah, don't drink it all," Slade said as he pulled the bottle out of the saddlebags and held it out to him.

Slade allowed Collins a few pulls of the bottle and watched as the man went in and out of consciousness.

"You still with me?" Slade asked.

"Off and on, Ranger," Collins muttered.

"This may sting a bit."

He then poured the whiskey onto the wound, and watched as rolling his head to the side, Collins grimaced with pain, as the alcohol burned through into the wound.

Finishing the bottle himself, Slade threw it away, then gathered some wood and started a small fire. He pulled his bowie knife from his boot sheath and placed the blade into the burning red-hot flames.

"Here's a piece of rawhide, bite into it," Slade said.

Ben Collins glanced over at Slade; an eyebrow raised ever slightly. It was an old, worn-out rawhide strip. "You want me to bite... into this?"

Slade looked at him for a moment, "Yeah," he replied with a quick grin.

"You'll let me know when you put the blade to me."

"Yeah, sure."

But as soon as the outlaw bit into the rawhide, Slade removed the red-hot blade and, without a word, burned the flesh at the bullet's entrance, fully cauterizing the wound.

With a howl of pain and the smell of burned flesh, Collins reeled into unconsciousness once again. Slade then did the same to the bullet's exit wound. After that, he tied a bandage around the wound.

John Slade stood, breathed deeply, and closed his eyes, as once again he'd cheated death. With his heart beating normally once again, he raised his head as his thoughts turned to his beloved Emily, gone now just a year. Will he ever meet someone like her? What does fate have in store for me?

"Only time will tell," he muttered to himself.

He left Collins and walked over to the dead bushwhacker.

Slade approached the outlaw who lay face down. He rolled him over and saw the bloody shirt where his slugs had passed through.

Kneeling, he searched the dead man's clothing; he failed to find anything to identify him. All he found was a ten-dollar bill. He pocketed the bill, then picked up the man's gun, tucked it in his gun-belt and turned to take care of the horses.

He built a larger fire, now that the one he'd started was burning itself out. He put on a pot of water to boil for coffee. Knowing Collins wasn't in any shape to ride, he just had to wait for him to come out of it.

Finally, Slade got around to cleansing his own flesh wound.

Once John Slade had settled in, he'd made sure Ben Collins wouldn't wake in the middle of the night and try to escape. So, he tied Collins's legs together and snapped a set of hand-irons on, effectively preventing any such attempts.

Laying on his bedroll, Slade fell into a restless sleep as the image of Emily's fleeting smiles and Josh and Lynn's tortured faces floated through his subconsciousness. And somewhere deep inside, he knew death was just a common way of life, which seemed to have taken his loved ones much too early. Then slowly his eyes closed, falling into that state of deep sleep as his tortured soul sought comfort, knowing those responsible for his plight had been dealt with.

A brief drizzle seemed to have a dampening effect on an otherwise temperate late morning as Collins and Slade rode just south of Austin.

Ben Collins didn't particularly like being tied down in his saddle or having his hands cuffed in front of him and his horse led behind the Ranger, worse, no hat to keep his head dry. And he voiced his displeasure, griping about the inhumane treatment he was getting.

But only one thought crossed Slade's mind as he shook his head. *So what?*

Pulling up the collar on his duster, he clenched the coat tighter around his neck, not allowing the rain to soak through his shirt and lowered his head, as the rain ran down his hat.

They lumbered through the now fast-falling rain, with no shelter in sight for miles.

After an hour of riding and what was left of the heavy rain turning into a drizzle, Slade and Collins had dismounted and were resting their horses just a few miles south of Austin under the protection of some large trees. In the far distance, the city was visible to the naked eye.

With Collins leaning up against a large tree Collins gazed over at the Ranger. "Been thinking, how did the Rangers get to know I was in the county and how did you find my trail?"

Slade, with gradual glances to the side, watched the outlaw and considered the questions.

He remembered back to when he'd received word from the governor's office, ordering his company to track and arrest wanted fugitive Ben Collins, wanted for the deaths of two law enforcement officers. Information was also received from the US Marshal in Waco Texas that Collins had previously been seen in the territory, but more so around the town of Bastrop. Considering it was only one outlaw,

Slade had decided to track him solo. No need to bring in a couple of Rangers. Besides, many of his Rangers were out and about on official business and weren't due back for a week. So, he didn't have a choice. He needed to act on this information pronto.

A day later, he'd packed his horse and set off after Collins.

"Got word you were about," Slade said as he shrugged his shoulders. "Been tracking you for over a week; then you made the mistake of stopping at a small cattle ranch where you stayed just long enough to get recognized. From there, it was easy enough to pick up your trail. It was clear enough that a blind man could've followed."

Collins smiled, nodding and raised his eyebrows. "Yeah. Reckon I overstayed my welcome alright."

Slade made no comment.

Collins was frowning at him.

"Damn!" he said. "But I thought I'd covered my tracks fairly good. Reckon not good enough for the likes of ya."

Again, Slade didn't say a word.

"You did a mighty fine job of doctorin' my arm," Collins said, adjusting his shoulder.

Slade glanced at the outlaw and smiled. Then he said, "Let's get moving, time's a-wasting."

With the sun pulling away from behind the clouds and the warm sun rays shining on an otherwise dry late morning, they arrived at the Ranger garrison.

Cold, wet, and hungry, they slowly rode through the garrison's main entrance. John Slade led his prisoner up to the Ranger's headquarters building and reined to a stop in front of his office, as several Rangers either rode or walked up to their executive commanding officer.

## CHAPTER 32

# JAMES WESLEY HATCHER
# OUTLAW

*Company "C" Texas Rangers Station, Austin, Texas*
*Late July 1882*

The sun was warm when Texas Ranger John Slade followed by ten Rangers riding in a formation of two's slowly rode through the station's main gate. Inching their way to the barracks building, he kneed his horse forward a little faster, waved his hat at his men and cut away from the formation heading to his bungalow.

The early morning wind picked up two small dust devils as they lifted sand into the air. The wind died down for the moment as it diminished in intensity and blew the sand devils away from Slade.

For the last three days, Slade, now having been promoted to Lieutenant, and his Rangers had been tracking a gang of four outlaws who were reportedly linked to the Hatcher Gang and credited with several stagecoach robberies, two train robberies, along with the murders of three innocent train passengers. Word was the four outlaws operated along the eastern side of the Colorado River and east of Austin.

At one point the Rangers picked up their trail, but then lost the tracks just east of the Brazos River thanks to a heavy rainfall that lasted for two days and erased all their tracks.

Reaching his bungalow's hitching post, Slade slowed, pulled up and tilting his hat back, gradually and with mild pain in his legs, dismounted his horse. Removing his saddlebags, he tossed them over his left shoulder and unsaddled his horse. He removed its bridle's headstall and bit, turned his horse's head, and slapped its flank. The big animal knew right where to go, as with a slow gait it trotted off toward the corral.

"Good horse," he said as he watched it amble away.

Picking up his saddle and harness and still shouldering his saddlebags, Slade turned and with the jingle of his spurs, headed toward the front door of what he called home when a young Ranger yelled out his name and came running toward him.

"Lieutenant Slade, sir," the youngster, no older than seventeen yelled out again. Coming abreast of the Ranger, he stopped. "Sir, the captain would like a word with ya sir."

He stood in front of the young Ranger named Josh Cummings, who stood as tall as Slade, but skinny as a beanpole, blond, dark tanned skin, and having a mild Eastern accent; the kid had volunteered for service just short of four months ago. He had no parents and was living with his uncle in San Antonio when he signed on the dotted line.

"Right ... now?" Slade asked. Dropping his saddle to the ground and removing his father's watch from his vest, he checked the time: 6:35. *What in Sam Hill does he need at this time of the morning?* He thought as he tucked his watch back in his vest pocket.

"Well, sir," Cummings replied dropping his eyes, "at ya convenience ... the captain mentioned."

"Advise the captain, I'll be there soon as I wash the trail dust off and have some breakfast."

Cummings swallowed hard and nodded, turned, and started for the captain's office.

Smiling and shaking his head, Slade picked up his saddle and slowly made his way to the front door of his bungalow. This is where he called home since the murder of his wife.

An hour and a half later, after a hot bath, a change of clothes and filling himself up with three eggs and a medium-rare steak with coffee at the station's mess hall, Slade meandered over to Captain James Franklin's office.

The Ranger wasn't sure what Captain Franklin wanted unless it was his report of the last few days on the trail. *Damn, that could've waited for later in the day, at least after resting and tending to my horse,* he thought shaking his head ever slightly.

With the morning sun not yet as bright and with the crisp morning air blowing gently on his face, Slade, once he'd arrived at Captain Franklin's office, walked through the wide-open door which Franklin kept open as usual to all, unless he was with a Ranger or with visitors. Taking another step, Slade stopped, closed the door softly behind him and without a word removed his hat.

Standing with his back toward Slade, Franklin was washing his face over a small basin, not yet having noticing Slade. As he turned around, he picked up a towel and started drying himself off and tossed it on his desk. Finally, he noticed him standing by the door.

"Well," Franklin said in his crisp Georgian accent, "What in sand blazes are you standing there for. Get on over here and take a seat John ... ya didn't have to wait for me to tell ya."

"Yes sir," Slade said as he walked over to the front of Franklin's desk, came around a chair and sat down. "I mean no sir ... you didn't," he mocked and added as he smiled at him conspiratorially almost in a whisper.

Captain Franklin was a blue-eyed, heavy-tanned, five-foot-nine-inch slim-built man of forty-four. Ten years ago, he and his family of two—his wife and seven-year-old daughter—moved from Atlanta Georgia and settled in Victoria Texas by the banks of the Guadalupe River.

Leaving his family for a day as he went hunting, a band of Comanches attacked his home, killed his family and stole twenty horses. But his wife gave a good accounting of herself, as four dead hostiles laid about the ranch. With the help of the Cavalry, they were able to find and take revenge on those that attacked his home. Later, he volunteered his services to the Texas Rangers.

With a noticeable sigh, Franklin came around to his desk. "Well now," he said taking his seat. "I see you came back empty-handed. So, give me your report."

Glancing at his captain and with a short smile, he replied, "Not much to tell, Captain. I tracked the owl-hoots for two days straight. Never caught hide nor hair of 'em though. Stopped off at two towns along the way for supplies and such but lost their tracks on the other side of the Brazos River."

A short pause ensued.

"I see," Franklin said as he moved his hands over to a pile of papers. Removing two telegrams stuck under several sheets, he kept one hand over them as he stared at his lieutenant and didn't say another word.

Slade continued. "One town we came to confirmed those we've been chasing were part of a larger gang operating east of the Brazos. One of the local marshals also confirmed rumors that they could be part of Hatcher's bunch. The marshal mentioned that four of his town's women have gone missing. Suspicions turned toward the bunch. Maybe they were possibly selling 'em over the border."

After a short pause, Franklin said, "The Hatcher gang, two of which you put six feet under and now the last of the remaining brother … it's why I called you in here."

With a raised brow, Franklin stopped and fixed Slade with an intense gaze with his piercing blue eyes. He said nothing. *As if two Hatcher brothers weren't enough. Now there's another with a gang of infamous desperadoes coming after my lieutenant. If that doesn't beat all, damn!*

Slade said nothing, just held eye contact with his captain. He suspected that there was something more here than just making his report of the last few days on the trail. He bided his time, waiting on his commander.

Franklin lowered his eyebrows and then held Slade's gaze for a moment with a certain concern for his lieutenant and leaning back in his chair said, "I'd received two telegrams the other day which should interest you very much, John."

Stroking his three days' growth of beard, Slade tilted his head to the side, gazed at his captain and without a word and his curiosity piqued, he waited to hear what all this was about.

Franklin hesitated as if he considered something else. But then he gently shook his head. "This involves you John, the Hatcher brother, his gang ... and Ben Collins."

"What about Hatcher?"

Franklin lowered his head and his voice and replied, "He's placed a bounty on your head."

Sitting forward on his chair, Slade said, "Very interesting. This would be funny if it wasn't so damn serious."

"Yeah," Franklin said clearing his throat. "The bounty is for two thousand dollars ... alive."

Slade shrugged as if this bit of information held no relevance in his life. "Is there anything solid on Hatcher?"

"His full name is James Wesley Hatcher, a tall son-of-a-bitch and the oldest of the three brothers," Franklin replied gritting his teeth. "While in El Paso, he got arrested for shooting and killing two local cowhands in a card game. They were waiting on the circuit judge when his gang busted him out of jail." Franklin paused. "On their way out of the jail they killed a deputy. It's unknown who did the killing. But it's said Hatcher was the murderer. He was last seen in Austin with his gang heading east."

"According to reports from several lawmen," Franklin continued. "Hatcher has a gang of eight to ten wanted fugitives. They identified two of the outlaws as the Stiles brothers, Sam and Rube, wanted in Victoria for killing a marshal and two other lawmen that tried to arrest 'em." Franklin paused and tried to catch up to himself—his thinking slower than his talking. Then he began again in a much lower voice. "Besides them, there's William Bill Daly, out of South Dakota, wanted since '79 for murder and another man named Ned Huddleston who goes by the nickname of Isom Dart, a man of color wanted in Wyoming for cattle rustling and who ran with Butch Cassidy and his gang. Marshal out of San Antonio reports the Stiles brothers and two others are responsible for several stagecoach holdups. I think those are the same four you were trying to chase down."

"Could well be them. I've heard of William Daly and Isom Dart, but not the others. A gang of murderers, rapists, cutthroats and bushwhackers, I imagine."

Franklin pursed his lips, pushed back his chair, and stood. As he came around toward the front of his desk, he fixed his gaze once again on Slade. "These men are dangerous, John. And now with a price on your head it could get even worse for you out on the trail."

Throughout this, Slade's facial expression remained rather passive. He glanced at Franklin, knowing they both had met up and fought some rather unsavory characters in their time; this was no different.

John Slade shrugged and nodded. "Reckon so. We just recently went up against bigger odds Captain ... and survived."

"Yeah, I remember that alright," Franklin said, remembering the ambush at Hatcher's hideout last year. It was a bloodbath! Most of his Rangers were killed or wounded. And the death of Slade's sister-in-law, Lynn Evans played upon his mind for a long time after. Had he not let her go on that raid she'd still be alive, but she wanted vengeance for her husband and sister, Emily, that were killed by Hatcher and his gang.

Stepping up to an old writing desk on the other side of the office, Franklin stopped, opened a drawer, and pulled out a bottle of Old Crow whiskey and two shot glasses and came back around to the front of his desk. Sitting back, he poured the whiskey into the two glasses half full and pushed one toward Slade.

Picking up his glass, Slade waited for Franklin to pick up his, and raising his glass in a toast he said, "Here's to living and dying," and downed his glass.

Tilting his head back, Franklin downed his drink and stared at Slade saying, "You sure have a morbid sense of life, John."

"It's kept me alive this long. Many have tried to kill me and failed, Captain."

"Yeah, I reckon."

"You mentioned Ben Collins," Slade asked. "Anything I should know?"

Filling his glass again, Captain Franklin downed his drink, cleared his throat, and leaning back in his chair then crossing his arms about his chest said, "Oh, yes, about that. Well, seems as if Collins got his day in court. According to the telegram I'd received yesterday from Marshal Anderson of San Antonio, they acquitted him of all charges. It had something to do about witnesses to the crime. And what that implies is unknown to me. But the interesting part is Collins wants to meet up with you in San Antonio if you're interested in meeting him. He says he'd be waiting at the Menger Hotel if you decide on the meet to thank you personally."

Slade straightened up somewhat and stared off to his side, his face uncomprehending. Then he locked eyes with Franklin. "Thank me for what, exactly?"

"That, you must find out for yourself, if you meet him there."

Standing and grabbing his hat, Slade said, "I have nothing to say to Ben Collins."

Franklin stared at his lieutenant as he took in Slade's comment. "Suit yourself, John."

"Is that all Captain?"

"Yes, go on get some rest."

Stepping outside into the hot glaring sun shining down in the early morning, Slade couldn't help thinking about Ben Collins and his request. He'd tracked Collins for over a week until he caught up to the outlaw. He remembered Collins' remark ... *damn, but I thought I'd*

*covered my tracks fairly good. Reckon not good enough for the likes of ya."*
Although, Slade knew if weren't for Collins being recognized at a small
cattle ranch, he would've missed his trial and his chance to arrest him.

On those days on the trail back to the Ranger station, Collins and
Slade developed a rivalry born out of mutual respect, more so for
Collins, than for Slade.

Suddenly, an idea grew in his mind. An idea that sounded crazy,
but if it worked, it would end the terror of Hatcher's bunch.

Turning back around, Slade headed back to Captain Franklin's
office. His idea growing and just when he stepped into his office, Slade
had it all figured out.

# CHAPTER 33

# BOUNTY HUNTERS

*Texas Ranger Station, Austin, Texas*
*Early August 1882*

The station saloon was a few hundred square foot log cabin with three rooms, single story, with a large wooden bar that served locally distilled whiskey and warm beer. Seven tables with four to five chairs each decked the central room, while the second room boasted a billiards table and off to the side were two bedrooms. A pot belly stove sat in a corner in the back of the saloon.

The tables and chairs were manufactured in Chicago and brought in by wagon. The owner, James Wetmore, who also served as the barkeep, kept a stable of four young saloon girls, refugees from far-away farms and paid them ten-dollars per week to keep the customers entertained. This was permitted of course, by the station commander, Captain Franklin.

The saloon was almost empty. All the Rangers still on duty could not enter the bar until late afternoon. Two dance-hall girls sat around one table in a corner and waited for the off-duty Rangers, cowboys, soldiers and a few railroad workers to stroll through the station and eventually make for the saloon.

On this day, only three strangers were at the bar.

They were about sixty years old, all professional bounty hunters who stood at the Ranger station's saloon bar drinking cheap red-eye rye whiskey. One of them stood apart from the rest. A tall and haggard man, wearing a gray Confederate cap with a full growth of white beard and mustache and carrying his iron low in its holster as he stared out a dirty side window, toward a bungalow across the dusty street as he sipped his beer.

The other two men, although smaller in stature than their comrade, were men that once seen, you couldn't forget their appearances. Both wore ragged, dirty clothing, sweat stained hats and short beards and mustaches as if they'd rode fast and far. Both carried twin Colt .44s Peacemakers slung low in their holsters and the other Colt was worn crossed holstered for easy quick as lightning style draw.

They'd arrived at the station about noon and decided to set up at the bar waiting to see if the *Ranger* left the safety of the station. If not, they would return at night, break into his bungalow, tie him up and then collect the two-thousand-dollar bounty. But this time it was different. This time he was wanted alive. They didn't consider themselves old and not having any other form of work, this was their living. But alive, now that was different.

Glass after glass they drank and they still didn't move. Their only concern was for the Ranger. Their horses were tied out front ready, so was their pack horse. They knew where to collect the bounty money and from whom; the problem was there were other bounty hunters and outlaws also gunning for the Ranger. Once they had him tied to his saddle, it would be on the trail where they could come under fire. But they'd come to that later.

First things first.

Twenty minutes later, the bounty hunter watching through the window, gestured to his comrades, and waved them over. Just then, Texas Ranger John Slade stepped onto a wide boardwalk flanking his bungalow, his saddle, pack-roll in hand, closing the door behind his bungalow.

Stepping onto the street, John Slade gave a low shrill whistle. Out at the corral, Slade's horse, a brown and white pinto, the same breed his father once had, heard the whistle and free of any restraints, raised his head, saw his master, and with a slow easy gait trotted over to him.

The three bounty hunters stepped away from the window, made their way out of the saloon and onto the boardwalk, stopped, and just stood, as they glanced now and then over to the Ranger. Cautiously, not to arouse suspicion, one by one they made their way onto the street and approached their horses.

The Rangers' station by now was a bevy of activity. Trappers, railroad workers and two covered wagons with families were coming into the station. A company of soldiers were making their way toward the station commander's office, just as John Slade, with his horse next to him, having saddled it and strapping on his bedroll, casually glanced over at the saloon; he noticed three hard looking men who had a profound interest in what he was doing.

*If I didn't know better, those three are bounty hunters*, Slade thought to himself. He knew the type. Plus, their gun holsters were strapped low. *If they weren't bounty hunters, then gunslingers. Maybe out for the reward*, he thought. "Well horse," Slade whispered. "Seems like we may have some company out on the trail."

Removing his gun-belt from around the saddle horn, he strapped it on. Then he swung onto his saddle, kneed his horse some, and pointed its head toward the saloon. As he approached, the three men saddled up and were turning away, heading out of the station, when Slade pulled up in front of them.

John Slade casually pulled back his shirt exposing his Ranger badge for them to see, then he pushed back the brim of his hat, stared at one then at all three, leaned slightly forward, and as he rested his hands on the saddle horn said, "You boys just passing through, or here on business?"

The closest man to him shook his head nervously turned and stared briefly at his comrades, then back at Slade. "Just passing through Ranger," he said. "Heading back to San Antonio."

"You men ... trappers?" Slade asked as he maintained eye contact with the three.

The man behind the first one that did the talking said in a calm, level voice as he locked eyes with Slade, "You can say that."

Slade was keenly aware of the tension mounting between him and the three hombres. He watched as one man gripped the handle of his gun loosely, ready for trouble if it came.

A long silent pause passed between them.

Slade stared hard at the man. A sullen, dangerous man, hardened perhaps, until the man dropped his eyes from the Ranger and his hand from his gun. "I see," Slade said, grinning as he slowly backed his horse away from them. "Well, y'all have a nice day now."

As they rode away, Slade said to himself, "Those three are going to be trouble."

It was late in the afternoon, as John Slade drew rein and slipped out of his saddle. Removing his hat, he placed it on the saddle's horn and reached for his canteen. Having slept earlier that morning after arriving with his Rangers from out chasing a pack of murdering outlaws, he was in a state of high alert. He hadn't seen a trace of the three who were at the saloon. But he felt quite confident he would ... soon enough.

He knew full well those three were bounty hunters and they wouldn't rest until they had him hogtied and draped over his horse.

Taking his hat, he poured water into it and gave it to his horse to drink. Then, sipping on the canteen, he stared out into the wide-open plains behind him. It was a wavering landscape of heat, sand and glaring sunlight that met his eyes. Yet he stared stony eyed, glued to one particular place out in the sand. Unable to see what it could be, he hazarded a guess—riders, maybe three of them, dogging his trail.

Then his mind wandered back to a second meeting he'd had with Captain Franklin.

"James, I know how this sounds," Slade said once he laid out his plan, "but I think it could work."

Shaking his head, Franklin queried, "What makes you think Collins will go along with it?"

"Well, not too many know that he was acquitted of the murders," Slade replied. "To many, he is still a wanted man. So, as far as him joining the Hatcher gang, well, there's nothing to lose, really. Either they take him in or not. If they do, then I've setup a place and time where he could meet up with me, so he can fill me in on all he's learned."

Still not convinced, Franklin stared long and hard at Slade and finally said, "Sounds too risky even for Collins. Don't know, John... I just don't know."

"He was a lawman before," Slade said, as he watched Franklin's hesitation. "He knew the dangers involved in the job, why not now too?"

Franklin nodding his head said, "I see your point John, but he was a wanted man for several years. What makes you think he won't go back to that way of living?"

John Slade cleared his throat. "Well," he said with bowed head, "I don't. It's a gamble I'll have to live with."

Franklin didn't answer right away.

More nodding from Franklin. "Okay, this is on you John. Remember, things don't always go as one plans. When would you go to San Antonio?"

Slade replied, knowing exactly what Franklin meant, "Later in the afternoon."

"Keep me posted," Franklin said. "And if you need help, I'm here for you."

"Thank you, Captain," Slade said and added, "About those outlaws I've been chasing. What can you do about them while I'm gone?"

"I'll send out a couple of Rangers," Captain Franklin replied. "See if they can pick up from where you lost them."

As Slade headed toward the door, Franklin shook his head and said, "You watch your step out there John."

"Don't I always sir," Slade said, smiling.

Franklin said, "Huh."

With the reluctant approval of Captain Franklin, John Slade set his plan in motion. First, he sent a telegram to Ben Collins stating he was on his way to meet him. Second, he notified the marshal in San Antonio of his arrival.

Now in open country and traveling to San Antonio, already he had some men after him. It was going to be a long ride.

Slade mounted his horse, turned on the saddle and once again stared back the way he'd just traveled and smiled. He let out a breath. "Reckon they'll catch up to me soon," he said to himself. Turning back, he kneed his horse forward down the trail.

James "Big Jim" Harper wore his old Confederate cap at an angle as he opened his binoculars and set his good eye toward the high ridge where the Ranger had stopped. The Ranger was just a speck on the horizon, but his trail was clear as day. They knew then that he was headed to San Antonio.

Harper was a former mountain man, standing six-feet tall, who served in the war of Northern Aggression, but had his belly full of the war and retreated into the mountains and then was classified as a deserter. Back in the 40s he'd made good money collecting Apache scalps, more than just skinning beaver, when he joined a band of hell-for-leather scalp-hunters, where they were paid by the Mexicans a hundred dollars for an Indian male, fifty-dollars for a woman and twenty-five for a child.

Now with his two compadres, Bill Watters and Todd Jones, both scalp-hunters themselves, they were bounty hunters who had never failed to bring in their man or woman. They made some good money, considering they'd been at it for several years and not one of them had suffered a bullet for their troubles. With mostly luck and determination, they always persevered. They never gave their prey a chance, they just outright shot and killed them. It was easier that way. Not having a so-called leader of the trio, they each knew how the others worked.

Harper considered the Ranger easy prey, leaving a trail a child could follow.

Harper turned toward Watters and Jones. "Let's get," he said. "He's on the move."

They had a plan, an outright easy plan, which they would put to use just after the Ranger made his camp. Like before, they were not taking any chances. If only they knew who the Ranger truly was, they would have taken another approach.

But they'd know soon enough.

The ride from Austin to San Antonio was about fifty miles, give or take.

With daylight still lingering, Slade pulled up on a small hillside and looked down at a gully that was only about four feet deep. It's where he'd cross several times before. He could make his camp here, he thought, but if those three bounty hunters were still on his trail, then this wouldn't be a good place to give an accounting of himself.

No, he'd ride into the fort and seek a helpful position more to his liking. Without a backward glance, he kneed his horse into a walk, rode down the hill, traversed the gully and got on a well-beaten trail that meandered to the fort.

Slade didn't hurry his horse. Slow and easy was the ride, not exciting his horse any.

A half hour later, he arrived at the desolate site, once called Fort Martin Scott. It had been abandoned back in '66, with no visible tangible remains of buildings, except for two structures, both with roofs. He'd hoped to make camp in one of them before dusk.

He still had a little over ten miles left before he arrived in San Antonio. Soon, he would follow the old Western Trail down into the valley and into San Antonio. By his reckoning, he should arrive there about noon. Time enough to meet up with Ben Collins later that afternoon.

With night slowly approaching, he rode well through the old fort until he came to what once was a General Mercantile store, which still had a roof and two front shattered pane glass doors.

He reined up and dismounted in front of the shattered doors and turned a wandering gaze down the way he'd come with an inquiring look in his eyes—have they picked up his trail? —he figured they had. He'd left it as plain and simple as possible to follow.

Draping the reins of his horse on his saddle horn, Slade turned toward the entrance and made his way onto what was left of the boardwalk as his horse followed its master into the structure. Slade didn't bother to stop it, already knowing it preferred the inside instead of out in the darkness. He didn't blame it one bit. *The horse had a mind of its own*, Slade thought.

Removing the reins from the saddle, Slade led his horse to a corner away from the entrance, then he looked around.

"What a pile of sticks," he muttered.

Dust and sand covered the broken wooden floor, broken down tables and chairs were scattered all around. The windows didn't have one pane of glass that wasn't shattered. Slade needed to build a small fire.

Gathering two chairs, he broke them down further and started a fire off to a corner. Then, removing his saddle and bedroll, he lay those down a few feet from the fire. He used his saddle as a pillow and then, removing his boots, he covered them with his blanket. Not enough to fool anyone for too long, but it was all the edge he should need.

Removing his Winchester from its saddle boot, Slade draped his gun belt over his left shoulder and started walking barefooted toward the rear of the building. His horse tried to follow, but Slade motioned it to stay. Stopping by a set of stairs, he decided to see what was around the outside of the building before he investigated the inside. He didn't want to be caught blinded by not knowing the complete layout of the building, inside and out.

· Then, making his way toward the back, Slade found a door laying half in, half out, barely on its hinges. With loud grinding sounds, he pushed the door enough so he could pass through; he made his way around the building and came upon a set of stairs leading up to a veranda.

With the light of the full moon and a sky full of stars, Slade made his way slowly up the stairs. At the top, he walked around the veranda and came to the front, just under the front doors. He then laid out on his stomach and setting his rifle pointing down toward the street, he waited.

He didn't have long to wait.

Having crossed the gully, the three bounty hunters dismounted and leading their horses, made their way quietly toward one structure, which apparently displayed the flickering light of a camp-fire.

"Stupid son bitch has a damn fire going just for us," Jones said.

"He's leading us straight to him," Watters agreed.

"Don't know," Harper said. "This guy is a Ranger. Why would he start a fire? Something's not right."

"He's stupid, plain and simple Jim," Jones said. "Don't overthink this. Besides, he doesn't even know we followed him."

"Reckon you're right," Big Jim Harper said.

"How you want to go about this Jim?" Watters asked.

"Two of you make your way around back," Harper explained. "I'll come up to the front and ask him nicely to surrender, give you enough time to get in and grab him."

"Yeah," Watters said. "We got it. We did this before."

"Yeah, but we killed *that* guy," Jones mentioned.

"Reckon we did at that," Harper chuckled. "Let's go, times a wastin'"

Through the stillness of the night, Slade heard an approaching horseman coming from his right, riding as if he didn't have a care in the world. Slowly, he made his way and reined in front of the doors just below him. Slade recognized the man. He was one of the bounty hunters he'd spoken to at the Rangers' station.

"Ranger, hey, Ranger!" Harper yelled out. "We know you're in there. We're here for ya. Come out peacefully or we come in."

Then from the veranda, Slade shouted down, "Where are the others?"

But just then, Watters and Jones rushed outside and stood beside Harper.

"That answers that," Slade said, grinning as he cocked the hammer back on his Winchester.

Harper stared up and spotted the Ranger, as Watters and Jones kept their hands on their guns, as did Harper. They didn't draw. They didn't know if the Ranger had a gun trained on them. They would be at a major disadvantage if he did.

Harper said, "Look, hombre, we need you alive."

"Well, I can't say the same for you three," Slade said. "You're going to have to earn that two thousand dollars bounty."

"No problem, you're shit to us, Ranger."

Slade just smiled. He knew any further words would be futile.

Then, without warning, Harper drew his iron from his cross-holster lightning fast. But as his gun cleared the holster, Slade already with a bead on Harper's gun-hand and before Harper's hand came across his chest, shot him in the face. Already dead, his body was flung backward out of the saddle when, with a loud thump, it landed on its back. His horse spooked, galloped away into the night.

Then all hell broke loose, as both sides opened fire!

It took Watters and Jones a split second to digest the fact that Big Jim Harper was dead, when they both drew their irons, but Watters was the slower of the two, and Slade watching the pair, noticed Jones pulling his Colt first and just when Jones took aim, Slade unloaded two rounds into his body, flinging him backward. And as his knees gave way under him, he collapsed to the ground, dead.

As his friend's body was being filled with rounds, Watters drew his Colt and while running into the building, fanned off four rounds into the veranda. As he ran, he saw by the light of the full moon, his slugs striking the veranda as a sliver of wood chips flew from under the wooden floor. But his shots were harried and wide. Running through the doors, he stopped and leaned against the wall, pulling bullets from his belt, and reloading his iron. Then he realized his two closest friends he'd known for years were dead. Dead, because they tried to bring in a bounty alive.

"Son of a bitch!" he muttered.

Slade, in the meantime, strolled back inside and leaning his Winchester by a wall, walked through an open door leading into a short hallway. Drawing his Colt .44, Slade cocked back the hammer on a live round and proceeded through the hallway and to a set of stairs leading straight down. His bare feet made no sounds as he proceeded down the stairs.

Watters, still leaning up against the far wall next to the entrance, didn't know what to do next and not knowing if the Ranger was coming to finish what was started, he took two steps in front of him and with his Colt by his side was ready to go out the back way and to safety, then to his horse before the Ranger knew he was gone.

Slade, by that time, was at the last landing when he heard footsteps approaching. Stepping out into the light of the still burning fire, Slade saw the bounty hunter, just at the same time Watters, taken by surprise, made out the Ranger.

It was Watters' slight hesitation that cost him his life, for just when they locked eyes on each other, Watters quickly raised his gun. Slade, with his gun leading out in front of him and with no qualms, fanned off three shots into the bounty hunter's chest. Watters' gun dropped from his hand as his body slumped to the floor and rolled onto his back, his life slowly leaving him as his blood leaked onto the wooden floor.

Texas Ranger John Slade calmly walked up to the man and kicked his gun away from him. Slade noticed the bounty hunter was breathing blood while his shirt was soaked with blood. Slade didn't give him much longer to live.

"God, Ranger," Watters said through clenched teeth, "please don't let me suffer, so finish me."

Without a word, John Slade raised his gun, cocked back the hammer, and shot him in the head. As Watters' face exploded, it drenched the floor with more blood. To Slade, it was the humane thing to do.

Shaking his head, Slade grabbed his gear, and with his horse, made camp in the other building. Maybe now he could sleep knowing there wasn't anyone else out there gunning for him tonight. Setting his bedroll and covering himself with his blanket, he soon was fast asleep.

# CHAPTER 34

# THE OFFER

*Mid-August 1882*

He kept his horse at a steady trot, eating up the miles, but conserving its strength. Slade knew that at this pace he'd make the northern outskirts of San Antonio sooner than expected. He wasn't hurrying his horse, knowing full well it was in great condition and capable of sustaining the pace for hours.

Just then, a rattler side winding across his path on the white desert sands halted and when it sensed the approach of the horse, continued its way; staring up at a cloudless blue sky, Slade watched a buzzard circling overhead waiting for its next meal.

With his latest model Winchester laid crossways on his lap, he'd earlier jacked a shell into the chamber and let the hammer down half-cock. He was riding through the badlands of Texas, that portion between Austin and San Antonio that invited bushwhackers, horse thieves, whiskey peddlers, outlaws, and marauders and having his rifle at the ready gave him an added advantage in case he crossed with trouble on the trail.

Texas Ranger John Slade's steed was a white and brown chestnut pinto with a height of less than five feet. It was at fourteen when young John Slade stumbled upon a dead horse in the open plains near Wild Horse Creek with a foal lying beside it.

As it lay stricken, unable to stand, Slade approached the little colt and having found no severe injuries, took it as his own and slowly nursed it back to health. From that moment, the horse and Slade became inseparable, except for the times during the war or when issued a horse by the Rangers. But one thing Slade never did was to name it. If he was to answer why, Slade would just shake his head and shrug. On his long travels and on more than one occasion, Slade would stop, water his horse and reward it with its favorite treats—sugar cubes and carrot sticks.

It was nearly noon when he branched over to the Western Trail and then another forty-five minutes that would take him down into the valley reaching San Antonio proper. The Western Trail was first traveled by Captain John T. Lytle in 1874 when he transported over thirty-five hundred head of cattle from Southern Texas into Nebraska and was continuously used thereafter for the movement of cattle and horses to markets into the Eastern and Northern states.

Established in 1866, it replaced the Chisholm Trail, which was abandoned in early 1882. The Western Trail ended at the town of Bandera Texas, best known for the Battle of Bandera Pass, when in 1841 John Coffee Hays and a troupe of Texas Rangers defeated a large party of Comanche Warriors.

During his long ride, Slade stirred restlessly at the memory of his late wife as a small tear flowed from his eye. Emily, his wife and that of Lynn Evans, her twin sister—both gone, but still so close to his heart.

Emily's smiling face, her voice sweet and tender and her joyful laugher always right there in front of him every waking moment. Then her dead lifeless eyes that no longer would stare at him, would infringe on his consciousness and the fateful night which slowly focused itself upon him; the night she was brutally murdered. And those of Lynn Evans, who was shot to death as she sought revenge on those that murdered her sister and her husband, Josh Evans.

Life has its consequences, so does death, he reasoned. But the sense of unreality was always short-lived as the pull of the living always seemed to bring him back to the present. "Life always goes on," he muttered. Yet, it'd been over a year since that tragic night, and still it felt as if it was only yesterday.

Reaching a small ridge, Slade pulled on the reins and slowed his horse. Dismounting for a few minutes, he reached for his canteen, then pulled the bandana from around his neck, soaked it with water and wiped at his sweaty face. Taking a swig from the canteen, he noticed it was almost empty.

His horse turned his head toward the canteen, probably wanting some water too.

"No more, horse. But there's more down in San Antone," he said. "For you and me."

Taking the reins in one hand and reaching for the stirrup with the other, Slade nimbly swung up onto his saddle.

He knew he was in broken country, as hills bottomed out in several steep rocky hillsides as he finally saw San Antonio down in the valley. Slow and easy, he let his horse take him down from the ridge as he set the pace once more.

A half-hour later and entering San Antonio from the north end, he rode down into the city and slowly made his way through the bustling streets packed with covered and uncovered buggies, as several shops were crowded with noonday shoppers strolling the crowded streets.

Three theaters, one on the far corner and two others across the street, were packed with patrons standing in line, waiting for its matinee opening to enjoy the plays put on by various traveling actors. It was a bustling city of commerce. Then, through the Iron Commerce Street Bridge, he passed the Riverside hotel. A few minutes later, he rode past the Menger Hotel, where he was to meet up with Ben Collins.

But first he needed to stop off at a nearby stable and get his horse boarded in.

Slade settled for a quaint little stable on the other side of Alamo Plaza, aptly named; *The Alamo Livery Stable*-Proprietor O.W. Toombs.

As he pulled up to the front of the stable, two buckboards with a hitch of two horses and four unsaddled horses were waiting for the owner of the establishment or his hired hands to take care of them. The customers were just milling about smoking and waiting their turn.

Slade, not wanting to wait around for anyone, dismounted and casually walked inside, as he called out for service, while from way back inside someone yelled in response, "Hold your horses, mister, be right with ya."

Smiling, John Slade dropped the reins to his horse by his side and kept on walking toward the sound of the man's voice, as his horse followed right behind him. A few seconds later, a bald, short, round man, wearing dirty black pants and black shirt, wiping at his hands with sweat dripping down his brow, came out of the darkness and paused three feet away from the Ranger.

O.W. Toombs was just opening his mouth, ready to put the customer in his place with a piece of his mind. But then, making eye contact, he quickly closed his mouth, noticing something quite disturbing in the manner the stranger looked at him.

Toombs didn't frighten easily, but this stranger was scary. It was his eyes. Even in the semi-darkness of the stable, he stared into the endless depth of the man's darkened eyes. He felt as if he was looking deep down into his soul and setting it ablaze.

There was pain and death in them. Toombs felt a sudden coldness sweep over him. Here was a dangerous man, maybe not to him, but to whomever crossed his path or crossed him. He wanted this man out of his stable.

"Yes sir," he said almost in a whisper, diverting his eyes from the stranger. "Take care of your horse for two bits and feed money."

As Toombs, not wanting to look into those eyes, started walking away, Slade stood in front of him and leveled his gaze down on the man. "Don't you want my money?" he asked.

"Oh," Toombs voice dropped, almost inaudible, swallowing hard and extending out an open palm.

From atop a ridge overlooking the crumbling walls of old Fort Gates, a guard stood watch, and from inside the old grounds, men and horses moved here and there as they finished setting up fortifications around a small section where two structures still stood, both with repaired roofs and doors.

Fort Gates, established in 1849 by the US Army as Camp Gates and by Captain William R. Montgomery and two companies of the Eighth United States Infantry to protect settlers on the Texas frontier from Indians, was abandoned in 1852.

It was located around what would become the city of Gatesville, on the north bank of the Leon River. The river provided cover from anyone attempting to gain entry through that end. A guard was also posted there, preventing anyone from sneaking up and attacking.

This was the new hideout for the Hatcher gang.

In a sullen mood, James Wesley Hatcher watched the activities his men were performing. Hatcher, silent and aloof from his gang, had no viable information on Texas Ranger John Slade's coming and going from the Ranger station. But that would be rectified before the day was over. He had plans, plans that when set in motion, would make him rich, while getting his revenge for the killing of his two brothers. The plans included cattle rustling, bank, and train robberies.

He'd already placed a bounty on the Ranger's head and by now the word was out that he wanted John Slade brought in alive.

He'd chosen the old fort because it was far away from any town; it was completely isolated. The ride to the closest settlement or town took about half a day. The ridge suited Hatcher well. It allowed his guards to overlook the entire surrounding area.

Building a medium size stable, a bunkhouse for his men and a small bunkhouse for him and his lieutenant and cousin Charlie Edwards, was done in a matter of a week with supplies and building materials brought in from surrounding abandoned ranches.

The late afternoon was bright and clear as a cool slight wind blew from the north, which kept the sweat off his brows. Hatcher had hired a Mexican farmer and his family, his wife and two boys to do the cooking. He was hungry and thirsty, as the work kept him busy.

From the corner on the veranda of his cabin, James Hatcher watched as his men worked. At the moment, he was waiting on Edwards to arrive to set up the next phase of his operations. From the bunkhouse, he watched Edwards step out onto the dirt path and start walking toward him.

As Edwards reached their cabin, Hatcher walked in, pulled up a chair and sat down in front of his desk, just as Edwards walked in.

"Charlie?" Hatcher said, staring up at his cousin. "Is everything arranged?"

Charlie Edwards peered down at his boss and remained standing by the door, letting the slight breeze flow into the cabin and onto his sweat filled face. "Yeah boss," he replied. "I gave the boys their assignments just as you wanted. A two-man team to rob the bank at Fort Worth, and another team to rob the bank at Round Rock."

"Good ... good man," Hatcher said. "In the meantime, I've received word that the Fort Worth to Cleburne train will carry a shipment of gold bullion tomorrow. The train leaves early in the morning."

Edwards didn't even argue the point that the men had been spread out thin. He knew better than to argue. "Who do you want to handle the job?" he finally asked.

Just then, standing by the door, Edwards stepped aside as Consuela, the Mexican farmer's wife, holding two plates of beef, beans, and biscuits, walked in, followed by her nine-year-old, holding a pot of coffee. Setting it on the table in front of Hatcher and not saying a word, she and her son turned and walked out of the cabin.

"Sit and have some grub, Charlie," Hatcher said.

Charlie Edwards nodded as he pulled up a chair and sat facing Hatcher, saying, "Thanks boss."

Pulling out his knife, Hatcher started cutting up his beef, shoved a forkful of meat and beans into his mouth and wiping his shirtsleeve across his mouth said, "Here's what I want, Charlie. Take three of the boys and yourself to take the train. Once that's done, you're to head out to the Houston Texas Central train line. I have it on good account that a shipment of forty thousand dollars in twenty-dollar gold pieces will be carried in a strong-box. You should be able to intercept it by noon."

Charlie nodded. "No problem boss, I'll get on it right away."

"Any word," Hatcher snapped. "On the whereabouts of John Slade?"

Charlie Edwards shifted uncomfortably in his chair. Hatcher stared straight at him. He knew the main reason Hatcher was here in the first place was to settle the score with Slade. And not having information to pass on to his cousin, well, that didn't sit well with him.

Shaking his head and pushing his plate away, Edwards said, "None, boss. But I just returned from town and heard that three bounty hunters were killed by Slade a while back. There'll be others after 'em I reckon."

Hatcher suddenly stood up and swept the room with an angry gaze. He glanced at Edwards, his eyes narrowing to pinpricks on his cousin. But then he relaxed. His anger subsided some, and calmly he said, "Two things, Charlie. First, have Tom Steele head out to the Ranger station and keep an eye out for Slade. I want to know when the Ranger leaves and whom he talks to. If I can't get straight at him, I'll try some other way. Second, let's up the bounty. Get word out that the bounty is now at twenty-five hundred."

"Will do."

"One other thing," Hatcher said. "When are you expecting Slim and the others to return?"

"Well, boss," Edwards replied. "Slim Evers, along with the two Stiles brother, Sam and Rube and Johnny McCloud are due back tonight sometime."

"Good." Hatcher sat back down and stared over at his cousin. "They should have taken the stagecoach and the two trains by now."

They met in the reading room of the Menger Hotel, in San Antonio's Alamo Plaza, which opened in 1859. The hotel built next to the battle grounds of the Alamo, had a capacity of fifty rooms, becoming an overnight success. It gained fame during the Civil War when it housed injured Union soldiers and many soldiers that were stationed in the city. It also became notorious while experiencing the turmoil that was the Texas Reconstruction Era.

It was renowned for its elegant barroom, billiards hall, and barbershop that were connected to the hotel. It had an almost regal appeal with its ornate mahogany tables and chairs, large mirrors on all walls, with fine crystal and sterling silverware. It boasted a certain Old English charm. Normally, John Slade would have preferred an open saloon, out in some dusty town in which to drink and converse, but this was the height of classiness, and he liked the opulence.

Once he'd stabled his horse, Slade took a room, with plans on leaving the next morning whether he was successful in persuading Collins to work for him or not.

Slade had a vision. He knew the only way to find out the location of Hatcher's hideout, and what Hatcher was planning and when, would depend on having someone inside the gang. And who better than an ex-outlaw and lawman like Ben Collins.

The Ranger, with a four-day stubble, wearing his black woolen hat, frock coat and white shirt, tan trousers, boots with spurs and with his two guns strapped around his waist, exited his room on the second floor, located just to the right of the stairwell.

Locking his room, he slowly looked toward both sides of the hallway, and with no one coming from either direction, turned, and walked toward the stairwell. At the bottom of the landing he walked past the signing desk, which was jammed full with arriving guests, with several small children running here and there, almost out of control and out of sight of their parents.

Shaking his head, Slade continued into what the sign over the door read: Reading Room. Pushing through the café doors, he entered and was met with the strong cigar, cigarette smoke, laughter and loud talking of a room jammed full of high-browed and expensively clothed patrons.

Glancing throughout the dimly lit large reading room, that boasted a high glass chandelier, with mirrors on the walls, chairs and several two cushion couches that lined the walls and tables throughout, Slade caught sight of Ben Collins sitting alone at a far-left corner table. Upon seeing Slade, Collins, wearing a white shirt and black vest with dark trousers and long wavy black hair, raised his hand toward Slade, trying to catch his attention.

Almost shoulder to shoulder, Slade walked through the crowd of people until he reached Collins' table. Coming to a stop in front of the chair, Slade stared across at Collins as he kept one hand on his cross-holstered Colt. Hearing the crowd's background noises and taking notice of Slade's gun-hand, Ben Collins placed both his hands on the table in a gesture that they weren't holding any guns.

"Collins," John Slade broke and said in a sharp voice as he tipped his hat, in more like a sign of respect than being sociable.

In front of Ben Collins was a half full bottle of whiskey and two shot glasses. One half full and the other empty, as if it had been waiting all this time for *him*.

Collins gave Slade a steady look and said, "Pull up a chair Ranger and pour yourself a drink."

These two didn't trust each other yet. Soon though, they would build a bond of trust that would work in both their favors.

John Slade pulled out the chair from under the table, removed his hat, placed it on top of the table and sat facing Collins. Taking the bottle, he poured the glass half full. He brought the glass to his lips and downed the whiskey in one gulp. Setting down the shot glass, Slade stared at Collins inquiringly, waiting for him to open up.

"So," Collins began, "I was surprised when I got your cable and that you accepted my offer to meet."

Slade smiled and laughed a little. "I was surprised too ... on your invitation. I never expected to hear from you again. Thought maybe you'd be heading to prison by now."

Collins became silent.

The reading room grew in patrons as they sat. They were surrounded by the high-pitched babble of those all around them. For a reading room, it was certainly very animated and loud, Slade thought.

Collins settled back in his seat and tipped his hat back. "Yeah, I reckon you were at that," he said. "I got lucky on the trail."

Slade favored Collins with another smile, knowing the true reason he was freed. "So, I'm here now."

Ben Collins sighed. "I just thought we could have a drink together and give you my thanks for not shooting me on the trail and not killing me when you had the drop on me."

Slade refilled his glass, but this time he just sipped at his drink. "About that, Collins. I have a problem."

Pulling a stogie from his shirt pocket, Collins lit it, blew the match out, inhaled the smoke and, staring over at Slade, tilted his head back and exhaled, "And you thought of me. Mighty generous, Ranger. This problem of yours ... does it involve me?"

"In a manner of speaking," Slade said. "Yes, reckon it does."

There was a brief silence as Collins glanced over at the Ranger. "Tell me about your problem."

Slade glanced across the table and didn't answer right away. He leaned back in his seat, rubbed his chin, and said, "I have a gang operating out somewhere in the foothills, led by an outlaw named James Hatcher."

Collins regarded the Ranger with a little amusement, shrugged and said, "I've heard about him."

"Interesting," said Slade. "Who from?"

"Newspaper," Collins replied, "has it he and a gang have robbed several stagecoaches, banks and such, killing a few people and a couple lawmen on the way. I read two Pinkerton agents were also shot and hanged while trying to arrest two of the gang members. And something about kidnapping some women and selling them across the border."

"That's one reason I'm here."

Collins frowned. "Hey now, is that Hatcher guy family to those that killed your wife a while back?"

"So, you heard about that. But yeah, the last of the brothers," Slade replied. "And he put a bounty on me to be brought in alive."

"Ya don't say," Collins said. "And what's the other reason?"

"Would like your help in finding out where their hideout is located."

"And how would I go about doing that, that's if I agree?"

"Join the gang," Slade said. "Find out what they have planned so we could help capture the outlaws in the act. Get the location of their hideout so we can put an end to them once and for all."

"Tall order, Slade," Collins said. "And what's in it for me, since I'm putting my life on the line?"

Smiling again, Slade said, "Two hundred a month until it's over, and any bounty on the outlaws you kill. Heard it said some bounties are in the couple of thousand-dollar range."

"If I were to agree," Collins said, sounding unsure that he would go along with the Ranger's plan, "how can I pass any of the information on to you?"

"There's a small new town called Killeen just south of Round Rock, where you can telegram me your information. Or if there is somewhere closer to the hideout that you can cable me from."

As he mulled it over, Ben Collins spied a man standing in a far corner staring over at them, but more so at Slade, with a slight smile on his face. The man seemed somewhat out of place in the reading room.

Collins glanced at Slade. "There's a tall stranger, grizzled and bearded, standing on the other side of the door, wearing buckskins, and packing irons low on his hip, staring dead at you, Slade. Anything I should know?"

Not turning, Slade said, "Bounty hunters have been on my trail. Took three out last time they came for my bounty."

"Where there's one," Collins said. "There's more Slade."

"I reckon. So," Slade added, "what of my request?"

"Sure," Collins replied, smiling. "I got nothing better to do."

"Then it's a deal," Slade said, standing and offering his hand out to Collins.

Also standing, Collins shook Slade's hand and said, "What do you want done with the stranger yonder?"

"Let's go see what his problems are," Slade said as he grabbed his hat and slowly made his way through the crowd, with Collins right behind him.

"Yeah, reckon I knew you'd say that" Collins muttered to Slade's back.

Just then, the stranger, seeing the two men walking over to him, turned, and walked out of the room and headed outside the hotel.

With Collins at his back, John Slade exited the room. As was his custom, Slade undid the thong to his two Colts, and cocked them both as he slowly turned toward the hotel's exit. Pushing through the doors, he stepped up to the veranda and stopped as his name was yelled out from the other side of the street, just as Collins stopped and stood on Slade's left side.

There were four of them, standing side by side with their hands on the butt of their guns, with one standing on the far left holding a shotgun. They had the common appearances of gunfighters as they slowly separated, leaving a few feet between them.

They knew who Slade was, and he wasn't coming with them yet. They were prepared as the four of them kept their eyes on the Texas Ranger's guns.

"John Slade, ya coming with us!" yelled out the stranger they saw in the reading room. "We don't want to kill ya, maybe wound ya. And unless ya drop ya guns and come along peacefully, we gonna kill ya."

Stepping out onto the street, John Slade stopped and faced the four bounty hunters just as Collins joined him on the street. Pulling back the sides of his coat, Slade exposed his two Colts as his hands swayed to the gun-handles.

"Stranger," the bounty hunter doing all the talking said, "we ain't got no beef with ya, so just walk away. This ain't your fight."

"Well," Collins said calmly as he undid the thong to his gun, "I'm making it mine."

The bounty hunter spat and said with sarcasm, "Suit yourself, hombre."

The four gunmen stared stony eyed at the two in front of them, as a dust devil was blown across the middle of the street, while a small crowd of onlookers gathered on the hotel's veranda, waiting to see who blinked first. Most had not seen a gunfight in town in the past, and to the young, this was their first, if it turned out to be so.

Grasping the butt of his cross holstered Colt, Slade said, "Pull ya irons or get out of our way, ya cum sucking dogs!"

It was the tall stranger that drew first, Slade saw it in his eyes!

He was slow, as Slade bent his knees slightly, pulling his two Colts so fast Collins didn't even know he'd drawn his irons and shot the talkative bounty hunter through the heart, and with his second gun firing as well, he shot his second bounty hunter in the head, just as one of the other bounty hunters drew and fired his gun.

The one with the shotgun brought it up in front of him, but just as he was about to pull the trigger, Collins drew and shot him in the head as his shotgun came to life; the buckshot sailed between Slade and Collins not doing any harm.

Slade turned his guns on the last hombre, who'd fired a shot grazing Collins' left shoulder and was preparing to let loose on Collins once again, when Slade emptied his Colt on the man sending him backward as each slug found its mark on the man's chest, dead even before he dropped to the ground.

The gunfight lasted less than ten seconds, as all four hombres lay dead or dying on the street.

From behind Slade and Collins, someone yelled out, "Drop ya guns and reach for the sky, hombres, this is the law!"

Collins and Slade both holstered their guns, raised their hands, and slowly turned. Standing there was the city marshal, a tall, trim, and erect man. He was wearing no hat and his hair was almost completely black—no white hairs visible. It fell over his broad shoulders. He was wearing only a white shirt vest and a pair of dark trousers and boots. Six of his deputies were holding rifles pointing straight at Slade and Collins.

"Glad you're here Marshal, name's Slade, John Slade, Texas Ranger and this gent here is my friend who came to help with these four bounty hunters."

Staring at Slade, the Marshal asked, "You got a badge, Ranger?"

Slade pulled the flap of his coat to expose the Ranger badge clipped to his shirt.

The city marshal, on the job for less than six months, said, "Let's walk over to the jail and sort this out, Ranger."

"No problem Marshal, glad to help," Slade said.

"So, you're the famous Ranger, John Slade, eh?"

Then, as the Marshal stepped up close to the Ranger and said, "Heard you were coming into town."

# CHAPTER 35

# COLLINS AND DUNHAM

*Mid-August 1882 San Antonio, Texas*

Still out in the street, John Slade turned his back to the Marshal and his deputies, as a few feet away, Ben Collins started walking toward the Ranger. Slowly shaking his head at Collins, Slade didn't want it to be seen as if they were the best of friends, just in the off chance any of Hatcher's outlaws were in town. That, he realized, could've put an end to his plan. Ben Collins immediately understood the gesture, as he stopped, turned, and walked back into the hotel. Nevertheless, the fact that Collins and Slade both took part in a gunfight may have doomed his plans anyway. Although he was taking a huge chance, Slade had no alternative but to continue with it.

Turning back around, Slade kept a steady eye about the crowd that had gathered in the middle of the street. Gazing left and right, and up and then down the street, he didn't see anyone suspicious that even resembled a gunfighter, bounty hunter or otherwise—just hard-working curious townsfolk. Breathing a quick sigh of relief, Slade started walking toward Marshal Jacob 'Jake,' Brand's jailhouse and office.

Ben Collins, while sitting in the reading room of the Menger Hotel, a newspaper in one hand and a lit stogie clamped down between his teeth, waited for at least an hour before he would set out. He realized that if anyone had been watching Slade and himself in the reading room, they may have wondered what the connection was between him and the Texas Ranger. The gunfight would've ended any plans of deception on joining Hatcher's gang. However, he was optimistic that no one had put two and two together.

Setting down the newspaper, Collins crushed out his smoke, yawned, then gazed throughout the reading room and toward the front entrance; he failed to see anyone paying the least bit of attention to him. Standing, he again casually gazed about the room once more, when suddenly he set eyes on a man who'd just walked through the swinging doors to the reading room. With squinted eyes, his head canted to one side as he released the thong to his gun. That man, Collins knew well, just stood there as his eyes scanned the room, but not catching sight of him.

The stranger was of medium height and skinny, wearing a buckskin shirt that extended to his knees and trousers too large for his frame. With his gun belt strapped onto his waist, the gun rode high on his left hip, and with a wide brim hat canted to one side, he looked completely out of place in the hotel. Collins figured Harvey Dunham was looking for something or someone.

Collins watched Dunham, an old mountain man and tracker walk over to the bar and leaned up against it. His gaze fell right onto Ben Collins, who was walking toward Dunham. With a wide crooked smile, Dunham recognized his onetime friend, Ben Collins. Harvey kept watching calmly, looking at Collins up and down and said as Collins approached, "Ain't ya a sight there youngster. Been a long spell since we parted last."

Stopping in front of him, Ben Collins only nodded as he looked into the eyes of a stone-cold killer. The last he'd seen of Dunham was in '73 when he and Dunham were tracking for a couple of Texas Rangers out after a few hardened hostiles terrorizing several settlers. Dunham killed two of the hostiles, scalped one, and was scalping another when Collins, disgusted with Dunham's inhumane behavior, tried to stop him. When Dunham refused to comply with Ben Collins' insistence to stop, Collins drew his handgun, and with the help of the two Rangers, stopped him. Collins remembered all too well that

Dunham cursed and threatened him, but nothing ever became of it. Now they stood face to face, and although Harvey Dunham hadn't placed his hand on his gun, the man's eyes said more than his words.

Ben Collins wasn't about to take any chances with the gunfighter. He hooked his thumb on his gun belt and keeping his hand about an inch away from his gun, he regarded Dunham for a moment. "What's an old man like you doing here." His voice soured. "Dunham?"

Dunham shrugged. "Not much," he replied. "Looking for someone, as it is." Dunham gazed around the room and with a small, bemused smile, his gaze fell back on Collins.

"Really? Who may that be?" Collins asked, frowning while glancing sidelong at Dunham.

The old man shrugged again and said, "Jasper by the name of Slade, a Texas Ranger. Heard tell he has a price on his head, which I aim to collect."

With a surprised look on his face, Collins asked, "You a lawman now, Harvey?"

"Why hell no, youngster," Dunham admitted. "I am making my living doing bounty work."

Collins nodded. "That's a change, Harvey. That work ain't much of living."

"Yeah, I reckon so," the old gunfighter said as he rubbed his beard, and asked, "What's you up to these days, Ben?"

With a thin smile, Collins replied, "Keeping a step ahead of the law."

"Heard tell you have a sizable price for your head too, boy," Dunham said and slowly added, "dead ... or alive."

Moving his hand closer to his gun, Ben Collins asked, "You aim to collect on it?"

The action wasn't lost on Dunham, and with a veiled smile he said, "Haven't decided. But Slade's the bigger bounty here, boy. Heard tell, the Ranger is in town. Maybe after him, I'll come looking for ya."

"Good luck with that." Collins, taking to a step back, started walking backward, not taking his eyes away from Harvey Dunham.

The barkeep slid over to the gunfighter and said, "You need to order a drink, mister."

"Sure, whiskey," Dunham said, still staring off at Collins.

Momentarily halting, Ben Collins shifted his gaze on Dunham, and said, "Oh, Harvey, ever come across a bunch of owl hoots operating out in the badlands?"

Harvey Dunham, with slow glances to and from his onetime friend, surveyed him closely. "Ah," murmured the trapper. "May have. The last bounty I fetched was a jasper who says rode with the Hatcher gang, one time or 'other."

"Much obliged."

Ben Collins didn't quite believe the old man's story. Dunham knew where the outlaws' hideout was located. Collins was sure of it. However, he wasn't going to let on to that fact. And the way the gunfighter was slowly itching his hand toward his gun, told Collins, Harvey Dunham was waiting for the right moment to draw and fire.

The bounty hunter continued to peer down on Collins as if to say *draw*. Instead, Dunham's voice lowered a little and said, "Watch your back, Ben Collins."

*There it was* ... a voice said inside Ben Collins' head.

Collins was sure Dunham was itching to have it out right there right then. Shaking his head ever so gently, he debated whether to draw on him and end it.

With his hand gripping the handle of his gun, Collins said, "If you aim to collect on me, draw your iron and let's settle this now!"

A silence fell on those in the reading room. All eyes of those present turned to the two at the bar, as word quickly spread around of a gunfight.

Slowly, Dunham crossed his arms about his chest and said, "Maybe later."

"I come across ya again," Collins said, "I'll shoot to kill!"

Dunham said nothing. He just turned his back on Collins, leaned on the bar, and downed his drink. He knew of Ben Collins' reputation with a fast gun. Nevertheless, he'd pick his own time to settle the score with him. There was plenty of time for that, he thought.

Ben Collins slowly walked out of the reading room and up to his room.

Keeping sight of Collins, and once he was out of sight, Dunham called over to the barkeep and said, "Pour me another whiskey."

Once the barkeep, a short, long-haired portly man, poured the drink, Dunham reached in his pocket and placed a two-dollar gold piece on the bar and pushed it over to him. "It's yours if you can tell me if you're seen a Texas Ranger named Slade come in here recently."

The barkeep didn't answer right away, he just stared at the man in front of him for a second. "Well, yes sir, don't rightly know his name," he finally said. "Saw the Marshal and a Ranger heading to the jail-house, just after the shooting about half an hour ago. That could be the Ranger you're asking about."

"Ya don't say," the gunfighter muttered.

"Sure enough."

Still holding down on the gold piece, Dunham asked, "What does this Ranger look like?"

Just then, the barkeep turned his gaze to the windows and observed the Ranger stepping out of the Marshal's office. "That be him right there."

Sliding over the gold piece, Dunham downed the whiskey and took a gander at the Texas Ranger. The gunfighter opened his eyes wide as a slow smile emerged on his face. "Got ya, son–of–a–bitch. You're mine now!"

The sun glared down from a cloudless blue sky, sending shimmering heat waves onto the streets of San Antonio, as John Slade stepped out of the jailhouse and Marshal Brand's office. Once he'd concluded his business, that of informing Brand of his purpose for being in town, Slade reached into his back pocket, pulled out a stogie, and lit a match to it. As he inhaled the smoke, he took three steps onto the edge of the street and stopped as he absorbed the sights and sounds of the bustling town.

The street in front of the Menger Hotel had thinned to a few shoppers with hardly a buckboard in sight. Throwing the match onto the street, Slade took another step, when from the other side of the street, he spied someone standing with a gun drawn and pointing straight at him. Slade thought that the sun was playing tricks on him. Shaking his head once, but he knew better. He also knew that if he drew his Colts, he probably wouldn't be able to defend himself. He undid the thong on his guns and casually kept his hands by the pistol grips.

"John Slade," Dunham yelled out, "you're a coming with me, so drop your gun belt slowly, hombre, and get your hands up!"

"Don't think I will," Slade yelled back. "You're going to have to shoot and hope you kill me before I put a bullet in ya head."

Dunham grunted his agreement. "Then, so be it."

At that very moment, Marshal Brand stepped out of his office and with his gun in hand leveled it at the stranger, as two of his deputies also with guns drawn stepped out from behind Brand and stood shoulder to shoulder with their marshal. Brand, recognizing the stranger, warned, "Put down your gun, Dunham. We won't have another gunfight in my town. Don't make me shoot ya."

A tense moment ensued.

Not knowing if Dunham was going to drop his gun back into its holster or shoot, the Marshal spoke to his two deputies and had them slowly surround the gunfighter.

Dunham saw what he was doing and yelled out, "This hombre has a price on his head, Marshal!"

Marshal Brand shook his head, shrugged, and said, "Not by the law bounty hunter!"

Four against one, the odds weren't in his favor as Dunham slowly holstered his gun.

Grinning, Dunham yelled, "My name's Dunham, Harvey Dunham, Ranger. I'll see you later."

"Not if I see you first," Slade retorted.

Both Slade and Marshal Brand watched Dunham walk to a hitching post by the hotel and approach his horse, and as he swung up to his saddle, he tipped his hat to Slade. And with a stern set to his jaw and narrow eyes, Slade saw anger and a grim determination in those eyes. Dunham, without another word, put spurs to his horse and at a fast gallop, rode east out of town.

The City Marshal stepped down to the street and stood in front of Slade.

"Much obliged Marshal," Slade said.

"You sure are right popular, Ranger."

"Reckon," Slade said and asked, "You know that hombre?"

"Unfortunately, yes," the marshal said, scratching his head. "He's come into town with a bounty once or twice. An old Indian fighter, gunfighter, and trapper. Now a bounty hunter. Ya gonna have to watch yourself 'round that jasper, Ranger."

"Thanks again, Marshal."

From his room overlooking the street, Ben Collins watched the events unfold before his eyes. At one point, he was set to help Slade. However, when he saw the Marshal and two deputies, he knew better than to interfere. Unless, of course, Dunham got stupid and drew his gun. He just wished Slade had shot and killed old man Dunham. Save him the bullet.

Ben Collins figured that if anyone knew where Hatcher's hideout was, it could very well be Dunham. He also reasoned that there was only one way to find out, that of tracking Dunham and hopefully have him lead him straight to Hatcher.

Hell, he thought, it's worth the try.

Collins was trying to kill two birds with one stone.

Stuffing his saddlebags with a few pieces of clothing, he stepped out of his room, locked it, and headed to the livery stables for his horse. He was bound and determined to track Dunham. If the old man didn't lead him to the gang, well he thought, he knew ways of getting him to talk. And if that failed, he'd put a bullet to the old rascal.

An hour later, as dark clouds formed and a brisk wind started blowing in, threatening rain, Ranger John Slade approached the outskirts of town. Turing in his saddle, he said goodbye to San Antonio and started once again on the ride back to Austin. However, unknown to him, Harvey Dunham began following Slade's tracks. And behind him rode Ben Collins, who'd had no knowledge Dunham was following the Ranger, as he too followed the old man's horse tracks.

## CHAPTER 36

# GUNSMOKE ON THE TRAIL

Slow was the trail he rode to Austin, and in no need to hurry the pace. John Slade rubbed his jaw frowning in thought. His chief concern was Collins and the man's ability to get into Hatcher's gang. When would it happen? He didn't know. However, he was confident the ex-lawman would fulfill his side of the plan.

Throughout the ride, something gnawed at the back of his mind. He felt a sense of apprehensiveness sweep over him.

Slade since childhood had the ability to feel trouble, blindsight as it was, that served him more than once during the war and now as a lawman. He could feel something or someone behind him before he set eyes on the person.

Now, he felt it again, strongly, and the last few miles heightened it; he could sense someone or something dogging his trail. Slade kept his horse at a trot, his senses fully alert. Then on impulse, he turned on his saddle but couldn't make out anyone behind him, except for a speck of dust far on the horizon. A rider, he thought. Or dust devil? He couldn't be sure.

With his Winchester laid crossways between his lap and the saddle horn he was ready for any eventuality. His gun was cocked and ready to fire. He was in the thick of the badlands, where he knew dangers lurked all around.

A half-hour later, he reached a lofty range of hills. As he rode up a narrow hill, he crested the top, came to a stop, and swung down from the saddle. Grabbing his binoculars, he placed the glasses to his eyes, stared down the way he came, and swept the countryside. He stopped and focused on a speck of dust, adjusted the sight, and through the darkness that was slowly spreading and the dark clouds looming, he made out the faint shadow of a rider on a dark horse, but still too far away to see who it was.

Slade frowned in the shadows of the late overcast afternoon as he kept gazing at the lone rider still too far away for immediate concern. Stroking the side of his horse, he jumped back onto the saddle. "Well horse, we may have company soon. The sun will slip down soon enough, and I reckon the evening chill gonna set in too. We're gonna have to find a place to bed down in a few." Swinging his horse's head back up the trail he rode at a slow gallop.

Ben Collins kept well behind old man Dunham, hoping he would lead him to the Hatcher gang. However, if he didn't know any better, he'd swear Dunham was following someone. Who could it be? He didn't know, nor cared.

*Whoever it is, I sure won't let him get close. I have other business with the bounty hunter.*

With knitted brows, Collins broke his horse into a hard gallop as it drove its hoofs deep into the soft ground, responding to the spurs digging hard into its flanks. Low in the saddle he rode, almost placing his head next to the horse's own. As he maintained a low profile in the saddle the horse increased his speed. With each minute, Collins drew closer to Dunham, who, yet, hadn't turned in the saddle looking back.

Moments later, just as Collins was gaining on Dunham, the old bounty hunter heard fast hoofs behind him and, as he turned on his saddle, he saw someone giving chase. Recognizing who it was, he remembered the last words between him and Collins; *"If I ever see you again, I'll shoot to kill."* Those words resounded in his mind. And then he spurred his horse faster and broke to his left, away from the trail and into some rolling hills, hoping to find a spot to bushwhack Collins.

From less than a third of a mile before reaching Dunham, Collins watched as the bounty hunter disappeared around a bend of a hill, as gunshots broke the quiet way up ahead and just around the bend.

At a fast gallop, and nearing the bend, Collins pulled up and dismounted on the fly, as he slapped his holster, drew, and hugged a boulder. Creeping slowly forward, he stopped and made out Dunham shooting up the hill at three men with rifles.

Dunham slipped down onto the ground, reloaded his iron, and came back up shooting once again when suddenly a stray bullet slammed into this right shoulder. As he yelped in pain, he thought he heard noises behind him.

Collins had the workings of an idea, which he immediately put to the test. "It could work," he said to himself. He called out Dunham's name, "Hey, old man, it's Collins, coming up behind ya, don't shoot."

Dunham whirled around and aimed at the danger he suspected from behind.

Stopping just enough so he wasn't seen or shot by the bushwhackers, Collins said, raising his hands, "Easy there, partner, just came to help."

"I'm doing just fine, youngster. Don't think I need of your help."

"Sure, you will," Collins said, keeping a sharp eye on Dunham's gun hand. "Unless they kill you first or ya die from loss of blood. I have an idea, though."

"What?"

"I'll work my way around 'em and catch 'em from behind."

Dunham quickly saw the validity of Collins' plan. Considering he was trapped. He couldn't take a step away from the boulder before he was shot, nor could he move to his side without exposing himself to hot lead. With a shake of his head, he stammered, "Okay, I'll keep them busy for ya."

Back at his horse, Collins drew his Henry Winchester model 1860, rounded the boulder, and like a hungry wolf on the prowl, made his way swiftly and steadily up the mountainside. Once or twice, he paused to get his bearings as the firing continued, giving him a rough idea of where the three shooters could be positioned.

Minutes later, the shooting paused, and Collins could hear voices from the three shooters. Turning into the voices, he steadily came to the top of the mount, stopped, and laid on the rock, aiming his rifle down at the three bushwhackers, drawing on a bead on them that would be easy targets. But he didn't like shooting them in the back, not his style. As he rose to his full height, he calmly said, "Hey, y'all having fun?"

Suddenly all three turned, giving Collins just what he wanted, face-to-face death. As fast as he worked the lever action of his rifle, he aimed at one, then on to the second; finally, the last of the outlaws had time to let loose a shot of his own that went wide off to Collins' right. However, they didn't stand a ghost of a chance to protect themselves before all three laid dead.

Collins jumped down from the boulder and ambled toward the three bodies. One by one, he searched them, took what little money they had, and salvaged some well-needed ammunition. "Yo, Dunham!" he shouted down. "Ya got no more trouble from up here. I'm coming down, so don't shoot me. Ya hear?"

"Yeah, I hear ya, youngster. How do I know ya won't shoot me?"

"I give you, my word."

Old man Dunham laughed. "Well, come on down and let's see if your word is any good."

Something in the old man's tone gave Collins pause. Would Dunham shoot him on sight even after saving his life? *Guess that's the chance I'll have to take.*

Once reaching the bottom of the hill, Collins came around the side of it, his rifle cocked and ready, just in case and saw Dunham sitting on the ground with his back to a boulder. With blood seeping down his shoulder, Dunham was in no shape to staunch the flow as he slowly looked up at Collins.

"How's that arm?"

"I think the bullet is still in there," he said, his face ashen. "Burns like hell."

Collins nodded and stared, saying, "Here, let me look at it."

Collins approached the old man and kneeled beside his wounded arm. He removed the buckskin jacket, exposing the injury. Collins then leaned him forward to get a look at the exit wound. He saw the bullet had gone clear through, which was good because he had no way to remove a bullet if it was lodged in there.

"The slug went clean through, old man, but I'll have to close the wounds, or you'll bleed to death before I get ya to a doctor."

With gritted teeth and down-cast eyes, Dunham responded, "Go on then, get it over with, youngster."

After building a small fire, Collins drew his bowie knife and placed it on the fire. Finding a twig, he had Dunham bite into it. And with the hot tip of the blade, he cauterized the entrance and exit wounds, while Dunham passed out from the pain and the smell of burned flesh.

Later, once he had the makings of a campfire, Collins brewed some coffee. With his saddle on the ground, he sat and stared at the old man who wasn't going anywhere tonight, as his mind planned for the coming morning, hoping that the old bounty hunter would get him to the gang's hideout. His thoughts also turned to Texas Ranger John Slade, and his plan.

Once he'd finished his coffee, he draped his blanket over him and was soon fast asleep.

# CHAPTER 37

## LUCK ON HIS SIDE

During the night, Collins was awakened twice by Dunham tossing and turning and yelling in his sleep. Collings figured he was having a nightmare. At one point, the old man shouted the name Rose. After several minutes, Dunham fell back to sleep and his yelling stopped.

Just as the sun peeked over the top of some rolling hills out in front of them, Collins started up the dying campfire and had a pot of coffee brewing along with biscuits and beans.

Moments later, Dunham woke with the scent of brewing coffee and hot biscuits on the pan. He sat up in his saddle and stared at Collins. "From all the things I've known of you Collins, never thought you knew your way around a campfire. Biscuits and coffee. The biscuits smell mighty good."

"How's that arm old man?"

"Some pain, but you did a good job of stopping the blood flow."

"Couldn't let you bleed out after saving your life."

Dunham shrugged. "Now what happens?"

"I'm trying to find where the Hatcher gang are hiding out. I've asked several people, but no one seems to know, or won't say where."

"What's your interest in 'em?"

"I want to join up and stay safe in numbers. While also pocketing some money."

Dunham rose and walked over to the campfire and sat across from Collins. "Happens I think I can help with that. I could take you there if that's what you want."

"That's exactly what I've been wanting since I came into this area."

Dunham nodded.

After a few minutes, Collins started wondering what the old man was doing riding out alone. Taking a deep breath, he asked. "So, what brings you out so far into the badlands?"

"I was tracking the Ranger named Slade, trying to collect on his bounty. Once he'd lay over his saddle, I was to take him to Hatcher… alive."

So far, after the initial team up with Dunham, everything seemed in place in learning Hatcher's hideout. The hard job now was getting the information out to Slade.

After breakfast, they broke camp, saddled up and rode due east.

As they kept their horses at a steady trot and riding side by side, Collins hummed as he wondered who Rose was that Dunham yelled out in his nightmare. "Meant to ask if I'm not prying, but last night in your sleep you yelled out the name Rose. Just curious old man, you don't need to say."

A dead silence.

Dunham shook his head, felt something go cold inside him. Then he said, not thinking too much about Collins' question, "Rose was my five-year-old daughter. I was out with a hunting party after some hostiles. When I returned, my cabin was attacked by Apaches. My wife and child were killed, and my cabin set on fire. After I buried them, I swore they would pay."

Collins turned to look at Dunham and all he saw was sadness and regret over an otherwise hard stone killer's face.

"I'm sorry, Dunham. I didn't know you had a family."

"Yeah, well no problem. You're the only one that knows."

He woke with a start and a yell on his lips.

Slade caught his breath as he stared at the early morning sunlight that caressed and warmed his face. His right hand had instinctively pulled his gun and pointed it out in front of him. Not seeing danger anywhere near him, he holstered the gun, rose from his saddle and removed his blanket from about his body.

Slade waited until he stopped shaking and had his breathing back under control before he took another step. His dream was always of Emily. The day she was murdered. Will he ever shake the dread of that day? He didn't think so. He could only hope that time would heal his broken heart.

After some hot coffee and hardtack, he broke camp, saddled up his horse, nimbly jumped into the saddle and led his horse toward Austin. "Not too far away now, horse. A few miles more and we'll be home."

Slade rode into the Texas Ranger Station about mid-day. Once he had his horse in the stable he walked toward his bungalow. A hot bath and a hot meal would revive his otherwise tired body. And then he would give his report to Captain Franklin.

Dunham led them up through several low laying hills that meandered through some rivers and creeks. The trail was fraught with a good deal of wildlife.

An hour and a half later they reached their destination. From on top a ridge that overlooked the crumbling walls of old Fort Gates, a sentry fired a warning shot into the air that stopped both men from advancing any further. "Turn around and go back the way you came, hombres. You have no business here."

"We're come to speak to your boss, Hatcher," Dunham yelled up at the sentry. "He knows I would show up."

"So, he's expecting you?" the sentry asked.

"Yes, yes, he is."

"Come on by then."

Hearing the shot, they knew visitors would be coming through shortly. Who it could be did not trouble him. Only a few knew where the hideout was located.

Hatcher and his two cousins, Charlie Edwards, and Slim Evers, stood shoulder to shoulder with their boss with lit stogies clenched tightly between their teeth. They weren't expecting anyone today, not until tomorrow, when his group he'd sent out for information returned.

Through the gap between the boulders, they saw two riders approaching. Collins and old man Dunham slowly trotted through the gap. Dunham made out Hatcher standing on the veranda with his two cousins with him. He turned his horse's head in that direction as Collins followed suit.

Edwards, standing next to Hatcher's left side, was the first to speak. "That's old man Dunham, the other rider is unknown to me. Dunham was here several weeks ago asking for exclusive rights to bring in Slade."

"Yeah, I remember that. I said no. Let's see if they bring us any good news," Hatcher responded.

Collins and Dunham were halfway to the cabin, when through the sunlight, Evers shook his head and pulled out his stogie. "Well, I'll be damned!" he muttered. "Boss, I think I know who the rider is. Seen him once or twice. He's a gunfighter and one time lawman, Ben Collins. Heard there's a large reward out for him."

Hatcher's eyes widened. "Yeah. I've heard of him. He killed a couple of lawmen and has been on the run for a long time."

"What do you think he wants?" Edwards chimed in.

"My guess is a place to lie low."

Moments later, both riders pulled up by the hitching post in front of the cabin. Dismounting, they tied their horses and stepped up to the boardwalk in front of the three outlaws.

Hatcher took a step forward. "Ah, I thought you said you would have Slade with you when you came back. And who is this hombre?"

Before Ben Collins said a word, Dunham responded. "Yeah, about that, I almost had the Ranger except I got bushwhacked. And if it wasn't for Collins here coming around when he did, I'd be dead right now."

Then all eyes shifted toward the stranger. The looks weren't lost on Collins. Guess it's time to put up, he mused. "The name's Collins, Ben Collins, I'd—"

"We've heard of you," Hatcher cut in with a wave of his hand. "You've been chased by a few bounty hunters. You've been in the newspapers and wanted posters for a long time. You've managed well for a man on the run."

"It's why I'm here. Could use a place to lie low for a while and maybe make payroll."

A moment of silence.

Collins suddenly felt a chill go up his spine. The look Hatcher gave him wasn't that reassuring. He waited and watched as Hatcher's gun hand moved up to his Colt. He felt that if he moved his hand up to his gun he'd be dead in seconds. He wasn't taking that chance.

Collins guessed he didn't impress Hatcher that much. He knew from the moment he accepted the deal from Slade that this would be a suicide run. Now three against one gun was the last draw. He didn't stand a chance of survival.

Tense seconds passed, and then faintly, Collins blinked and saw Hatcher's hand slide down his side, empty-handed. "Let's go inside and talk about it."

Hatcher stood to the side and let the two men step into the cabin.

# CHAPTER 38

# WITHOUT A SHOT

It didn't take long for Collins to get a feel for the place.

After Hatcher approved his stay he walked his horse to the stables and set out for the bunkhouse. He found an empty bed by the back entrance, which suited him just fine. He'd decided to wait until after supper to look the place over, without arousing too much suspicion about what he was doing.

He placed his hat and gun belt on a wall peg by his bunk and laid back on his bed until supper was announced. And that would be soon according to the talk in the bunkhouse.

Collins glanced around the room. A noisy card game of five players sat around a table in the center of the room, while a few just laid in their bunks. Several of the outlaws he recognized by their wanted posters, and others he'd not seen before. So far, his status as a free man hadn't reached the ears of the outlaws in the room. With luck, he should be out tonight, making it a moot point.

It didn't take long for supper to arrive. For moments later, a Mexican woman and an eight or nine-year-old child brought in supper and drinks. The food was a mixture of fried chicken, baked beans and biscuits. Collins filled a plate and sat back on his bunk.

Two outlaws, Bill Daly and Johnny McCloud, who Collins knew by reputation, strolled up to him and halted a few feet from his bunk. "Say?" Daly asked. "Ain't ya Ben Collins?"

Collins slowly put down his plate. His guard went up, and he was on full alert. Did they know he wasn't a wanted man anymore? He glanced at his guns—they were too far to reach—he wouldn't make them before he was shot or taken prisoner.

Collins' only recourse was to continue with his gambit. He inhaled deeply, exhaled. "That's me. Can I help you?"

"You're famous in this neck of the woods. Glad to meet you. I'm Bill Daly, and my friend here is Johnny McCloud."

"Ya going to be around much?" McCloud asked.

"I certainly hope so."

"Well, welcome to the gang," Daly said.

A sudden calm came over Collins. He glanced at the retreating outlaws with a faint shake of his head.

After supper, and with daylight still flickering, he strapped on his guns and donned his hat. Out in the open, he moved from one corner to the next. There wasn't anyone about to challenge him, so he kept searching.

He was looking for places he could use to slip away from the place come sundown without being seen. It would be his only chance. He wasn't coming back once he'd left the hideout. His part of Slade's plan was for him to get the location of the hideout and he'd accomplished that.

Suspicion would be aroused if he tried to leave the same way he'd come, through the gap and the main entrance with the sentry who would have questions he couldn't answer. So no, that was out of the question.

He was in an old Army fort, and by experience, where there was the main entrance there usually was a back gate—so he started looking for it.

Thirty minutes ticked by and he wasn't any closer to finding the back entrance to the fort. With the sun quickly fading in the west, he had little light to see where he was going and what he was doing.

He estimated that he'd walked a fairly long distance as he hugged the side of some crumbling walls, when suddenly, and under a canopy of green, as he made his way around a slight bend, he reached out to the other end and couldn't feel anything there, just space. Strolling toward the other end he stopped at what appeared to be the remains of a wooden barrier he estimated extended across for perhaps the same width as the main entrance.

This was the back gate!

He tried opening the gate, but it was shut tight. He'd need his horse to open it.

Now with only the bluish moonlight casting down, Collins walked back around to where he started, taking his time not knowing if someone had followed him. Then he stopped. Kneeling, he made himself a small target, as he made sure no one was out that could identify him and arouse suspicion.

Not knowing how long he'd been searching and coming out of the dark passage of the rear gate, he was greeted with a starless, pitch-black night. The passage was overgrown with tall trees and overhanging branches that sealed the sun, moon, and stars from shining through completely.

With no one in sight, Collins made his leisurely way to the stables. His luck was still holding as he entered the stalls. He was alone. Saddling up his horse, instead of riding out, he decided to walk the horse. Hoping to keep the hoofs from creating too much noise that would attract attention, especially since sounds are usually louder at night.

Following the high mountain ranges and the crumbling walls of the old fort, and through the starless dead of night, Collins led his horse as he soundlessly walked on, when suddenly, he stopped and quickly dropped into a crouch. He heard voices and saw lighted cigarettes not too far from where he'd stopped.

"Well, I ain't gonna stay here all night. I have to go and relieve Bill up at the entrance."

"Fine, I'll head back to the bunkhouse. Whatever noises I heard; I don't hear them now."

Collins was still far from the two men. He heard a horse ride out at a slow gait toward the main entrance. Moments later, he heard the second outlaw ride back and disappear into the bunkhouse.

That's when Collins realized how close he'd reached the bunkhouse.

After backtracking some, Collins finally arrived at the bend which would take him to the back gate. Still leading his horse, he continued through until he arrived at the wooden barrier. Collins untied the rope from his saddle, then he tied one end to the saddle horn and wrapped the other end to the spot he thought would get the job done.

Collins patted his horse's head and eased it forward a little at a time, then stopped. There was a slight grating noise. He waited for several moments, but no one came out to investigate. He eased his horse until he could make out a hole in the barrier. Stepping up to the hole, Collins could now open one side of the gate with enough room so he could ride through into the other side. Retrieving his rope, he waiting a few moments to make sure all was clear.

Minutes later, with a boot in the stirrup, Collins climbed onto the saddle and slowly led his horse through the opening. He kept the large animal at an even gait as he broke free to the other side. With darkness all around, he spurred his horse forward.

The door burst open and a young corporal with a cable clutched tightly in his hand, assigned to Company C of the Texas Rangers, Austin Station, with duties at the Western Union Cable office, ran out and headed to the bungalow assigned to Lieutenant Slade.

Arriving at the bungalow, Slade heard someone at the door before anyone knocked.

"The door ain't locked, come on in," Slade said from the living room where he was reading a book.

"Telegram for you, sir. Just came in," the Corporal said.

There would be only one person who Slade was expecting a cable from, and that was Ben Collins.

Thanking the young Ranger, Slade read the cable twice. He knew where Old Fort Gates used to be. Getting dressed, he went to inform his captain.

"You think Collins is being straight with us about the hideout, John?" Captain Franklin asked.

"Yes sir, he even included the location of the sentry for us. With twelve or more outlaws unaware we're coming."

"I have only six available Rangers," Captain Franklin said. "John we're stretched too thin as it is."

"Yes, sir."

A short silence followed.

"I'll send a cable to Captain Snelling, the commanding officer at the Army Eighth Cavalry Regiment out of Gatesville," Captain Franklin said. "See if he can help."

"Captain, you need to stress to Captain Snelling that we need to do this tonight before sunrise tomorrow and before they discover Collins was a traitor. With the element of surprise in our hands this is our only chance to get them all in one place."

Three hours later, a troop of fifty cavalry soldiers led by Captain Matthew Snelling rode into the Texas Rangers' station. They were followed by three wagons and a Gatling gun being pulled by a fourth covered wagon.

In the commanding officer's quarters, Captain James Franklin, Captain Matthew Snelling and Lieutenant John Slade sat with glasses of wine and bread over an open fire. After introductions had gone around, Franklin said, "Matthew, thank you for coming over so quickly."

"It was my pleasure Captain," Snelling said. "Plus, I was getting bored at the fort. So tell me, what exactly do you want us to do and do you have a plan?"

"I'll let Lieutenant Slade answer that."

Slade, with a pad of paper, drew a rough outline of the interior of the crumbling fort. Then, he drew two structures. "What we know is this. According to our man who infiltrated the gang, the structure closest to the main gate is Hatcher's, which he shares with two cousins. The second structure built well away from Hatcher's is the outlaws' bunkhouse."

Examining Slade's drawing, Captain Snelling asked, "Do you have a plan on getting inside without being seen, Lieutenant?"

"Yes sir," Slade responded. "That's where you and your soldiers come in. I see you're loaded for bear. Why the Gatling gun, Captain?"

"Good question, Lieutenant. Not knowing initially now many of the outlaws we were talking about, I thought it prudent to bring it along. Now that I know how many we're up against, I could use it as a deterrent weapon. Anyway, that's my plan. I wouldn't want to use it unless I had no other choice."

After discussing the tactics with the captain, they gathered their men and explained where they were going and what they were facing. With the Texas Rangers following the Army soldiers, they started the long ride to old Fort Gates.

They arrived in the dead of night. But with a gas lantern, a trooper led the way for John Slade once they arrived at the site Collins had described in his cable. Minutes into his search, he found the opening.

Captain Snelling detailed two soldiers to find and eliminate the sentry described by Collins. According to Slade's plan, they would wait until that was accomplished before they even proceeded through the gate. They would be keeping the noises down to a minimum. Two other sergeants were assigned the next step in the mission, and with their group of fifteen soldiers each, they waited for the commander to give them the move-out signal. Their mission, to surround the structures and accomplish the movements soundlessly. Then shoot anyone trying to escape through the back or side of the structures.

Fifteen minutes later, one soldier returned to the camp, after eliminating the main entrance sentry guard, while the second, as ordered, became the Army's sentry.

Captain Snelling took over from there.

On foot, he led his soldiers to the opening into the hideout proper. Still too dark to see clearly, he still could make out the two structures. And then, the commander gave the word to the two sergeants to proceed toward the structures.

In neither Hatcher's cottage or the bunkhouse, no one heard the approach of the US Army Calvary or the Texas Rangers. Once Captain Snelling was satisfied the structures were surrounded by his soldiers, he called on the wagon with the Gatling gun, front, and center.

Slowly it came and halted between the two structures, about fifty yards. The gun had already been armed and ready to fire before moving it into location, avoiding the loud noises it would take to load and make it ready.

The rest of the soldiers and the Texas Rangers were spaced side by side on either side of the Gatling gun, in reserve as it made a formidable line of defense.

Inside the bunkhouse, someone heard movements and noises and looked out the window with disbelief and shock. He woke everyone and then they heard the ultimatum being given. Captain Snelling yelled out, "This is the US Army Calvary and the Texas Rangers, we have you all surrounded. Surrender and we will not use the Gatling gun and no soldiers will be shooting into your bunkhouse or the cottage. You have five minutes to decide."

In the bunkhouse, there wasn't a bit of confusion to the man. They all immediately dropped their gun belts to the floor and one by one stepped out of the bunkhouse, with their hands raised. The same was being done by Hatcher and his two cousins. Once they saw his gang was giving up, they had only one choice to get out of this alive: surrender!

With the prisoners kept covered by the Calvary, John Slade took the lead. He and his Rangers moved in two iron-barred prisoner transport wagons and loaded the prisoners up without a fight.

Not a single gunshot was fired during the mission.

The newspapers would later call it a resounding victory for law and order in Texas.

# CHAPTER 39

# THE END TIMES

*John Slade Ranch, Austin, Texas,*
*June 1916*

It was a warm summer morning at the Slade ranch.

The sprawling five-bedroom, two-story log-built home on forty acres of plush green farm-land had been finished to cement the owner's large growing family. Out of the cattle and horse business, and retired from law enforcement, John now enjoyed having his family all in one place.

John Slade, at age seventy-two, sat casually on the veranda in his favorite rocker, enjoying the sunshine after a hearty breakfast with the family. Married for the last twenty-three years, his wife Clara Jones Slade with their two adult sons, Gary, and Mark Slade, both in the real estate business, with their three children, John's grandkids, John smiled at his role as a grandfather.

Earlier, John was sitting with his back to a built-in bookcase, in his reading room with a writing tablet on the desk. He needed to finish writing his recollection of his days as a Texas Ranger while it was still fresh in his mind. These would be his life stories. He wanted his family to know about the man that he was and the tragic life he'd led before having such a beautiful family.

From time to time, he would stop and glance around the room, as a memory of his first love had crept into his consciousness. It was her face, that of Emily. Tears fell. He picked up a handkerchief and dabbed at them. Then he remembered the fire that killed his parents. All this he wrote. Those memories were still quite vivid for a man his age, and he gave thanks for it.

He'd read about the end of Hatcher and his gang, when several years ago, they tried escaping from prison and every single one of them was gunned down in their brazen attempt.

Wiping the last of his tears, he leaned back in his chair, as his mind drifted to the memory of Ben Collins. For several years the two had become good friends. Then, according to the newspapers, in 1906, Collins, a lawman for the Bureau of Indian Affairs, was killed by an outlaw named Jim Miller in retribution for another killing.

Enjoying his two boys teaching his grandkids to ride a horse, John Slade stepped back inside the house and ambled slowly toward his reading room once more. He was feeling tired and dizzy. He needed to put away his letters and catch up with a nap.

Slowly he sat in the leather chair and gathered his notes and letters when suddenly, he closed his eyes. He felt a shortness of breath, and his eyes closed. His head fell forward. He gently laid it on the desk and let nature take its course.

This was a good death, surrounded by family, at home peacefully.

## THE END

# ABOUT THE AUTHOR

Victor M. Alvarez was born in Puerto Rico, at nine his family moved to New York City and he was later drafted into the U.S. Army. He received airborne training, ranger, military police schools and later jungle warfare training. His military awards range from Jump Wings, Vietnam Cross of Gallantry, awards of the Purple Heart, Air Medal, and Army Commendation Medal, among many other awards. He makes his home in New Smyrna Beach, Florida.

## NOTE FROM THE AUTHOR

Word-of-mouth is crucial for any author to succeed. If you enjoyed *Two Guns Across Texas*, please leave a review online—anywhere you are able. Even if it's just a sentence or two. It would make all the difference and would be very much appreciated.

Thanks!
Victor M. Alvarez

We hope you enjoyed reading this title from:

# BLACK ROSE
## writing™

www.blackrosewriting.com

Subscribe to our mailing list – *The Rosevine* – and receive **FREE** books, daily
deals, and stay current with news about upcoming
releases and our hottest authors.
Scan the QR code below to sign up.

Already a subscriber? Please accept a sincere thank you for being a fan of
Black Rose Writing authors.

View other Black Rose Writing titles at
www.blackrosewriting.com/books and use promo code
**PRINT** to receive a **20% discount** when purchasing.

www.ingramcontent.com/pod-product-compliance
Lightning Source LLC
Chambersburg PA
CBHW010730100726
47899CB00009B/2996